MW00770097

ELEMENTS OF CHEMISTRY

CAPTURE (PART 3)

PENNY REID

PROLOGUE
A MOLECULAR COMPARISON OF GASES, LIQUIDS, AND SOLIDS

-Six months post-breakup-

"I DON'T KNOW how to do this, Kaitlyn. You're going to have to help me."

"Do what, Dad?"

The phone was silent for a beat before he said, "Talk to you about your mother."

I grimaced and picked at an imperfection on the kitchen table. Four months ago, when Sam and I had moved off campus, we furnished our apartment with thrift store purchases. The shellac was peeling away from the Formica and I was making it worse.

"I don't know what there is to say." I shrugged, biting my lip to keep my chin from wobbling. The truth was that I missed her. My dad and I had been talking regularly over the phone, but I hadn't been participating in our Sunday meetings for the last six months and I missed having a connection with my mother.

"I think she hurt you. Am I right?"

I shrugged even though he couldn't see me. Part of the reason I hadn't contacted her was definitely because she seemed to be indifferent to my feelings about breaking up with Martin.

The other part was because of my fear she'd be disappointed in me. During my summer of discontent after my breakup with Martin, I'd decided to switch majors—from chemical engineering to music—and take the fall semester off school.

Taking a semester off school was the Parker family equivalent of giving up on life. I'd made the decision rather flippantly, and without consulting my parents. However, my determination to change majors had deeper roots and was the impetus behind my current gainful employment as the piano player in a special events band.

After a week of psyching myself up, I'd auditioned in July and was now officially a paid musician. The group played mostly weddings. They also performed at Bar and Bat Mitzvahs, swanky business receptions, and office parties anywhere between Boston and New York City. My evenings and weekend afternoons started filling up fast, especially when we'd have to travel into the city for a job.

Being around music almost daily—either as part of the band, or the time spent alone composing—made me realize I had to pursue it. I had to live it. It was my passion and ignoring what gave me happiness and peace was unacceptable.

Instead of admitting the whole truth about why I was avoiding my mother, I said, "I don't even really understand why I'm so upset with her. She didn't do anything. Not really. And I know she had good intentions. It's just...I feel like she doesn't care about me sometimes, I guess."

"Well, you're wrong. She does care about you. She loves you."

"Then I don't think I understand what love is. I thought I knew. I thought it was this great thing where two people support each other and work together to solve problems. I thought it was about trust and loyalty, being honest, kind, being a team. But now I have no idea. In fact, I'm doubting that love exists. Maybe, as a society, we made it up to explain and justify our unhealthy desire for co-dependence."

He was silent for a moment and I knew he was thinking about what I'd said, processing it. One of the coolest things about my father was that he listened to understand, not to react.

"I actually agree with you to a certain extent, if I'm understanding your meaning correctly. We humans, most of us, are co-dependent and it's often unhealthy. It's up to the two people within the relationship to keep the co-dependence healthy. But, you are assuming there is only one kind of love, Kaitlyn. I can tell you there are as many kinds of love in the world as there are stars in the sky."

"That was very poetic, Dad."

"I bet you didn't know I used to write poetry for your mother."

This made me start and I sat up straighter in my chair. "You did?"

"Yes. And it was pretty good, for a medical student who was infatuated with an unobtainable ice queen. It made her melt…a little."

I heard the smile in his voice and it made me nostalgic for his sweet sappiness.

"What happened?"

"I asked her to marry me, not expecting that she would say yes, but she did. So we got married, and I was in very deep infatuation-love with her. She was so…good. So driven. She was talented at inspiring people and surprising them with how smart she was—because she is, she's brilliant. And she's very charismatic."

I thought about this for a second, mildly horrified that I was attracted to guys who were like my mother.

He continued. "But then I became disillusioned because she belonged to the world just as much as she belonged to me. And I didn't like that."

I considered this for a moment, thinking about my father being jealous of the world. I couldn't imagine my father being jealous at all. He was so…nice. Even tempered. Sweet.

"What did you do?"

"I told her I wanted a divorce. I told her I couldn't be with someone who was always putting me second and that I'd made a mistake."

I sucked in a sharp breath. "Why did I not know about this?"

"It happened before you were born."

"What did she do?"

My father sighed, as though he were releasing memories from long ago. "She begged me to stay, which shocked the hell out of me, but she did. She offered to leave politics and even went so far as to drop out of her commissioner's race without telling me. She tried to make herself into a different person, because she didn't want me to go. She didn't want to lose me."

"That seems...very unlike her."

"It was. It is. But love—the kind of love she felt for me—makes people do crazy things. It twists them up and can make them question their own choices."

"So, you stayed, obviously. But then how did she get back into politics?"

"I realized I was ruining her with my jealousy. She tried to change for me, and not for the better. The parts of her I loved the most—her brilliance, charisma, goodness, fierce desire to correct injustice—these were not compatible with my jealousy. And I also realized that she didn't belong to the world, and she didn't belong to me. She belongs to herself. We all belong to ourselves, until we have children. Then our children lease us for as long as they want."

I exhaled a laugh and shook my head.

"Never doubt that your mother loves you, Kaitlyn."

Feeling ashamed as I contemplated my father's wise words, I forced myself to stop picking at the Formica.

My father continued, "But she does everything in the extreme. In your case, she respects you and trusts you in the extreme, so she trusts that you'll come to her when you're ready. Meanwhile she's bitten off all her fingernails."

I thought about this for a stretch, feeling a bit of panic at the thought of facing her and being a disappointment.

"What if I'm never ready?"

"Then that would make you stupid, and you're not stupid. You're stubborn, but you're not stupid."

"I don't know how to do this, Dad. How do I make things right?"

"Come home for Thanksgiving. Talk to your mother. Or yell at her. Just do something with her. You two need each other and I can't take another Sunday call without you, so call in for the next one. Just...be brave."

4

[1]

-SEVEN MONTHS POST-BREAKUP-

"**B**ETWEEN YOU AND me and the tree, I think we should have our own Thanksgiving before you leave." Sam was folding our clean laundry while I sorted through my desk, purging it of old classwork and notes. I'd decided to go home for Thanksgiving and was leaving in three weeks for the long weekend. I had an abundance of restless energy. I used the energy to clean my room.

My father was correct. It was time for me to make things right with my mother.

I'd rejoined the Sunday calls at the beginning of October, yet none of us had broached the subject of my months-long absence.

As well, she and I hadn't spoken yet about my decision to take a semester off school, and I was glad. When I brought it up on a mid-October call, I'd tried to explain and defend my position. She told me to wait.

My mother had said, "You need time."

And she was right. I'd needed the time to figure things out without dwelling on the fact that I must be a disappointment.

"Is your mother going to make Tofurkey again?" I asked Sam.

Her only response was to make a gagging sound.

I chuckled at this. Her mother was a strict vegan. Sam loved steak.

"Hey Sam, do you think I could get a job at your restaurant? Not as a server of course, since I don't have any experience, but maybe I could bus tables or wash dishes."

I was re-enrolling at the university in the spring, but now as a music major. I'd applied and auditioned for the music program, probably setting my graduation date back by two or more years. As well, this meant likely losing my academic scholarship. My dad had offered to pay for tuition; therefore I was determined to get a second job, pay for my living costs, and pitch in for the school expenses.

"I can ask..." She peered at me for a long moment, biting the inside of her lip as she considered me. "But have you thought about maybe applying for a job at The Bluesy Bean? I hear the lady there only hires musicians as baristas because she makes them serenade the customers."

I chuckled. "Ha ha, that's funny."

I tossed a stack of papers into the paper bag I'd set aside for recycling and then shifted my attention to the bookshelf. I had so many textbooks. I thought I'd need them for reference; I should have just sold them back for cash. The room fell into silence, which wasn't unusual for us these days.

Which was why I was surprised when Sam blurted, "So, I think it's time that you talk to me about what's going on with you."

I glanced at her over my shoulder, and found her watching me with her hands on her hips.

"What do you mean?"

Her jaw was set, her eyes narrowed into determined slits. "I mean, you didn't speak to me—or anyone else—for months, until you got that job with the band last July. Hell, even when we picked out this apartment it was like pulling teeth trying to get you to voice an opinion. And don't get me started on the weird, angry acoustic guitar music."

I gave her an apologetic half smile. I knew this conversation had to happen eventually. Sam had been so patient with me. I was better, so much better, and now was as good a time as any to bring everything out into the open, to clarify my headspace over the last few months.

I faced her, crossing to the bed. "I know. I'm so sorry about the angry acoustic guitar music."

She continued like I hadn't spoken, as though some dam had broken and she needed to get all her thoughts out. "I know you don't like me mentioning *his* name."

I rolled my eyes at my dramatics from months ago, when I'd told her I never wanted to speak of Martin Sandeke ever again; but it also made me realize I'd been greedy with my thoughts.

"And then you joined the band and started drinking Red Bull. Next you decided to change your major and take a semester off school—which I'm totally for, by the way. It's just that you never talk to me about anything. You're in your head all the time. And I want to know, it's been almost eight months since the two of you split and I think it's time for you to tell me. Are you over *him* yet? Is Kaitlyn back? Is it okay for me to ask you questions and voice my unsolicited advice?"

I took a deep breath, gazed at her affectionately, then patted the spot next to me on the bed. She eyeballed me, then the bed, then plopped down beside me.

"Okay," I started, trying to figure out how to give her a Cliffs Notes version of what I'd been going through. The words would be difficult, so I decided to use terminology with which I was most comfortable. "Let me start from the beginning, with the solid state of matter."

She lifted one eyebrow at me, her chin falling and issuing me a look of disbelief. "Solid state of matter? What are you talking about?"

"Let me finish. So, after M-Martin and I broke up—"

"So we can say his name now?"

"Just listen. After Martin and I broke up, I admit I did not take it well. I was an immovable mass of low energy. I kept thinking that if I didn't think about it, then I would never have to deal with it."

"So, you were in denial."

I laughed a little at her apt simplification. "Yes. Basically, I froze everyone out. I was a solid. This lasted for a long time, because I'm stubborn. As well, you know I like my pity parties and self-recrimination soirées."

"Yes, it lasted two months. You went to class, sometimes you went to your jam sessions, but mostly you just hid in the closet."

I cleared my throat, remembering this dark time, and grateful I'd moved past it. "So then this brings us to the liquid state of matter. You know how I started loosening up once we moved into the apartment?"

She nodded. "Yeah, but you still wouldn't talk to anyone. You just sat in your room listening to Taylor Swift's angry-girl music."

"Yes, but I was angry. I wasn't frozen anymore, I was just really, really pissed off. I think the new apartment was the catalyst for my shift in state from solid to liquid. It felt like a new start. Away from the dorms, away from the college atmosphere. It was a reminder that life existed beyond school. I was only nineteen—almost twenty—and, I realized that I have decades left on this planet. I couldn't keep hiding in closets..."

I reflected on my feelings at the time. Yes, I couldn't keep hiding in closets, but this thought made me angry. I'd been happy hiding in closets before Martin had ruined everything and scratched my itch.

I hated him for it.

During my liquid state I'd redoubled my efforts to avoid all mentions of, or references to, Martin Sandeke. I wasn't ready to accept he existed in the world, and yet might as well be Hercules as far as I was concerned. I would never see him again—never in person—but maybe in a magazine or in the news. Our breakup had been my choice and it was the right decision, but it still pissed me off.

As well, I wasn't ready to accept that *I* certainly no longer existed to *him*.

Sam sighed. "So, this angry phase, this *liquid state* as you call it—this is when I tried to get you to read that fitness magazine interview Martin gave over the summer?"

I nodded. "Yes. Sorry for snapping at you about that."

She shrugged. "It's okay. I get it. So, if I recall my high school chemistry correctly, the gas state comes after the liquid state."

"That's right. Though I like to think of it as the nitrous oxide, aka laughing gas, phase—otherwise known as the *I-don't-give-two-poos* phase."

"Oh! That's when you started drinking Red Bull and boxes of wine. I still can't believe you're drinking the demon liquor even though you're not yet legal. Shame on you."

I tried to give her my best *girl, you crazy* face. "Sam, you're the one who buys me the boxes of wine. You're my supplier. But I make no apologies and I have no regrets. I've discovered I like my boxes of wine and I'm not giving them up for the next six months before I turn twenty-one. They're stackable, like Tetris. All beverages should be stackable."

"I agree, beverages should be stackable, it saves on shelf space. And it's not my fault I'm older than you are and enjoy enabling your illegal activities, especially if it means I'm not drinking boxed wine by myself. But back to you and your states of crazy, the boxed wine phase was when you started going to those music meet-ups. I remember that phase."

"But, if you remember, it was around this time that I decided to take the fall semester off school and switch my major to music."

"And you started hanging around those druggies at the Fourth Avenue bar. But that only lasted a week."

"Yes, it only lasted for about a week." I studied Sam for a beat before continuing, marveling at how perceptive she was and how lucky I was to have her as a friend. "I'd made a deal with myself: I would be carefree and act my age. If I were carefree then I would forget about Martin and be happy."

"The boxes of wine do seem to make you happy," Sam agreed.

What I didn't say, because it was difficult to admit my irresponsibility, was that everything became a joke. I didn't *need* Martin. I didn't need anyone. I could live outside the closet of obscurity just fine on my own. I needed nothing.

"You're right though, it wasn't sustainable for me. I'm far too practical and reclusive. Firstly, Red Bull tastes like excrement."

"It does! Right?"

"And secondly, as much as I enjoyed the time I was actually playing music, I had no patience for druggies."

Watching people actively choose to destroy themselves felt like watching Martin choose revenge over living his life free from his father. It was during this time I recognized revenge was Martin's drug and he was an addict.

"So, solid state is denial. Liquid state is anger. That makes the gas state the bargaining stage."

I cocked my head to the side, studying Sam. "What do you mean?"

"The five stages of grief," she explained matter-of-factly. "Next is depression."

I looked at my friend for a long moment, realizing she was right. She was *so* right. The next state was depression.

"Oh my God, you're right." I gave her a sad smile. "Yes, otherwise known as the plasma state of matter."

Sam's gaze became sympathetic as it held mine, her features softening with compassion. "Toward the end of the summer, when you started crying again."

"You heard that?"

"Yes. I heard the crying. And the sad music you were composing in your room. It's beautiful, by the way. Much better than your Red Bull-slash-gas-slash-bargaining phase music."

I gave her a soft smile. "Thank you. It was very…cathartic. It allowed me to reflect on the months that came before it. But mostly I think I was trying to wrap my mind around how and why I'd allowed one week—one solitary, singular week—to completely change the course of my life."

Why had I given Martin Sandeke so much power over me? And why was I continuing to give him power? I hadn't seen or spoken to him since that terrible day on campus. He hadn't once tried to contact me, but I hadn't expected him to try.

And yet…I missed him. I thought about him and our week together all the time.

Sam's mouth turned down at the corners and she gave me a sincere and sympathetic look. "Kaitlyn, you fell in love with Martin over that week. You trusted him…you slept with him."

I nodded, glancing down at my fingers. "I know…"

I know I missed the depth of feeling, the loss of control, the surrender to passion, the being lost and found all at once. Being seen. He was still wrapped around my heart and I had no way to evict him. I wasn't sure I could.

I added, "I know that, before Martin, before our week together, I'd been repressed, stuck without knowing it. But then after we split things were even worse."

Sam pulled me into a hug as I continued my confession. "He became my compass, my beacon. And before him, I'd been a girl desperately trying to follow the footsteps of expectations even though the shoes didn't fit."

"And he helped you see beyond family expectations?"

I nodded against her shoulder. Over spring break I'd started to become a woman who was excited about forging her own path.

I pulled away from my friend, but continued to hold her hand. "Then I left him and he left me. We abandoned each other before I'd discovered what I wanted or who I was. My compass was gone. I couldn't go back to hiding in closets even though I tried."

She chuckled at this, adding, "Boy, oh boy, did you ever try."

I smiled at her. "But the closets don't fit anymore. Nor do I know how to move forward blindly. I want to be something else, someone else, not Kaitlyn Parker who hides in closets and does what everyone expects."

"But not everyone has the benefit of a compass or a guide. Most people go blindly into their future."

I nodded again. "Yes. I figured that out."

I'd figured out that people did this by trusting their heart.

"Well, we've already covered denial, anger, bargaining, and depression. Does this mean you've moved on to acceptance?" Sam gave me a wide, hopeful smile that made me laugh.

"Kind of." I shrugged, my gaze moving over her shoulder as I focused my thoughts. "Think of it this way. The fifth state of matter is a theoretical state—"

"Really? We're still using the chemistry analogy?"

I continued as though she hadn't spoken, because the word *acceptance* didn't feel quite right. "One could argue the fifth state of matter isn't theoretical, that it's a class of states that occur under unusual or extreme circumstances, like Bose–Einstein condensates or neutron-degenerate matter."

"I have no idea what you just said."

I pressed my lips together so I wouldn't laugh, but returned my gaze to Sam. "But for the purposes of my stages of grief, I'm going to label the fifth stage as quark–gluon plasmas. It's a state of matter that is believed to be possible, but remains theoretical…for now."

"Theoretical?"

"Theoretical because my fifth stage of grief has to do with me getting over Martin, which I admit hasn't happened yet. And it also centers on finding my purpose, but using only myself as a compass."

"You can also use me as a compass, you know. I'm very good with the aforementioned unsolicited advice."

If I hadn't realized it before, I realized now that Sam was a singularity of awesomeness. "I know, and I will. But it's more than just moving on from Martin. It's a stage where I become comfortable in my own skin, happy with where I am, what I'm doing, and who I'm doing it with."

"So, it's theoretical."

"Yes." I nodded, finally returning Sam's hopeful grin. "It's still theoretical. But it's possible."

[2]

I FOUND MY mother in the garden.

She was home for the Congressional Thanksgiving recess. Growing up, I'd always thought it funny that the US government took a *recess,* like little kids took recess in primary school. I imagined the Speaker of the House hanging upside down on monkey bars and the majority leader shaking down junior senators for lunch money.

I knew we'd be seeing each other because it had been on the Sunday agenda for the last month. I'd been mentally preparing for this meeting. She'd said I needed some time before we discussed my months-long absence from her life and my decision to take a semester off school.

But the time had come. I needed to talk to her about it, even though it was messy and unsettled. I needed her to listen without trying to fix.

When I found her in the garden, I announced to her back, "I want to be a musician. I want to pursue music and major in it and I don't want to be a scientist or a politician."

My mother turned as I spoke, stared at me for a beat, her forehead wrinkling slightly, probably because I wasn't prone to outbursts. Then she nodded and said, "Okay."

I waited for her to continue, maybe add a, *But you're on your own...* or *But when you come to your senses...* or something similar. She didn't.

When she just continued looking at me, my suspicions burst forth. "You think this is a phase, right?"

My mom took a deep breath, glanced briefly at the ground, then returned her gaze to mine. "Maybe. Maybe not."

"You're disappointed in me? Because I took off this semester? Because I'm not following in your footsteps? Because I'm—"

She held up her hands and cut me off. "Kaitlyn, stop. Stop. Stop putting words in my mouth. I'm not disappointed in you. I'm disappointed in myself."

I frowned at her, studying my mother in her navy pants suit, and light blue shirt, and the little United States flag on her lapel. Finally I asked, "Why?"

"Because you obviously need my support and I have no idea how to give it to you." She crossed to me, her eyes searching, then pulled me into an unexpected hug.

When she spoke next I felt her chin move against the side of my head. "I'm not...I've never been very good at being maternal."

I laughed, partly because I hadn't expected her to say it and partly because it was true.

She squeezed me. "I'm good at being rational, methodical, and solving problems with logic and analysis. But, try as I might, I've never been able to figure out how to provide the comfort that you've needed. And I'm sorry."

Every one of my internal organs flooded with the warmth of relief that accompanies hope. I squeezed her in return, unable to help myself. "You're forgiven."

She stepped back, but her hands remained on my arms. She was clearly frustrated. "I don't know how to help you or be what you need, Kaitlyn."

"Can you listen?"

"Yes. Of course."

"Without trying to problem solve or find a superior solution to my issues?"

She hesitated, her eyes narrowing, looking incredulous. "You mean, just listen?"

I nodded.

She stared at me, appeared to be firming her resolve, then said, "For you, absolutely."

[3]

-NINE MONTHS POST-BREAKUP-

"**A**RE YOU EVER going to go out with Fitzy, or what?"

I let my befuddlement show on my face by widening my eyes and looking from side to side.

All I wanted was a bottle of water.

"What you talkin' 'bout, Willis?"

I enjoyed asking my bandmate this question, mostly because his name was actually Willis. Usually no one my age had any idea that the question was a reference to a 1980s TV show I used to watch with my dad called *Different Strokes*.

Willis glanced over his shoulder to where Abram the bass player, Janet the lead guitarist and saxophonist, and Fitzgerald our singer and second guitar—aka Fitzy for short—were finishing the sound check. Since Willis held my water bottle hostage, I followed his gaze and found Fitzy watching us. When he saw our attention focused on him, Fitzy averted his blue-eyed stare and began messing with his mic stand, his shaggy brown hair falling adorably over his forehead.

Willis turned back to me, leveled me with his dark brown eyes. Like the rest of us, Willis was dressed in a tuxedo, bowtie, cummerbund, the whole get up. Unlike the rest of us, Willis was in his mid-forties and never minced words.

17

Unfortunately, he chopped his words instead, usually with a dull blade or a mallet. Willis's thoughts were often sporadic and hard to follow; as well his analogies didn't quite make sense.

"Listen, Cupcake. He's got it bad for you, like a porcupine and a balloon. Now, I don't care what y'all do in your free time, but I'm tired of losing good people because you kids can't keep your seatbelts fastened. We lost Pierce, our last pianist, when Janet and he refused to work together after six weeks on a mattress tour. They drew straws and he came up espresso—you see?"

I nodded, trying to follow. "So, Janet and Pierce, your last piano player, were a thing? And it didn't end well?"

"It *never* ends well." Willis narrowed his dark brown eyes and pressed his mouth into a flat line. He was bald, his head completely shaved, and the collar of his dress shirt didn't quite hide the tattoos on the back of his neck. This didn't affect our squeaky image since he was our drummer and sat at the back of the stage. Also, he was my boss.

Willis lowered his roughened voice—made gravelly by years of smoking and drinking and laughing too loud—and squinted at me until his pupils were barely visible. "Musicians are like lightbulbs, they burn hot and bright, but can't be screwed more than once. If you two need to get it out of your system, that's fine. But you're a great kid, real goddamn talented, pretty, look good on stage. But Fitzy is also pretty and will be hard to replace—you get my meaning?"

"I think so. You don't care if Fitzy and I get together, but you don't want it to impact the dynamic of the band. Right?"

He nodded, looking irritated. "Isn't that what I just said?"

"Yes, absolutely. I understand loud and clear. Not dating bandmates is one of my life rules."

What I didn't vocalize was that Willis didn't need to worry. Although Fitzy was super hot, super nice, and super talented, I felt no attraction to him beyond the surface of his skin and the attractiveness of his voice. This was because Fitzy wasn't very bright.

If he were an actual lightbulb he'd be a twenty watt fluorescent. Hard to look at—because he was so pretty—but too dim to make a noticeable difference in any given room.

Abram the bassist, however, was a completely different story. His face wasn't classically good-looking—with his long brown hair, hazel eyes, big jaw, and hook nose—nor was he book smart. But he was tall and broad and manly-handsome. As well he was shrewd, and wicked sharp. He had a razor wit and twisted sense of humor.

He also always had one or two women in the audience who waited for him after our sets. It didn't matter if we played a country club wedding outside New Haven, a dive bar in Queens, or a high-rise in Manhattan. Without fail, he never went home alone. As well, at times his jokes were shaded with bitterness; it was easy to see he was jaded.

I was undoubtedly attracted to Abram—the talented, witty, sexy bassist. But I wasn't attracted to Abram—the serial dating king of the bitterness squad.

I'd come to the conclusion that intelligence was my catnip, followed closely by charisma. And, thanks to my romantic history, I'd realized that just because a person was intelligent and charismatic didn't mean they were good for me. The brighter the brain, the greater the gravitational pull, the more wary I was.

Therefore, Fitzy was harmless.

And furthermore, I was careful to stay out of Abram's orbit.

What I needed was a nice guy who understood my jokes. Someone who was friendly rather than charismatic. Someone who was bright, but wasn't so brilliant he was blinding.

"Get on your perch, lady bird. It's almost time." Willis walked past me to his place behind the drums.

I grabbed my bottle of water and followed Willis to the stage. Avoiding Abram's level stare, I gave Janet a friendly head nod and waved at Fitzy. He waved back, giving me a big, white, perfect smile.

Tonight we were playing a Christmas party at a New York City location we knew well. It was a converted fire station, now a moderately sized concert venue—very popular spot for weddings and office parties. I liked it because the interior was original red brick with cool Norwegian-looking tapestries lining the walls, likely placed purposefully to help with acoustics.

Also, the stage was set back from the dance floor. Though I'd been playing publicly for several months, being close to or surrounded by the audience still felt overwhelming. I liked being in the back, with the piano between me and the audience.

The set started with the basic cocktail hour fare: heavy on the piano, vocals, and saxophone; light on the drums. We would play five sets, each growing progressively louder and edgier as the older crowd left, leaving the young people who wanted to dance.

Nothing was special about this event. I had no expectations, indications, or signs from above (or below) that this event would be any different from the dozens of other office parties I'd played over the last several months. I was cool. I was collected. I was fine. I was doing my thing and wondering if I still had bacon in the fridge, because I had a severe hankering for a BLT.

Then, amidst my bacon preoccupation, my ponytail holder snapped during the fourth set and the bobby pins I'd placed to fasten my bun were no match for the weight of my hair. I was forced to perform the remainder of the set with curls in my face.

It was irritating and distracting. As well, and inexplicably, the snapped ponytail holder was the catalyst for an intense and abrupt wave of self-consciousness. The sensation started with a nagging tingle on the back of my neck. I ignored it. It persisted.

I lifted my gaze to Abram and found him watching me with a smirk. I rolled my eyes and turned my attention back to my fingers as they flew over the keys, writing off the tingle as Abram-related. A moment later I glanced back at Abram, feeling irritated I could still feel his stare, but he wasn't looking at me.

Yet, I felt eyes on me. I felt watched. It was a weight, like a hand, and I couldn't shake the impression. My heart thudded uncomfortably in my chest as I scanned my bandmates. I found them all focused on their instruments.

I told myself I was being silly, but the feeling persisted. It was unnerving, like walking down a dark hallway and hearing the echo of footsteps.

When the set was finally over, I twisted my hair over my shoulder and out of my face. I glanced at the audience as I stood from the piano, scanning the crowd for the source of my discomfort, half expecting to find nothing.

But I did find something.

I found blue-green eyes on a familiar face, dressed in an immaculately tailored suit, with a tall brunette on his arm, a drink in his hand, and his penetrating gaze firmly anchored to mine.

[4]

RESONANCE STRUCTURES

"I'M SORRY, WILLIS. I need a minute…I don't feel well." I was sitting on an upturned bucket backstage, my hands on my knees. My voice was weak and I truly, truly did not feel well.

Janet was rubbing my back and Fitzy hovered nearby with a plate of food. Abram was leaning against the far wall, his feet crossed at the ankles, his hands shoved in his pockets as he watched me.

Seeing Martin again—just *seeing* him across a crowded room—had been so much more flustering and mind-bending than I could have predicted. My thoughts on repeat were:

He's here.

He's here with someone.

I kind of still hate him.

But I hope he doesn't hate me.

I think I'm still infatuated with him…

Surprisingly, the loudest and most pressing thought: *He's seen me naked.*

Martin, plus my dad—when I was an infant—were the only two men in the entire world who had seen me naked. Really, only Martin actually counted, because I didn't have boobs or pubic hair or a girl

23

shape when my dad used to give me raspberries on my tummy. Plus, he was my dad.

Only Martin...

That pressing thought served to confuse me and increase the potency of my awkward feels. Perhaps I needed to fix that. Perhaps I needed to find another guy and show him my girl stuff, widen my audience, so that being in the same room with Martin didn't turn me into a skeevy, nudity-obsessed wacko.

Perhaps diluting the meaningfulness of intimacy would lessen the impact of his presence. Then I could look at him and think, *Hey, you're one of the guys who has seen me naked. So what? Who hasn't seen me naked?*

"Do you think you can play? It's just one more set," Janet asked softly, pulling me from my thoughts. She was a nice girl, very maternal, with a heart entirely too soft. A direct contradiction to the image she projected with her dyed black hair, pale skin, icicle eyes, and copious piercings.

I nodded and closed my eyes. I could play. I would play. I just needed a minute to stop my hands from shaking.

I wondered if there was a broom closet nearby where I could chill out for five minutes. I wouldn't hide all night, just until it was safe. Maybe Fitzy could join me and I could show him my boobs.

"Jarring, unsettling, startling, alarming, disconcerting, distressing, disquieting."

A pause followed my mumbling, and then Willis asked, "What are you doing?"

"She's chanting synonyms." Abram's voice carried from across the room. I opened my eyes and met his gaze. He was watching me with interest. "It calms you down, yes?"

I nodded, frowning. He was entirely too shrewd.

Willis grunted. "Well, okay. That's...as weird as a loan shark with debt. But we got another ten minutes before rodeo time."

I held Abram's gaze for a moment longer, then stood—a little wobbly on my feet—and turned to Willis. "I think I'll take a short walk."

Fitzy leaned forward and began to volunteer, "I'll go—"

But Abram lifted his voice and talked over him, "I'll walk with you. Come on. Let's go."

The tall bassist pushed away from the wall and crossed to me, wrapped his hand around my arm just above the elbow, and pulled me out the back door.

"Be back in five minutes!" Willis called after us.

"We'll be back in seven," Abram countered, steering me down the alley to the street and away from the stink of the dumpster.

I pulled out of his grip when we reached the sidewalk and folded my arms over my chest, not really feeling the cold of the last November evening because my mind was racing, trying to keep pace with my heart. I was definitely not going to show Abram my boobs. That would be like jumping from the frying pan into the beer batter, then back in the frying pan.

When I saw Martin across the room, I just stood there, my fingers still on the edge of the baby grand piano. It didn't feel real and I was sure he was going to disappear if I blinked.

So I didn't blink.

Eventually, Fitzy pulled me off the stage and I had no choice but to blink. Yet when I looked back and Martin was still present—still standing at the bar with his beautiful date next to him, surrounded in a thick cloud of arrogance, still staring at me—I almost blacked out.

He didn't disappear. He was real. And he most definitely saw and recognized me.

"You feeling better?"

I realized Abram and I had already walked a block and a half. The distance was a surprise. "Yes. I feel better. We should go back."

Lies, all lies. I didn't feel better. I felt like throwing up. *Will the drama never stop?!*

We continued forward.

"Sometimes you sound like a robot when you speak." He didn't appear to be annoyed as he made this comment; rather, it was simply an observation, maybe meant to distract me.

"Do I?"

"Yeah. Mostly when you talk to me."

"What can I say? You bring out the artificial intelligence in me."

I heard him chuckle as he took my arm again, bringing me close as we skirted a crowd of rowdy young men, all dressed in New York Knicks jerseys, likely on their way home after a game at Madison Square Garden. When we were past the boisterous crowd, I moved to pull my arm out of his grip, but he didn't release me. Instead he tugged me into a small doorway and turned me to face him.

"So, who's the guy?"

I lifted my eyes to his, found him studying me with moderate interest. Moderate interest for the perpetually sardonic Abram felt like a laser beam pointed at my skull.

"What guy?"

"The guy at the bar. The stockbroker, or hedge fund manager, or whatever he does."

I squinted at Abram, setting my jaw, but said nothing.

He lifted a single eyebrow and I noticed he had a scar running through the center of it. The scar paired with his hooked nose—likely broken more than once— and long hair, gave him a rather ruffian-like appearance, a pirate prone to fights.

"Ex-boyfriend," he stated. He'd clearly pulled the answer from my brain with his ruffian voodoo.

I grimaced. "Yes...kind of."

His lips pulled to the side as his eyes skated over my face. "Kind of?"

"We need to get back." I didn't move.

"Are you afraid of him?"

I ignored this question because it was entirely too complicated for me to answer. Instead I said, "It's been five minutes at least."

"Did he hurt you?"

I closed my eyes, leaned back against the brick of our little cave, and murmured, "We hurt each other."

We were silent for a stretch and I felt his gaze on me, but I hardly noticed. My mind and heart were twisted up in a battle of wills, and yet neither of them had decided what to do, how to feel, or what to think.

"Come on, let's go."

Once again, Abram encircled my arm with his long fingers and tugged me down the street. This time I made no effort to pull away. Once we reached the first stoplight, he slipped his grip from my arm to my hand, lacing his fingers with mine. Even in my fog I definitely noticed. Usually, I would have withdrawn by crossing my arms over my chest in the universal body language code for *not interested in you touching me*, but instead I let him hold my hand. I let myself take some comfort from the connection, even if he wasn't really offering any.

Honestly, I had no idea what to think about Abram, whether he was actually offering comfort, why he was holding my hand...so I didn't think.

Soon we were back in the alley and entering the back door of the venue. Willis was the only one left in the backstage area; he stopped mid-pace as we entered. "You're late as a Chevy to a fuel efficiency contest. It's been ten minutes."

"We're not late. We're early," Abram drawled, squeezing my hand then releasing it. He crossed to the cooler and pulled out a Coke while I sunk back to the bucket I'd been sitting on earlier.

"Early? You said you'd be back in seven minutes. It's been ten."

"Yeah, but I meant fifteen." Abram paired this by lifting his broad shoulders in a shrug, then adding an unapologetic and crooked smile.

Willis turned his scowl to me. "Are you ready?"

I opened my mouth to respond but Abram cut me off, "No. She threw up twice during the walk. She can't play, unless you want her tossing chunks all over the stage."

Again, I opened my mouth to interject. This time Willis cut me off. "No, no! You stay back here, I can't have glitter at a confetti party." He rubbed his bald head and stomped toward the steps, muttering as he went, "We'll figure it out."

"You're welcome," Abram said between swallows of Coke, bringing my attention back to him.

"Why did you do that?"

"So you'll owe me one."

This only served to intensify my frown. "I don't owe you one. I didn't ask for your help."

"Fine. Then I did it because I'm a nice guy."

I shook my head. "You're not a nice guy."

He grinned, looking positively wolfish. "No. I guess I'm not. But you're a nice girl. You bring out my altruistic side."

"Hmm…" I squinted at him and said nothing else, but I felt a little bit better.

This, this right here, this exchange between Abram and me was likely the source of my improved spirits. If I'd met Abram last year I likely would have run in the other direction. But now I was talking to this smart, charismatic, undeniably hot musician and hadn't once considered that I might be reduced to a blubbering fool.

I was officially *adulting*.

I was engaging in discourse with a guy to whom I was attracted, but whom I would never consider dating. Bonus: I wasn't trying to change the subject to musical theory, or some other tactic meant to distract.

Abram mimicked my squinty stare—though his was joined by an amused smile—and tossed his empty Coke bottle in the trash. "Wait for me after the set, I'll take you home."

"No thanks, I'm taking the train."

He stopped in front of me on his way to the stage and straightened his bow tie before sliding his long-fingered hands—bass-player hands—down the front of his suit jacket. The suit wasn't tailored very well and was baggy around his middle. Obviously he'd sized up so the shoulders would fit but hadn't invested in tapering it to fit his torso.

"You'll wait. Remember? If you're too sick to play the piano, then you're too sick to take the train."

"I live in New Haven. That's a long drive."

He shrugged, turned, sauntered to the steps, and called over his shoulder, "I like long drives."

I heard the recorded music cut off and Fitzy announce the last set followed by an upbeat number. I stayed on my bucket, my arms folded across my stomach, for three and a half songs, considering my options and trying not to think about Martin.

I ultimately decided I would think about Martin, but not yet. I'd wait until I was at home, just in case thinking about Martin made me cry. Also, thinking about Martin often led me to compose music. I was not above exploiting my memories of him or the feelings associated with unexpectedly seeing his face in the crowd for my own purposes. I liked to think of it as *channeling my angst.*

Yes, thinking about Martin later with a blank sheet of music and boxes of wine and tissues was definitely for the best.

Furthermore, I decided Abram could enjoy a nice, long car ride all by himself. I was going to take the train.

I pulled on my jacket, hooked my bag over my shoulder, grabbed another Coke from the cooler, and left via the backdoor. I didn't feel it necessary to leave a note; rather I would call Willis in the morning and apologize for flaking out.

I was ten steps from the backdoor when I saw him, or rather, the silhouette of him. The city lights were at his back, his face cast in total shadow.

I stopped. Everything stopped, or slowed, or suspended. It was a moment out of time, a singularity.

Then Martin moved and everything started again.

My heart slammed against my ribs, making me flinch and flush as he straightened away from the corner of the building. And I regretted my decision to postpone thinking about Martin. I should have sorted through my feelings inside, because now the momentum of my emotions choked me, leaving me defenseless. I couldn't actually form words. Martin hovered at the end of the alley, waiting, like he expected me to speak first.

But what could he possibly want to hear from me? We were together for one week and we'd ended badly. I'd purposefully avoided all mention of him—online and elsewhere. Even so, I couldn't help but know some details. Those details told me he'd withdrawn from college last semester and moved to New York. I guessed the rest—he was doing splendidly as a boy wonder venture capitalist.

Our mutual silence stretched and I grew certain he definitely expected me to break it, like we were in the middle of a conversation and it was my turn to speak, the ball in my court. Eventually it must've become obvious I wasn't going to be the one to modify the state of our conversation inertia.

He cleared his throat as one of his hands came to his jacket and he touched the front of his coat.

"Parker," he said. I felt the single word in my bones, though it sounded like a casual greeting. But it struck a chord because I never thought I'd hear his voice again.

I shifted on my feet, also cleared my throat, and tried to mimic his unaffected intonation. "Sandeke."

Another long moment passed where neither of us made a sound or movement. It was a bizarre situation to find oneself in for many reasons, not the least of which was all the busy goings-on surrounding us—people rushing by on the sidewalk, cars and buses and taxis whizzing behind him. I heard and felt the subway beneath my feet, the muffled music behind me, horns blaring, sirens whining. But we were still and silent.

Then abruptly, walking toward me, he said, "Do you need a ride?"

I shook my head. "No. No, thank you."

"I have a car. Do you live in the city?"

"No. I'm still in New Haven."

"I see…"

He stopped, now some five feet away. His gaze traveled up then down my body and he stuffed his hands in his pants pockets, his exquisite eyes remote and guarded when they landed on mine. I could see him clearly now beneath the light of the alley, and what I saw made my chest ache with the unfairness of him. I couldn't help but devour his features, recommitting his face, both familiar and unfamiliar, to memory.

He looked older, more like a man, and there was a new hardness in his face. He also might have been an inch taller, or maybe not. Perhaps he just carried himself differently. I didn't know how it was possible, but he felt even more imposing than he had before, and the gulf between us felt wider than ever.

This was hard. My heart hurt.

I thought I'd matured, grown from a repressed girl into a woman with an adequate amount of aplomb, worldliness; but I could see now that I still had a long way to go. Or perhaps I was always going to be part doofus. Perhaps it was in my genetic makeup to be a perpetual kid. Just standing near him made me feel like an imposter, like a poser trying to play grown up.

He was inspecting me. I could see the calculating gleam in his eyes; I was a problem that needed to be solved. I felt the heavy heat of embarrassment surge uncomfortably from my chest to my neck. Old Kaitlyn raised her hand and suggested I should hold very still and close my eyes until he got the message and left me alone, or thought I'd transformed into a large rock or a living statue.

Old Kaitlyn sure was a nut.

Whereas new Kaitlyn suspected that the chances of making it through the next ten minutes without bursting into tears were about three percent. New Kaitlyn was also very frustrated because she wanted to be over Martin Sandeke. She wanted to be able to see him without becoming an emotional pendulum.

However, both new Kaitlyn and old Kaitlyn wanted nothing to do with drama or angst or unwinnable arguments. I was over being a hot mess and wallowing. I had no idea why he was here, but every instinct told me to extract myself as soon as possible if I wanted to avoid future pitiful behavior.

I decided to embrace new Kaitlyn's frustration. Old Kaitlyn's suggested antics would get me nowhere. Whereas I could channel frustration into something useable, maybe even transform it into false bravery.

"Well, I'll see you around." I gave him a flat smile, thankful the alleyway was dim because it would mostly hide the impressive blush burning my cheeks, nose, forehead, and ears.

I moved as though to walk past him, and he quickly countered by stepping to the side, blocking my path. "Do you want to get a drink?"

"Oh, no thanks. I have a drink." I held up my Coke as evidence, trying to keep my voice steady and polite.

The corner of his mouth tugged to the side. "I meant, do you want to go somewhere to drink? Coffee?"

My eyes cut to his. "What about your date?"

"What about her?"

"Well, would she come with us?"

His gaze searched mine. "Would you be more or less likely to say yes if she did?"

This question hurt my heart and sounded like a riddle, so I ignored it. "Nah, I have work in the morning and I'm pretty tired."

"Work? Another show?"

"No." I pressed my lips together, not wanting to admit I was basically restarting college in the spring, and worked as a singing barista at the Bluesy Bean. But then I decided I was being a ninny and had nothing to be ashamed of. Martin had always been meant for a different world than mine. We were opposites, we always had been, always would be.

I lifted my chin and glanced beyond him as I explained, "You know that coffee shop with the blue bean hanging over the door? The one next to the row of bars on Crown Street?" I forced myself to meet his gaze again, adding, "Well, I work there now. I'm one of the singing baristas." I was pleased I was able to admit this without a fresh wave of embarrassment. As well, my voice sounded conversational and entirely normal.

His eyebrows furrowed, transforming his achingly handsome face into a sexy scowl. "You're working at a coffee shop? Why?" he demanded.

I shrugged. "Why do people work? To make money."

"Did your mother cut you off? After—"

I interrupted him, not wanting to hear what came after *after*. "No. Not at all. Nothing like that. I just—"

I stopped myself from explaining, abruptly wondering why we were talking at all. What was the point of this exercise in masochism? I had a nine-month-old wound that felt remarkably fresh. A dull ache had set up camp in my chest and was expanding, inflating to my throat, and pressing against my ribs.

"Listen." I sighed as I glanced beyond him again, my eyes beginning to sting. Now that the shock was wearing off, looking at him was becoming increasingly difficult. "I need to go. I have a train to catch."

"I'll drive you."

"No, thank you."

"Parker, let me drive you."

"No."

"Why not?" he asked quietly, sounding less pushy than curious.

I was about to respond with the truth, that being around him made me feel like I'd made no progress over the last nine months; that I was at a minimum infatuated with him if not still completely in love with him; that I had no desire to cry in his car. I had no desire to cry anywhere ever again.

But we were interrupted by the sound of a door closing, sauntering footsteps, and Abram tossing his arm over my shoulder.

I glanced up at my bandmate, confused by his sudden closeness. "Because she already has a ride," he drawled.

[5]
ACID-BASE EQUILIBRIA

I T TOOK MY brain five stunned seconds to engage and realize the ramifications of Abram's appearance and announcement. In the sixth second I pushed Abram off and away.

First of all, the implication was clearly that we were together.

In order to clarify, I announced loudly, "He's not my boyfriend. We're not dating."

Secondly, Martin was no longer looking at my face; he was looking at the spot where Abram's hand had rested on my shoulder.

And thirdly, my life was officially a cliché. I wondered if there were some unseen director just around the corner saying things like, *Okay, cue the new love interest. That's right, we want him to walk onto the scene at the worst possible moment.*

"But you still want me to give you a ride?" Abram asked, his tone chock full of zealously good-natured solicitousness.

"No. I don't want a ride. I don't want any rides. No rides for this girl." I pointed to myself with my thumbs, burning a brighter shade of red.

Martin's eyes flickered to mine and narrowed. I was being scrutinized.

Abram chuckled and nudged me flirtatiously with his elbow. He turned his smile to Martin. Martin was not smiling.

"Hi. I'm Abram. Katy's *bassist.*"

I shook myself and realized I'd made no introductions. "Right. Martin, this is Abram. He plays bass in the band. Abram, this is…Martin."

"Pleasure to meet you, Martin," Abram said, like it truly was a pleasure and offered his hand.

Martin's glare focused on the offered hand—the same hand that had seconds ago rested on my shoulder—then he lifted his gaze to Abram's. He reached forward and accepted Abram's hand for a shake. It was one of those weird, man handshakes that last too long, and where the hands turn a little white at the knuckles.

After several seconds I couldn't take it any longer. This was Martin Sandeke, grand Jedi Master of the short-tempered fist fight. *Ye Martin of old* never needed a reason to lose his temper. Granted, I hadn't seen him in almost nine months. But the last thing I needed was Abram with a busted jaw or—worse—a hurt hand. Willis might never forgive me.

So I reached forward, pulled them apart, and tugged Martin toward the street. "Aaaand we're done. Martin, would you be so kind as to drive me to Grand Central station?"

"You've got an impressive grip for such a pretty stockbroker," Abram yelled after us.

"I'm not a stockbroker, asshole." Martin's voice was low and belied the intensity of his irritation; I could feel hesitation in his steps, like he wanted to turn around and show Abram the meaning of an impressive grip, so I linked my arm through his and increased my pace.

Abram's laughter followed us as far as the street and I turned right even though I had no idea where his car was parked. Being so close to him was disconcerting and set my heart racing. We made it to the end of the block before Martin used my hold on his arm to stop us and pull us to the corner, out of the pedestrian traffic.

"Where are you going?"

I released him and took a step back, grateful for the space. "I don't know. I just wanted to get you away from Abram."

Martin's gaze swept over my face. "Why? Does he bother you often?"

"No, not at all. He's fine, and we get along fine. I think he was just trying to be helpful, in his own weird way."

He was still scrutinizing me as he shifted a step closer. "You two...ever...?"

I released a pained sigh when I understood what he was asking, deciding the evening had taken a sharp turn in the direction of completely preposterous. I closed my eyes, fought the urge to cover my face.

I won. I didn't cover my face. But I did take a minute to collect myself before saying, "That's none of your business. You said you didn't mind giving me a ride to the station." I opened my eyes but didn't manage to lift my gaze above his chin. "Will you please take me to Grand Central station so I can catch the train home?"

I could tell he wanted to say more, he wanted to yell, scream, and rage, and I couldn't wrap my mind around the implications of his short fuse, why he might be angry. I reminded myself that this was Martin Sandeke, who always expected people to jump when he said so, who'd never had a problem yelling at females and males and turtles and grass and furniture. I braced for his tantrum.

Instead he took a deep breath, silent but visible in the rising and falling of his chest, and nodded. "Yes. It would be my pleasure to give you a ride to the station."

I squinted at him, at his oddly polite words and tone. "Martin...?"

"Parker."

"Is there anything else you'd like to say before we're within the confines of your automobile? Anything loud perhaps?"

He shook his head and pulled his leather gloves out of his coat pocket, his tone soft, gentle even. "You should wear these. It's cold."

"You want to say something. What is it?"

"Weren't you the one who always told me..."

Martin reached for one of my hands and I lost my breath when his skin came in contact with mine. I'm not going to lie, my pants went a little crazy, and my heart did a flip then thumped uncomfortably—all signs I was still intensely in lust with him. He hesitated, his thumb drawing a gentle line from my wrist to the center of my palm, then he slid the large glove over my fingers with more care than necessary. They were warm from his pocket.

When he'd slipped both gloves in place he lifted his bewitching eyes and finished his thought. "I can't always have what I want."

* * *

THE CAR RIDE lasted less than fifteen minutes and was spent in wordless silence. Of note, it was also spent in a super fancy luxury automobile. I didn't know the make or model, but the dials were in Italian, the seats were buttery-soft leather, and when he accelerated it made a really satisfying *vroooom* sound.

I'm not ashamed to admit I took off one of the gloves just so I could caress his taut…leather seats.

When we arrived at the station I turned to him, taking off the second glove, and said benignly, "Thank you for the ride."

He gave me his profile as he nodded, his tone casual and polite. "No problem, any time."

Confused by his weird politeness, and feeling remarkably empty though my heart had set up camp in my throat, I placed his gloves on the armrest between us and opened the door to leave.

Then he said, "I read The Lord of the Rings."

I paused, my car door half open, and twisted to face him. "You did…?"

"Yes." He cleared his throat then met my stare; his was guarded, bracing. "I did."

"What did you think?"

"It was good…" Martin's eyes lost focus and moved to the headrest next to my face. "Slow at first. I thought they were never going to get out of that Hobbit village."

"Ah, yes. It only took them ten thousand pages and three thousand verses of elf songs."

He smirked. "Give or take a thousand."

I smiled, glanced down at my fingers where they twisted the strap of my bag.

I was surprised he'd read it and wasn't sure what it meant, if it meant anything. I was still pondering this revelation when his next words shocked the heck out of me.

"I don't think Frodo was responsible for the destruction of the ring."

My gaze jumped to his and I found Martin watching me attentively, again as though he was scrutinizing me. I struggled with my bewilderment for several seconds at his referencing our conversation from so many months ago.

Finally I managed to sputter, "You...you think Sam is ultimately responsible then?"

"No," he answered thoughtfully and then paused; he seemed to be memorizing my expression before continuing. "I think one couldn't have done it without the other. I think Frodo needed Sam as much as Sam needed Frodo, maybe even more."

I don't know why, but my eyes misted over even though I wasn't in danger of crying.

I gave him a soft smile, letting him see my pleased astonishment, and agreed quietly, "I think so, too."

We stared at each other and I felt something pass between us. I surmised it was closure because it felt peaceful and good. We'd shared a beautiful week. Because of him I was on a new path, a path I loved. He'd woken me up, even if I was kicking and screaming the whole time, and even if it broke my heart in the process.

Maybe we weren't meant for each other, but I finally realized that our time together wasn't a waste. It changed me and I would always be grateful to him for that, even if we'd parted under painful circumstances.

"Thank you," I said suddenly, breaking the moment.

"For what?"

I realized I couldn't say, *Thank you for waking me up to my passion* without sounding wacko, so instead I said, "For reading the book, I guess. And for the ride to the station." I tossed my thumb over my shoulder, my hand landing on the door to push it farther open.

"Right." He swallowed, glancing behind me. "You're welcome."

"I should go."

"Right." He nodded, giving me a flat smile and his profile.

"Goodbye, Martin."

I paused for a second, waiting for him to say goodbye, but he didn't. His jaw was set and his eyes were studying his rearview mirror. So I opened the door all the way and climbed out of his fancy car, shut it, and turned to Grand Central station.

I didn't hear him pull into traffic, but I didn't look back to check. I'd already spent too much time looking backward.

[6]

CONCENTRATIONS OF SOLUTIONS

S AM LIKED TO go '80s dancing on Thursday nights with several of her tennis pals. I'd never gone with her because I had no level of confidence in my non-ballroom dancing skills. But part of my theoretical state included opening myself up to new experiences, but not being so open-minded that my brain fell out.

Therefore, on Thursday night when Sam asked me if I wanted to go '80s dancing, I said yes.

I discovered that club dancing was basically just moving around however the heck I wanted; furthermore, I discovered it was a lot of fun. Sure, weird guys would sometimes sidle up to our cluster and try to cop a feel or insinuate themselves in the circle, especially since girls outnumbered the guys in our group. I quickly learned how to avoid stranger danger behavior by latching on to one of the three male tennis players who tagged along until the uninvited dude moved on.

This worked perfectly until the end of the night when Landon, one of the three tennis guys, asked for my number. I panicked and gave it to him as Sam watched on with an amused smirk.

As soon as we were back in our apartment, Sam started sniggering.

"What?"

"You're a good dancer," she said, eyeballing me.

"Thanks…?"

"What did you think of Kara?"

I had to really, really concentrate to remember which of the girls she was referencing. "Was Kara the one with pink hair?"

"No, Kara was the one with the Dungeons and Dragons mini dress."

"Oh! Kara, yes. I liked her."

"Well, she's looking for a place to stay next semester. How do you feel about another roommate?"

"Would we move?"

"Yeah, but I think there's a three-bedroom becoming available in our building sometime in February."

I scrunched my face, wrinkling my nose. "Can I think about it? You know how particular I am. Can I meet her a few more times? Hang out? See what she thinks of the chore chart and angry acoustic guitar music?"

"Sure. That makes sense. I'll set something up after New Year's." Sam began eyeballing me again. "Speaking of you being particular— sooooo Landon, huh?"

I gave her a pained look. "I didn't know how to say no. He's the first guy in my twenty years on this planet who has ever asked for my number."

"Technically he's not the first."

I grumbled, but said nothing.

"You didn't have a problem saying no to Martin last year in chemistry lab when he asked."

"But I thought Martin was a jerk. It's easy to say no to a jerk. Plus he never helped with tabulations so I felt no guilt. Landon seems like a nice guy. It's hard to say no when a nice guy asks so nicely, and he spent most of the night helping me keep creepers at bay."

"So you gave Landon your number because he was helpful and nice?"

"I don't know…maybe? I feel like I should reward his nice behavior." I hung my jacket up in the hall closet, noting I had two jackets on the rack and the rest were Sam's.

Sam shook her head, walking past me to the kitchen and calling over her shoulder, "When he calls don't go out with him. He's actually a douche canoe. And he's a big baby on the court."

"Then why did you invite him?" I followed her, abruptly in the mood for Cheesy Poofs dipped in Nutella.

"Because he's tall and menacing looking. His face reminds me of the eagle news reporter from the Muppets."

"He does have thick eyebrows, I should give him the name of the lady who waxes mine." I crossed to the cabinet and searched for the ingredients for my junk food fix. I was still down seventeen pounds from last year. I'd gained some back over the summer, but running around at the coffee shop and playing gigs at night kept me busy and cut into my cookie time.

"They're like caterpillars sitting on his face, I bet they're fuzzy... but forget Landon for a minute. What I want to know is, does this mean you're finally over Martin?"

I lamented the contents of the cabinet pitifully, partially because there was no Nutella and partially because I hadn't told Sam about my run-in with Martin over the previous weekend.

"What's wrong?"

"There's no Nutella, and I'm in the mood for Cheesy Poofs dipped in Nutella—"

"That's disgusting."

"—and I saw Martin last Saturday."

"Whoa! Wait, what?" She spun on me, her mouth open, her eyes wide.

"There's no Nutella—"

"Don't be clowning me. You know I want to hear about Martin, not your Nutella woes. You saw him? Where? When? How come you didn't tell me?"

I grabbed the Cheesy Poofs from the cabinet and turned to face her, feeling weary and wary of the subject already. "I don't know why I didn't tell you. I guess I needed to...no, that's not right. I think I didn't tell you because we kind of gave each other closure and I needed a few days to process it."

Her eyes abruptly narrowed. "He gave you 'closure'?"

"Yeah. At least I think he was trying to. Anyway, it doesn't matter. Seeing him was a total fluke. He was at a gig we were playing in New York. We talked a little, he drove me to the train station, then we said goodbye."

Actually, I said goodbye. He didn't say anything. But I'd assumed his goodbye was implied. As such, I felt comfortable with my version of the story.

Sam looked me up and down, her face twisted in a way that betrayed her disbelief and/or confusion with my story. At length she said, "Huh...that's weird."

"Why is that weird? Honestly it was kind of nice. We were both *adulting* like adult adults who behaved like adults."

"It's weird because of that one interview he gave in the fitness magazine over the summer. I think it was in Men's Health. Did you ever read that, by the way?"

I shook my head, taking a bite of a poof and lamenting the obnoxiously crunchy sound it made; I spoke around my chewing, orange cheesy food dust puffing from my mouth like a cloud. "No. Never read it."

"Hmm..."

I ate another poof as she studied me. *Crunch, crunch, crunch.*

I was just about to stuff my face with another when she said, "It's about you, you know."

"I... What?" I did not eat the poof. Instead I held it in front of my mouth as I frowned at my best friend.

"The interview, it's about you. Well, not the whole thing. Just...half of it."

I choked on nothing and could feel my eyes bug out of my head. "Wait, what? What? Why? What?"

"If you're feeling over him then it might not be a good idea to read it."

I stared at her, my mouth opening and closing as I struggled for words. Finally I settled on, "What did he say?"

"Are you going to read it?"

"Should I?"

"Are you over him?"

Was I?

Not knowing how to answer, I ate the suspended cheese-rice-puffed-food. This time the crunch felt satisfying instead of obnoxious, like an exclamation mark.

"Don't read it," she said suddenly.

"Maybe I want to."

"Then read it."

"Maybe I shouldn't."

She grinned. "Then don't."

* * *

I DIDN'T READ Martin's interview. At least, I hadn't read it as of Saturday night.

Friday and Saturday were busy; we played four gigs. Two afternoon holiday parties in Boston, one evening wedding in Yonkers, and one crazy late night Bat Mitzvah on Saturday in New Haven.

As well, I had a very odd conversation with Abram after the third set at the Yonkers wedding; it started with him saying, "What you need is a rebound guy."

I glanced over my shoulder, found him standing just to my right, facing me, his mouth curved in its perma-smirk.

"You mean for basketball?"

His smirk became a grin. "No. Not for basketball. For getting over that stockbroker douchebag."

I scrunched my face at Abram and sipped my Coke. "What are you talking about?"

He shifted a half step forward, lowering his voice. "A warm body, someone who's good at kissing and fucking. You need a rebound lay."

"*Oooohhhh...*" His meaning finally sank in, which only made me nervously gulp my Coke. My eyes grew wide as I tried to look everywhere but at him and my brain attempted to figure out how to extract myself from this conversation. His comment sounded a lot like, *Hey,*

I'd like to have sex with you to help you get over your boyfriend. Use me.

"I'm not offering," he clarified, correctly guessing that my abrupt bout of anxiety had everything to do with my assumption he wanted to be my rebound guy. I relaxed a bit, but then he added, "Though I wouldn't mind being the guy after the rebound guy."

I choked on my Coke.

He laughed, a deep, baritone laugh that sounded more sinister than merry, and he patted my back. "Hey, are you okay?"

I nodded, sucking in air through my nose, then coughing again.

"Did I surprise you?" His dark eyes were warm and still held his earlier laughter.

I continued nodding as his hand stopped patting my back and switched to stroking it instead. I shivered, because his hot palm and capable fingers against the thin material of my tuxedo shirt felt good and was sending little tingles along my spine; as well he was standing in my personal space, his magnetic maleness making me a bit dizzy.

I stepped away and caught his arm, halting his movements.

"So, I'm...that is to say, I'm—"

"You're not over the douchebag," he supplied, which wasn't what I was going to say; nevertheless it was the truth.

"No. I guess I'm not." My voice was raspy from my coughing fit.

"Then take my advice and get laid. Let someone else make you feel good. Hell, I bet Fitzy would cream himself at the thought."

I winced. "I don't like the idea of using people." Plus I didn't like the idea of having sex with someone when I wasn't in love, but if I'd said that to Abram, I assumed he would make fun of me.

"You need to. Sure, be upfront about the arrangement. Let him— whoever him is—know that it's a no-strings kind of thing. But do yourself a favor, and find a rebound guy. Otherwise it'll be years before you get over your ex."

I studied Abram for a long moment, releasing his arm and leaning away, wanting to really see him. He wasn't teasing; in fact, he appeared to be speaking from experience.

"How many rebound girls have you been with, Abram?"

His smirk was back, but it was somehow less sharp. "I've lost count."

"And have they helped?"

"Yeah. I mean, they *have* helped. I'm not nearly as miserable and pathetic as I was before..." He trailed off, and his smirk waned, his eyes turning serious. "But I'm not going to rebound forever."

"When will you stop?"

"When I see someone who's worth hurting for again. Someone worth the risk." He lifted his hand and tucked several strands of hair behind my ear, his fingers lingering on my throat. "Or she finally sees me."

* * *

By the time my alarm went off on Sunday morning for my shift at the Bluesy Bean, I was cursing Sam for telling me that Martin's interview was about me, or half about me.

I was also cursing Abram for planting strange ideas in my head—about a rebound guy, about him as a potential post-rebound guy. I was all mixed up. I was attracted to Abram, but hadn't allowed those feelings to deepen beyond passing interest. But what if I let myself actually get to know him? What if I *liked* him?

I was relieved to find my co-worker Chelsea already on the register when I arrived.

"You're early," she sang, giving me a bright smile.

"I thought I was late."

"No. Ten minutes early. It's been really quiet so far." She pulled her long, thick, blue-tinted braid over her shoulder.

I fastened my apron and took stock of our milk supply. "If today is anything like last Sunday, we can expect a mad rush with all the Christmas shoppers."

"That means Christmas carol requests. You'll have to sing with me." Chelsea gave me a wink and a smile.

I gave her a smile that likely looked more like a grimace. "Oh...yay."

She laughed, then turned her attention to the front of the store where two early morning customers had just entered.

I kind of loved Chelsea...from a distance. I think everyone loved Chelsea from a distance. She was charming, incredibly talented, clever, and crazy fun. As well, she had one of the most beautiful soprano voices I'd ever heard. She was also thrice divorced at the age of twenty-eight. Given the Marilyn Monroe resemblance of both her face and body, men loved her. They loved her a whole lot.

But I suspected Chelsea loved the stage and the thrill of admiration. When she wasn't singing for wages at the local community theater, she was singing for tips at the Bluesy Bean, flirting with her legion of admirers. I was grateful that she craved the spotlight; her willingness to be the center of attention allowed me to settle into a comfortable zone.

And speaking of zones, since starting at the coffee shop three weeks ago, I found it was easy to zone out while making lattes and cappuccinos. Cooking in general, and making coffee specifically, was a lot like chemistry lab. Thus, as I set to work, I was able to meditate on the carousel of pros and cons circling around my brain.

Pro - if I read Martin's interview, then I could stop obsessing about whether or not I should read the interview.

Con - if I read Martin's interview, I might start obsessing about the content of the interview.

And so the day proceeded in this way and all was well. More precisely, all was relatively normal until just after the mid-afternoon rush died down. I was cleaning up the mess associated with coffee grounds and drippings accumulating over time on a tile floor when I heard Chelsea say under her breath, "We've got a Chris Pine at twelve o'clock."

Chelsea had a labeling system for men.

She told me she was looking for a Brad Pitt (older version) or a Chris Pine (younger version). Someone charismatic, beautiful, smart, wealthy, and dedicated to a cause other than himself. I asked her if she'd ever considered looking for a Neil deGrasse Tyson or a Francis Collins. Someone who wasn't necessarily physically stunning, but whose brain and goodness more than made up for any external lack of overt attractiveness.

She'd snorted at me, rolled her eyes, and said, "If I have to have sex with the guy, I don't want to have to do it in the dark all the time."

It was an interesting perspective...one which I found disturbing. On one hand I understood why attraction was an essential element of chemistry between two people. But her inability or unwillingness to appreciate attractiveness beyond the skin and see the person as a whole made me feel a little sorry for her.

Presently, curious about her Chris Pine, I straightened from my task and tried to nonchalantly glance over the coffee makers. That's when I spotted Martin walking into the café.

My eyes widened in surprise and I ducked back behind the espresso machine, shock and a strange panic keeping me motionless for several seconds while I had a silent argument with myself:

What in the name of the cosmos is he doing here?

Perhaps it's a coincidence.

What am I supposed to do???

...just act normal.

What's normal?

I briefly considered staying hidden for as long as possible, but then I realized it would be weirder to suddenly appear once he ordered his drink than to gradually straighten now.

Maybe I could pretend I was cleaning the floor...which is what I was doing just moments ago, before he walked in.

Or maybe I could actually finish cleaning the floor.

This idea seemed to make the most sense, so that's what I did.

Unfortunately, cleaning the floor only took me five more seconds. So when I straightened, I struggled to act normal. I didn't know what to do or where to look and had abruptly forgotten how to breathe and stand with my arms at my sides. Yet even as a fierce blush lifted to my cheeks, I was determined to make the imminent encounter as benign as possible.

"Welcome to the Bluesy Bean. What can I get you?" I heard Chelsea say using her husky voice.

I decided I just needed to go through the motions of normalcy, do what I would normally do. So I picked up the towel I'd been using to mop the floor. I turned and deposited it in the bucket under the sink, then moved to wash my hands.

"I'll have a large Americano." Martin's voice caused a shiver of awareness to race down my spine. I endeavored to ignore it.

"Room for cream?"

"No."

I finished washing my hands and turned back to my machine, refilled the espresso grounds, and set the dial. In less than ten seconds I was going to have to reach over and grab his cup and I would be fine. I didn't know why my heart and brain were freaking out so much.

"Really? How about sugar?" In my peripheral vision I saw Chelsea leaning on the counter. She often did this to take full advantage of her low-cut top.

"What? No. No sugar."

"Oh. I was just curious how you take your coffee. I like mine sweet and creamy."

There was a distinct pause, a thick silence difficult to ignore. It lengthened, grew, then suddenly felt untenable. So I glanced up and found Chelsea watching me, her eyes narrowed in confusion. Then I glanced at Martin. He was watching me, too.

His stare was pointed, like he'd been watching me for longer than a few seconds and was waiting for me to look at him.

All at once I felt caught.

"Oh… Hi, Martin." My acting skills were pathetic, but I tried my best at genuine surprise. It might have helped that I was feeling a little out of breath.

"I was hoping you'd be working today." Still looking at me, he passed Chelsea a twenty.

Her eyes bounced between us, narrowing more.

"That's right, I forgot. I told you I worked here."

"Are you going to make my coffee?" He grinned, leaving his twenty on the counter for Chelsea to pick up, and floated closer to where I was mostly hidden by the machines. But I wasn't really hidden from him because he was so tall. He could easily see over the row of contraptions. Realizing this, I stopped twisting my fingers and reached for a large cup.

"Yes. I am your barista at this fine establishment. It is my pleasure to make you coffee." I lamented the fact that, due to my uneasiness, I sounded like an android.

He must've noticed my odd speech pattern too, because he asked, "Do you always talk like that?"

"Like what? Like Mr. Roboto?"

"No, like awesome."

My lips parted and I blinked at him, his comment catching me completely off guard. When his eyes began to dance and his grin widened, I realized he was using our past to tease me. This might have pissed me off two weeks ago, Martin thinking he had the right to tease me about anything, but the fact that he'd given me his gloves when I was cold and read The Lord of the Rings somehow made his teasing not...bad.

"You're weird," I blabbered unthinkingly and shook my head at him and his bizarre teasing. But I had to twist my lips to the side to keep from returning his contagious smile. "Why are you here, weirdo?"

He seemed pleased with my name-calling and drifted closer until he was directly in front of me, only the machines between us. "I want to talk to you. Do you have a break soon?"

"Umm..." I stalled by commencing coffee creation; I flipped the brew switch and moved two doppio cups under the dual espresso dispenser.

I was way overdue for a break. Chelsea had taken three, and I'd taken one. I glanced at Chelsea, found her watching us with a frown. It wasn't an angry frown or a sinister frown; rather, it was a *the world has ceased making sense* frown. Her brain was obviously working overtime trying to figure out how I knew her Chris Pine, aka my Martin Sandeke.

"S-s-s-sure. Let me finish your Americano and I'll make myself some tea. Go grab a table." I tilted my chin to the one by the window, in the center of the café.

"Good. Will you please bring me a muffin? I haven't eaten since breakfast."

I could only nod and stare at him, again caught off guard by his conversational tone—like we were old friends—as well as the use of the word *please*. The smile he gave me before he departed was softer, smaller, but somehow more devastating than his others. As I watched him ignore the spot I'd indicated in favor of a very private table in the corner, I mulled over his strange behavior.

The smiling.

The teasing.

The manners.

The lack of bluntness and demands.

It was all very disconcerting.

Disconcerting, distressing, confusing, alarming, perplexing, odd...

* * *

"You make good coffee." Martin sipped his hot beverage, his eyes watching me over the rim.

"Technically I just press the buttons." I was having difficulty relaxing beneath his gaze, so I fidgeted with my tea cup and spoon.

"Parker, just take the compliment and say thank you."

"I won't. I won't take it because I don't deserve it. The machines make good coffee, as do the bean growers and bean roasters."

His face told me he thought I was being ridiculous. "Fine, then you're an excellent button pusher."

"Thank you. I accept the compliment and acknowledge that I excel at pushing buttons."

"Especially my buttons." He paired this with a smirk and an eyebrow lift.

I huffed, irritated I'd walked right into that verbal trap, and yet reluctantly amused by the word play. "Very funny, Sandeke."

His smirk became a smile. Then he laughed and my heart gave a little leap.

Suddenly, it was nine months ago and we were on a plane headed for the island. I was faced with the heady sight of a happy Martin. It was a reminder that happiness on Martin was a revelation of beauty and physical perfection married to excellent and infectious good-mood vibes.

But this time I didn't laugh. My heart felt tender and wary of this Martin, because he was so easy to like. So I crossed my arms over my chest, protecting myself from the onslaught of his magnetic charisma, and waited for his laughter to recede.

When he saw I wasn't charmed, his smile faded and he straightened in his seat, clearing his throat as though he were about to speak.

I spoke first, wanting to get right to the point. "Why are you here? What do you want to talk about?"

He must've read something in my expression, perhaps a hardness in my eyes that told him I was low on patience, because when he spoke next, everything about his demeanor changed.

His eyes grew sharp, the set of his jaw rigid, and his shoulders leaned back in the chair, making him appear taller, more imposing, and yet relaxed at the same time. Based on this body language and what I knew about power dynamics from watching my mother, I surmised we were about to enter into a negotiation.

I was quickly proven correct.

"I want to discuss the terms of our friendship."

I stared at him, careful to keep my face devoid of expression, even though I wanted to yell, *WHAT THE HELL ARE YOU TALKING ABOUT?*

Instead I said, "What friendship?"

"The one you promised would always be mine if I ever wanted it, no matter what happened between us."

This made me blink several times, succeeded in cracking my calm exterior, but I managed to say in a steady voice, "You can't be serious."

"I am. I'm completely serious. You promised I would always have *a safe place* with you, and now I want that safe place."

53

This was the Martin I remembered. This was the unyielding, demanding, blunt boy that had stolen then broken my heart.

I gritted my teeth and willed the rising tide of so many different emotions to stay buried. Obviously anger was the first, the strongest to swell in my chest and try to choke me. Again, he must've seen something shift or build in my expression because, and to my astonishment, he leaned forward and his austere business façade yielded, his eyes turned beseeching.

"Listen, I'm not here to take more than you're willing to offer. Obviously you can tell me to go fuck myself. All I'm asking for is a chance to be your friend. Because, even though things between us didn't end well, I still trust and respect you more than anyone I've ever met. You are," he paused, gathered a deep breath, his gaze searching as it skated over my face, "Kaitlyn, you are incredibly honorable, and reasonable, and good. I could really use your advice. I could really use some honorable and good in my life."

"But not reason?" I questioned, stalling, not sure what to make of this impassioned speech.

"No. I have plenty of reason. But without honor and goodness, reason isn't worth much."

My lips parted in surprise and I felt my mask of indifference slip at his shockingly wise words. He looked earnest and focused and I knew I was already teetering on the edge of acceptance.

But the acrid taste of past heartbreak and the bitterness of his previous betrayal held me back, keeping my altruistic instincts from taking over.

And something else, something petty and entirely based on vanity.

When we had this conversation in the past, at the cottage on the island, he'd told me at the time that he could never be indifferent enough to be my friend. That he would always want me too fiercely to settle for just friendship.

If he wanted to be friends now, that could only mean he'd become indifferent to me. He didn't want *me* anymore. And that made my vain, selfish heart hurt. This realization stung, because I couldn't imagine being able to achieve the same indifference toward him.

"You don't have to answer me now." His gaze and tone were steady, sensible.

I wanted to tell him he'd hurt me too deeply, that this newfound indifference toward me that allowed him to ask for friendship was hurting me now. But I couldn't. Because that would be giving him the knowledge he still had power over my feelings.

Instead I opted to make the decision his and, by doing so, I hoped it would push him away. "Let's say I only agree to be your friend if you tell the world your father is an evil asshole and that our families were never close, that he never had influence over my mother. What would you do?"

I didn't expect Martin to grin, but that's what he did as he quickly replied, "Parker, I already did that. I did that, like, two months ago."

Again I felt my mask slip and I blinked at him in astonishment. "You did?"

"Yes. The interview was in the Washington Post. Haven't you read any of the interviews I've given?"

I shook my head and answered honestly, "No. I haven't. I've been avoiding them."

"None of them?" Something like dawning realization cast a shadow over his features.

Again I shook my head. "No. I didn't…" I took a deep breath and forced myself to continue the thought, "I didn't want to know about you. I didn't want to know what you were doing."

This was mostly because given how well and unaffected he'd looked the last time I saw him, and how wretched and heartbroken I'd been, I assumed he'd quickly moved on with his life, maybe even dated other women. In fact, given the fact he had a date last week at my show, I was now certain he'd dated other women.

I didn't need to see magazine spreads and page sixes of Martin Sandeke, the most eligible bachelor of the universe, hitting the town with his legion of admirers.

Meanwhile I hadn't been able to move on.

He stared at me for a long moment, his grin waning into a pensive frown.

"Are you going to read them?"

I shrugged, tried to look unaffected. "Probably not."

Martin's open gaze morphed into an irritated glare at my statement.

Abruptly he said, "I searched everywhere trying to find out about you, what you were doing, how you were. That's how I found your band."

"My band? Wait, what?"

"I hired your band to play that party last week. Well, my PA did. It was for a group of startups focused on rural technology education initiatives. It's a new project of mine."

I didn't hear anything after, *I hired your band to play that party last week.*

"Why would you do that?"

"For the same reason I'm sitting here right now." Martin sounded like he was on the border of exasperated and angry.

My gaze drifted to the table between us as I tried to sort through this mountain of surprising information. He hired my band? Why? To have the opportunity to talk to me? But then he brought a date to the event? What the what?

But before I made it very far, he stood, drawing my attention and focus back to him. He'd pulled out his wallet.

"Listen, you take some time. You think about it. Here's my number."

I accepted his card without looking at it as I was too busy staring at him with muddled incredulity.

Dumbly I said, "You have a card?"

"Yes. It has my personal cell phone number. If I don't hear from you I'll stop by again next week."

"So...you what? Have other business cards that have a different number on them? Ones without your personal cell phone number?" Leave it to me to be caught up in the details.

His frown intensified, as though I'd asked a trick question, then he eventually responded, "Yes. My other cards have the number of my PA. So what?"

"You realize you're a twenty-one-year-old with two different business cards, right? And a PA. And likely a corner office someplace." This was all coming out of my mouth stream of consciousness, as I was thinking and speaking at the same time.

He blinked at me, shook his head like he didn't understand my meaning, like *of course* he had a corner office.

"That makes you both impressive and ridiculous. Please tell me your towels aren't monogrammed."

Martin set his jaw as he recognized my meaning, but I could see the reluctant smile in his eyes as he peered down at me.

"They are monogrammed, aren't they? And you've probably taken to calling them 'linens.'"

His lips pressed together in a firm but rueful line. Martin crossed his arms and said, "Is this what I can expect from our friendship? You giving me shit about my linens?"

"Absolutely," I said, then indicated to his wrist with my chin, "and your fancy watches."

"So, is that a yes?" he pushed, lifting a single eyebrow.

"It's a…it's a maybe."

[7]

AVOGADRO'S NUMBER AND THE MOLE

N OW THAT I was working, I typically didn't have a chance to look at the agenda for the weekly family call until ten minutes before I was supposed to dial in. We'd shifted the time due to my new work schedule, which was nice. But it also meant I was rushing around just before, and I never seemed to have enough time to review the materials.

This wasn't usually a problem. However, today, five minutes before I was supposed to call into Skype, I read the agenda and I spotted a new item.

Benefit and Campaign Fundraiser - Kaitlyn to perform.

I frowned at the topic. But there was nothing to do about it, no reason to ask for clarification ahead of time since our meeting was just about to start. So I highlighted the line and wrote a big question mark on my paper copy of the agenda. Then I opened the Skype session and dialed in.

"Hello?" I heard George, my mother's PA, on the line. He hadn't activated the video yet.

"Hey, George. It's Kaitlyn."

"Yes. I see you. Let me switch on the video." I heard some rustling as he added, "Your mother is on the phone with Senator Peterson, trying to talk him off the ledge. She'll be right back and then we can get started. Your father was called into surgery."

"Sounds good." I scanned the rest of the agenda. Everything else looked fine. Once his face popped up on my computer screen I asked, "Hey, George. I have a question about one of the new items on the agenda, the one about the benefit and fundraiser."

"Oh, yes. Your mother has a campaign fundraiser coming up in May. The week after is a benefit concert for Children's Charities. Both are in New York. She thought it would be good for you to perform at one or both."

I saw my expression in the little box located in the bottom right corner of my computer screen. I looked just as surprised as I felt. But what my expression didn't show was the spike of panic. The idea of performing in front of a crowd of people who knew who I was, who my mother was, held absolutely no allure for me. Being just another member of a random band meant I was anonymous. But being Senator Parker's daughter, on stage in front of hundreds or thousands of people sounded horrible and terrifying.

"Really? That seems strange." My voice cracked a little.

He shrugged, scratching the top of his bald head. "No. Not if you think about it. You've always been gifted with music. I remember when you were thirteen and you taught yourself all of Beethoven's sonatas without sheet music. When music was just a hobby for you, asking you to perform would have been an exploitation of your private life. But now that it's your chosen career, this will be beneficial for you both."

That's what I liked about George, he was a straight shooter, never minced (or chopped) words, just said things plain and simple.

My mother popped into the picture and gave me a wide smile as she adjusted the computer so they were both visible. "Did George tell you about William?"

"Yes, Dad was called in," I said.

"Since he can't make it today we'll skip over the house stuff and hold it until the next meeting," my mother clarified, still smiling warmly. She looked so happy to see me.

"Sounds good." I smiled back.

This was only our second week using Skype instead of a dedicated conference line (with no video) and I really liked it. I liked seeing my mom and dad (and George); it made them feel more real. I liked they could see me and see I was doing well.

"We were just talking about agenda item four," George said, drawing my mother's attention to a piece of paper he had placed in front of her on the table.

"Oh, yes." Mom glanced at me, her smile even wider. I could see the excitement in her eyes. "Let me tell you about this, I think it's a great opportunity for you."

"George already filled me in on the basics. You want me to perform in front of people for a campaign fundraiser and for a benefit, both in New York in May?"

"Yes, well, that's the gist of it. There will be a large number of industry professionals present, people from Broadway and Hollywood at both events. I know you have your little wedding band, but I also know you're capable of so much more than that. Just think of it as a way to network and make connections for your career."

I tried to keep my face from betraying the pang I felt when she'd said *little band*. I know she didn't mean anything by it, because—to her—it was a little band. Whereas for me it was a giant leap of self-actualization.

I had to clear my throat of emotion before responding. "Would I be performing with others? As part of an ensemble? Would there be practices leading up to the performances?"

"No. You'd be solo, and hopefully playing one of your own compositions if you can have that ready in time. I'm sure it won't be a problem for you." She was distracted as she answered because her cell phone was ringing again; she didn't see me sit back in my chair or the color drain from my face.

"I'm so sorry, Kaitlyn, but I have to take this call." She turned an apologetic and frustrated gaze to the computer screen. "We'll hold the rest of the agenda until after the holidays."

I nodded, relieved I would be given a reprieve from having to give her an answer. She stood up again as she answered her cell phone, leaving George and I on the call.

"Next week is Christmas," George noted absentmindedly. "Did you mail your packages yet? Do you need me to send you a shipping label?"

"I'll mail everything on Tuesday, before I head to New York. A label would be nice," I answered distractedly, trying to imagine myself playing one of my own compositions in front of industry professionals. I grimaced, feeling slightly sick. It's not that I lacked confidence. It's that I disliked people. I especially disliked people looking at me with expectations and judgment. I just wanted to play music.

"Sounds good. I have the address of where you'll be staying next week in Brooklyn while you're up there playing shows. According to our last call, you are planning to stay with your bandmate, Janet Deloach, and her two friends, the Mr. Bergmans. Is that still correct?" George asked, obviously running down his list of questions.

"Yes."

"Your father will be calling you this week just to talk. He expressed his extreme disappointment that he had to be absent from today's call and wished me to tell you that he loves you and misses you very much. Is the calendar you send for this week still valid?"

I smiled at my dad's words—as read by George—and answered his question, "Yes. There haven't been any changes to my calendar."

"Okay, then I think we're finished." He glanced up and gave me his trademark, flat and friendly George smile. "Merry Christmas, Kaitlyn."

I mustered up enough wherewithal to return his smile with one of my own. "Merry Christmas, George."

Then we ended the call.

* * *

"SAM, CAN I ASK YOU A QUESTION?"

"Do it." She was studying her menu. We'd opted for Italian tonight; she could never decide between the lasagna and the chicken carbonara.

I put my menu down and folded my hands, readying myself to ask a question that had been forming in my mind for the last several months.

"When did you feel like it was okay—like, it was appropriate—for you as a girl or a woman or whatever, at what age was it that you felt comfortable, or wanted to dress and act, and I guess be perceived as—"

"Spit it out already. Just ask the question."

"Fine. At what age did you feel like you wanted to be sexy?"

Her eyes darted to mine, grew wide, and she stared at me from across the table.

"Is sexy a difficult word for you to say out loud?"

I shook my head. "No. But it's a difficult concept for me to contemplate and not be confused. I don't think I fully understand sexy."

She nodded thoughtfully, her eyes drifting back to her menu.

We were on our Monday night date…with each other. We'd started doing this after we both secured employment over the summer. It was an excuse to get dressed up because otherwise I would spend all my time in either a tuxedo uniform, or baggy jeans and a men's concert T-shirt.

I was trying to explore the concept of traditional femininity— perfume, makeup, matching lacey undergarments, dresses, jewelry, pretty shoes—because I didn't want to dismiss dressing up having never given it a real chance.

Yes, I recognized that "traditional femininity" was historically steeped in misogyny. However, I also recognized deciding to eschew traditional femininity because of chauvinism was just as flawed as subscribing to lace underwear just because men seemed to like it.

I wanted to explore this part of myself for me, not in spite of or because of another person. If I was going to change my style or add to it, I wanted to do it because of how it made me feel. Not because I wanted to make someone else feel better or view me differently.

At least, that's how it had started. But after seeing Martin last Sunday, and realizing how hurt I'd been by the fact he now viewed me as a platonic friend, I was starting to wonder if I had deeper, subconscious motives for exploring my femininity.

An example of one of my less than healthy thoughts: *Maybe if I'd been sexier and more traditionally girly, Martin wouldn't have been able to get over me so fast.*

So…yeah. Not healthy. Which was why I still hadn't looked up or read any of Martin's interviews. I didn't want him to be the motivation for my decisions.

Of note, I still hadn't decided what to think about Martin's offer of friendship or about wearing makeup and frilly garments.

Regarding the clothes, at first everything itched and I felt like my movement was restricted. After a while though, after four girl-dates, I began looking forward to glamming it up, and found myself noticing other peoples' makeup and clothes with appreciation.

"Hmm," she said at last, still studying her menu. "That's a really interesting question."

I took a sip of my water and waited for her to answer.

"Do I want the lasagna or the carbonara?"

"The carbonara."

"Okay. Decision made." She placed the menu on the table and closed it, giving me a searching stare. "So you want to know when I started to feel sexy or when I started wanting to feel sexy?"

"Were they different ages?"

"Yes."

"Then tell me when you started wanting to feel sexy."

"I guess I was fourteen."

My mouth fell open. "Fourteen?"

"Yes. Or maybe thirteen, or twelve. I remember wanting to be sexy like the girls in the magazines."

"What magazines?"

"Vogue, Glamour, Cosmo."

"You read Cosmo at twelve?"

"Yes. When did you start reading Cosmo?"

I sputtered for a moment, then admitted, "Never. I've never read Cosmo."

"Most of it is garbage, meaningless fluff, stupid stuff. But they sometimes have brilliant articles and short stories. Also, it's how I learned to do the cat-eye."

"You mean that black eyeliner thing?"

"Yeah. They had step-by-step instructions with pictures."

I thought about this, the fact she'd been twelve when she'd first wanted to be sexy. Meanwhile I wasn't sure if I wanted to be sexy, even now.

"Do you feel like twelve was too early? Too young?"

She shrugged, wrinkling her nose. "I don't know. I got my period at ten. Five hundred years ago women were getting married at fourteen or fifteen. In some parts of the world they still do."

"But in modern times and western culture, our context being the here and now, do you think it's too early?"

Sam squinted at me. "Yes and no. On one hand, I think it's natural to be curious about sexuality. But on the other hand, I think girls are caught in this terrible net of perpetual disappointment. We're not really allowed to talk about sex, or ask questions about it, or be interested in it. If we are interested and if we like it, then we're labeled as *easy* or *sluts*. If we're not interested, then we're frigid and repressed...we're prudes. It's like, we see images of women being objectified every-where. And then we're told to act and dress like a man at work and school, or else no one will take us seriously—even other women won't take us seriously. Basically, women are fucked."

"That's depressing."

"Yes. Yes it is. How about you? When did you first think about being sexy?"

I gathered a large breath and shook my head slightly. "I guess the first time I thought about being sexy was when I was seventeen."

"Wow."

"Yeah. So that makes me a frigid, repressed prude?"

"Yes. Absolutely. And I'm a whorey slut. Why seventeen?"

"Honestly, it was only because I could never get Carter—"

"Your gay boyfriend."

"Yes, my gay boyfriend who I didn't know was gay. I could never get him to do anything but kiss me, and only in front of other people.

He never wanted to do anything when we were alone together. I thought maybe it was because I wasn't sexy."

Sam watched me for a bit, considering this, then asked, "But... didn't you ever want to be sexy for yourself? Just to feel good?"

"What do you mean?"

"Like, put on a new outfit or eye shadow? Not because someone was going to see you, but just because you wanted to dress up and feel pretty?"

I began shaking my head halfway through her second question. "No. Never."

"Hmm..." she sat back in her chair and inspected me, then pressed, "And you're sure you like guys?"

My mouth fell open in startled outrage and I leaned forward to loudly whisper, "Sam, just because I'm not a girly-girl doesn't mean that I...that I'm—"

"That you prefer mares to stallions, I get it. I just don't understand it. I always thought you wanted to dress that way because you didn't like attention."

"What way?"

"You know, frumpy."

"I dress frumpy?"

"Kind of, actually, yes. Yes, you dress frumpy... frumpily... whatever."

"Because I don't wear form-fitting clothing or clothes that bare my skin and highlight my body?"

"Kaitlyn," she gave me an *oh, come on* look, then continued, "baggy, shapeless clothes that cover your body is the definition of dressing frumpish. Hell, your tuxedo for work makes you look hot in comparison, as at least it shows off your ass."

I opened my mouth to protest but then realized she was right. Baggy T-shirts, oversized jeans with the cuff cut off...on most days I dressed frumpily.

Do I want to dress frumpily? Should I even care? What is wrong with me that I never realized I dress like a frump?

As if seeing my internal struggle, Sam quickly added, "If you want to dress in baggy clothes then dress in baggy clothes. If you like it, then to hell with what everyone else thinks, including me."

"But, I don't… I mean…I—"

"Ladies? Are you ready to order?" Our waitress chose that moment to return to the table, giving me a brief reprieve from trying to verbally untangle my thoughts.

"I'll have the lasagna and she'll have the lobster ravioli." Sam picked up both of our menus and handed them to the server. I usually didn't mind that she ordered for me, because I always ordered the same thing.

But for some reason, this time I was incredibly irritated by her assumption I would order the ravioli. What if I wanted the steak? Or a salad?

"Actually," I interjected, giving the waitress an apologetic smile, "I'll have the duck ziti."

Our server nodded, like it was no big deal, then left us to our discussion.

Sam lifted an eyebrow at me as she raised her water glass to her lips, saying before sipping, "The duck ziti, eh?"

I nodded firmly. "That's right. The duck ziti."

"Not the lobster ravioli?"

"No. I'm tired of lobster ravioli."

She studied me for a long moment, replacing her glass, crossing her arms, and narrowing her eyes. I mimicked her stance and her glare.

"That's fine. Don't get the lobster ravioli if you don't want it. Try duck ziti, try the steak."

"I will."

"But just know, no matter what you order and no matter what you eat, it's your decision. If you want the lobster ravioli every day for the rest of your life, there is nothing wrong with that. Don't change your order just because you think you're supposed to, because society tells you it's weird to order the same thing every time. You have to live with your entrée, not society, not me. You."

"But how will I know whether I like the duck ziti if I don't try it?"

She paused, considering me, her mouth a flat, thoughtful line. Then she sighed, saying, "I guess you won't. I guess you do have to try the ziti. I just don't want you feeling pressure to change, because you're pretty awesome just how you are. It would make me sad if you started ordering steak when you really want ravioli."

"This analogy has officially gone too far. We both know we're talking about my tendency to hide. It doesn't matter if it's a closet or it's baggy clothes. I can't keep hiding from new things."

"But, you're not. Look at you, you're all dressed up. You have your eyebrows professionally waxed and shaped. You're in a band. You're a singing barista. You try new things."

"Yes. At a snail's pace I try new things. When I feel completely safe, I try new things. When I'm with you, I try new things." I gave her a small smile, leaned forward, and put my hand on the table, palm up. She fit hers inside mine and returned my grin.

"Sam, you're a good friend. I want to try new things, even when those things don't feel entirely safe. I want to try new things before I'm even certain I want to try those new things. It's time for me to take some risks."

"You're not talking about drugs, are you? Because, smack is whack."

I laughed and rolled my eyes. "No. I'm talking about buying a T-shirt that fits. Maybe a new dress, so I don't have to keep borrowing yours."

What I didn't add, because I hadn't yet told her about seeing Martin at the coffee shop, was that trying new things also included agreeing to a friendship with Martin Sandeke.

THE NEXT MORNING Sam was out of the apartment.

Even so, I shut the door to my room in order to achieve maximum privacy. I was going to call Martin.

I'd thought about making the call from the bathroom, just in case Sam came home unexpectedly, but I decided that was taking things a bit too far.

I gathered several deep breaths as I psyched myself up. Then, feeling an odd surge of courage, I grabbed my phone, tapped in his number, and lifted the cell to my ear.

It rang three times.

I was trying to figure out whether or not I should leave a voicemail —should it come to that—when it was answered.

"Hello?" asked a female voice on the other end.

I frowned, glancing at the card he'd given me, wondering if I had the wrong number or if I'd been given his PA's phone number instead.

"Hi. Hello, um—I'm sorry. I think I might have the wrong number. I'm calling for Martin Sandeke."

"No. You have the right number." Her accent was British.

"Oh. Okay. Is this his PA?"

"No. This is Emma Cromwell, his partner. Who is this?"

Partner. Partner? Oh! ...partner. Well, barnacles.

I closed my eyes and released a silent sigh, felt my stomach fall painfully to my feet. I sat on my bed and cleared my throat before responding, "I'm...Parker."

"Kaitlyn Parker?" It might have been my imagination, but she sounded a little irritated by this news.

Which meant she knew who I was. That was just lovely. Now I felt like an evil usurper. Here I was, the ex-girlfriend, calling *her* Martin. I was pretty sure that if I were in a committed relationship, I wouldn't want my boyfriend's ex calling him.

How did I even get here?

I nodded, then realized she couldn't see me, so I said, "Yes. Kaitlyn Parker. If now is a bad time, you can just have him call me later. But no rush."

"He's just getting out of the shower, so I'll have him call you back when he's not busy."

I nodded again, my heart joining my stomach, beyond my feet, falling down to the center of the earth. "Sure. Like I said, no rush."

"Mmm-hmm. Goodbye."

"Good—" I didn't get to say 'bye, because she'd already ended the call.

* * *

I WAS COMING to recognize I was probably still very much in love with Martin. Maybe I always would be. This thought made me want to cry, but I didn't.

Instead I decided to go shopping because I had Christmas presents to buy. If there was one thing I'd learned over the last nine months it was the importance of going through the motions. Sam called this: Fake it 'til you make it.

This last week leading up to the big holiday was going to be crazy busy. We had two or three gigs a day, starting tomorrow. Last minute office parties, hotel feature events, themed weddings, and holiday brunches. As they were in New York, I was planning to stay in the city for the week with Janet (my bandmate) and two of her friends.

I was an efficient shopper, mostly because I'd always been ambivalent to shopping. I quickly grabbed the items on my list and was finished, ready to head back to the apartment after two short hours. But for the first time in perhaps my entire life, I didn't want to go back to the apartment and be alone. So I window-shopped for a bit.

Strangely, window shopping turned into store buying, and after another two hours I was back at the apartment with three new pairs of women's jeans, several fitted but delightfully nerdy tops, four matching bra and panty sets—because they were on super sale—and two new pairs of shoes. I also bought myself some cozy socks with Abraham Lincoln on the calves, because he was my second favorite president.

Once home, I unpacked then repacked my bag, deciding to take some of my new stuff with me, then went to the kitchen in search of hot chocolate.

That's when my phone rang. I didn't look at the number before answering because I was still thinking about how much I'd enjoyed my morning. I was floating in my new-clothes-euphoria.

"Hello?"

"Kaitlyn?"

*Aaaand...*now I was crashing back down to earth.

"Hi, Martin." I endeavored to ignore the familiar ache in my chest.

70

"I hoped this might be your number. You called earlier? You should have left a message."

This gave me pause, but then I started speaking and thinking at the same time. "I did leave a message."

"Really? I didn't get a voicemail."

"No, I left a message with your…" I tripped over the word, but then forced myself to say it. I knew it was better to rip the bandage off than to try to peel it back slowly. "I left a message with your girlfriend."

He was silent for a beat, then asked, "My girlfriend?"

"Emma."

"Emma? No. No, no, no. Emma is not my girlfriend. She's my partner."

"Partner, girlfriend, significant other, sensei—whatever."

"No, Kaitlyn." I heard him laugh lightly, like he was both relieved and anxious. "Emma is my *business* partner. We've never…we're not like that."

This gave me pause. I was fairly certain Emma had sounded irritated on the phone earlier when she'd discovered my name. Perhaps I'd been imagining it.

"Anyway, you called?"

"Yes. I did. I called." I glanced around the kitchen as though it might help me figure out what to say next. My mind hadn't quite reconciled the fact that Emma wasn't his girlfriend; my heart and stomach were looking to me for direction on whether to soar or switch places, and I had none to offer.

Should I feel happy? Relieved? Ambivalent? Unsurprisingly, the kitchen offered no guidance.

I must've been quiet for too long, because Martin asked, "Are you still there?"

"Yes. Sorry, I'm here. Yes, I called. I wanted to talk to you about the terms of our friendship."

"Our friendship?" I heard the smile in his voice.

"Yes. I was thinking, you and I…I mean, even though we only spent a week together, I feel like—on some level—we became friends.

71

And I liked our friendship, I liked you." I closed my eyes, winced, and covered my face with my hand, feeling mortified and glad he couldn't see the monster blush creeping up my neck.

"I liked you"...really? You are so bad at this.

But then Martin surprised me by saying, "I liked you, too. If you remember, I liked you a lot."

This made me laugh my relief, pleased I wasn't the only one risking part of myself and my pride.

I answered quietly, "Yes. I remember." Now I was blushing for an entirely different reason.

"So, terms?" He prompted, "What days of the week do I get custody? And for how long?"

"Custody?"

"When do I get to see you?"

"Martin, we don't need a schedule. If you want to see me or talk to me, just call me."

"What about today?"

Again I glanced around the kitchen; it had no advice to offer.

I sputtered, "Uh...well...I guess...sure. If you have the time. I'm heading up to where you are in a little bit, as we have a show in the city tomorrow morning."

"I'll take you out to dinner tonight."

Going out to dinner felt too much like a date. I didn't think I was ready for anything that my heart might misconstrue and pin hopes upon.

"Or we could meet at the MET and grab a bite there." The cafeteria at the Metropolitan Museum of Art had great food and was extremely public. Plus, it felt like a neutral spot, like something platonic friends would do together.

He was quiet for a few seconds and I could almost hear him thinking. Finally he acquiesced, "Sure. That's fine. Where are you staying tonight?"

"In Brooklyn, with my bandmate, Janet, and a few of her friends. We're actually staying there all week. I have, like, three shows every day this week."

"You're not going home for Christmas?"

"No. I went home for Thanksgiving. Plus the Christmas season is a very lucrative week for the band. I promised Willis I'd be available."

"Willis?"

"My boss."

I heard the creak of leather, like he was shifting in his seat, and when he spoke his words sounded measured, carefully casual. "You could stay with me, if you wanted. I have plenty of room and I'm in Manhattan."

My heart sped up at the offer. *Hmm, let me see. Spend a week with Martin on an island. Why did that sound so familiar and hazardous?* It actually sounded amazing, at least my pants thought so…but also like a really, really terrible idea.

"No, thank you. I wouldn't want to soil your linens." I was pleased to hear him laugh at this while I continued, "But that's really nice of you to offer."

"I'll pick you up from the station."

"No need. Janet and I are riding over together, then we're dropping our stuff off in Brooklyn. I'll take the subway to the MET and meet you there for food."

"The offer still stands." I could tell he was grinning. "Feel free to stay with me anytime."

I realized I was grinning too, like a love-sick goof.

And I also realized that this, a friendship with Martin, was either going to help me get over him and be my best idea of all time, or I was going to fall even harder and it was the worst mistake I would ever make.

[8]

PHASE CHANGES AND HEATING CURVES

URNS OUT MY worst idea ever of all time was deciding to stay with Janet and her twin, aspiring actor friends.

As soon as we walked in the door I knew something was amiss, mostly because of all the drug paraphernalia scattered around stinking up the studio—including, but not limited to bongs, bags of weed, bent and burnt spoons, lighters, syringes, and what I was fairly certain was the hydrochloride salt form of heroin.

One of the twins was passed out on the couch. The other was on the floor, shooting up.

I paused in the doorway just long enough to absorb the general splendor of these idiots ruining their lives before turning around and marching back down the last flight of stairs we'd just hiked up.

"Katy, wait. Where are you going?" Janet called after me, but did not follow.

"I'm leaving."

"But—wait, wait a minute." Now she was following me. I'd made it to the second landing before I felt her hand on my arm making me stop. "What do you mean you're leaving?"

I faced her, my eyes darting back to the open door, her bags still in the entry. "Just that. I'm leaving. I'm not staying with druggies."

Her lip curled as her eyes moved up and down, as though she were seeing me for the first time. "Is this because your mother is a politician? Are you afraid of ruining her rep? Or are you just being stuck up?"

"I guess I'm just being stuck up. This has nothing to do with my mother. Even if my mother were a singing barista, I wouldn't spend one second more in that apartment. I don't like drugs. I don't want to have anything to do with them."

"Come on, they're not bad guys." Her expression softened and she smiled warmly. "Come back—we'll order a pizza and ignore them."

I shook my head before she finished speaking. "No. It's one of my life rules. I have no tolerance for drugs or for people who do drugs."

"Does that mean you have no tolerance for me?" Janet stood straighter, her chin lifted in challenge.

"Do you do drugs?"

"Hell yes."

I shrugged. "Then I guess you have your answer."

Her mouth opened in shock and I took advantage of her momentary stunned surprise to walk down another two flights of stairs.

I heard her call after me just before I exited the building, "Good luck finding a place to stay the week before Christmas, every place is booked. And don't come back here with your judgmental bullshit!"

The door slammed behind me, cutting off any additional tirade she might be flinging in my direction. I took a deep breath, filling my lungs with icy air, and reminded myself, *just because I don't feel calm, doesn't mean I can't be calm.*

I walked toward the subway station, holding my sleeping bag to my chest and shifting the weight of my backpack. Even though I'd packed relatively light, the bag was still heavy. Janet was right. Finding a place to stay for the night was going to be nearly impossible, especially a place I could afford.

I basically had two options.

I could call my parents and ask them if I could borrow money for a hotel room. I really, really didn't want to do that.

I wasn't going to live my life having my mother and father support *my little hobby.* It wasn't a hobby to me. I wanted to be treated like an adult. I was making my own decisions about my future, I should be able to make my own way. I would accept their help with tuition, but then I promised myself I would be on my own in all other facets of my life.

The second option was catching a train back home tonight, then catching another train back to the city early in the morning. This wasn't a great option either since it was going to be incredibly expensive to take the train back and forth every day, not to mention exhausting.

Debating my options, and knowing ultimately I really only had one option if I wanted to be truly self-sufficient, I took the subway back to Grand Central Station.

Once I was no longer underground, I texted Martin.

KAITLYN: *Sorry. I have to cancel our MET meet up. I'm not staying in the city and need to try to catch a train back home before they're all sold out. Maybe next time.*

I WAS STANDING in front of the departures board when I felt my phone vibrate, alerting me to his response.

MARTIN: *Are you already in the city?*
Kaitlyn: *Yes, but my arrangements fell through, so I'm going back home.*
Martin: *Don't go. Stay with me.*

I STARED at this message for a full minute, my heart accelerating then dipping then twisting as I thought about this potential solution I hadn't considered. Earlier, from the comfort of my living room in New Haven, this suggestion had seemed ludicrous. Now, faced with the reality of a train ride back home and another in the morning, this idea felt a lot more plausible. We *were* friends after all.

Maybe I was staring for longer than a minute because Martin texted again.

MARTIN: *I'm hardly ever at my place. You'd basically have the apartment to yourself.*

I FELT like this last message was an unbreakable code...

If he was hardly ever there, did this mean he had a girlfriend? Emma the business partner wasn't his girlfriend, but he didn't deny *having* a girlfriend. What about the brunette at the gig last week? Maybe she was his girlfriend.

Did he spend the night at this theoretical woman's place all the time?

Could I be any more psycho and weird about Martin Sandeke?

Feeling like I needed to know for certain whether he had a girlfriend before I agreed to spend a night in his apartment, I debated how to respond to his latest text.

If he had a girlfriend then I was leaving for home tonight and the answer was a firm no. I didn't want to see him with anyone else...ever. As well, how fair would it be to this hypothetical girlfriend if I was lusting after her boyfriend for a week while in his apartment? It wouldn't be fair at all, and it was against the cool-girl code.

But I felt strange about texting him and asking him, so I tried to cleverly extract the information instead.

KAITLYN: *Does this mean you're a workaholic or is your social calendar just impressively full of hot dates?*

Martin: *A workaholic. My social calendar is mostly work stuff.*

Kaitlyn: *So, you're out late only because of work?*

Martin: *Usually.*

Kaitlyn: *Any other reason?*

THERE WAS a significant pause in his text messages. I waited, watching the clock on my phone. I was about to do a google search for "Martin Sandeke girlfriend" just to put myself out of my misery when he finally responded.

MARTIN: *Are you more or less likely to stay the week if I have a girl-friend? Because I can get one if I need to.*

ONCE AGAIN I was staring at my phone, surprised by his text. But I shouldn't have been surprised. Martin had nerves of steel and balls of titanium. Before I could text him back, he sent another message.

MARTIN: *There is no one. Stay with me. It'll be the most exciting thing that's happened since I bought a PS4.*

HE DIDN'T HAVE A GIRLFRIEND...!

I couldn't help myself, I did a jig, right there in front of the departures board at Grand Central Station. It was an instinctual, involuntary jig.

After the fact, I recognized I did a jig for no reason because nothing was ever going to happen between us again. He'd had his revenge on his father. He existed in his universe of one. He'd moved on. And I wasn't likely to trust him enough to let anything happen. Regardless, the fact he was single felt like a victory, so I did my jig.

I read his message again and my attention caught on the very last part.

Kaitlyn: *Wait, you have a PS4?*
Martin: *Yes.*
Kaitlyn: *Do you have any Lord of the Rings games?*
Martin: *Yes. Middle-earth: Shadow of Mordor.*
Kaitlyn: *What's your address? I'm on my way.*

* * *

MARTIN LIVED IN the Upper West Side. Finding his building was no big deal and was basically a relatively short subway ride with one transfer. When I arrived, the doorman seemed to be expecting me because he greeted me as *Ms. Parker* and ushered me into the lobby to the desk of a friendly concierge. Her name was Mae and she was extremely cheerful.

"Aren't you lovely, dear? Mr. Sandeke called ahead and said we should be expecting you. I'll show you up to his apartment."

"Oh, I don't mind waiting until he gets home."

"Nonsense, dear. He was particular about you going up right away. Besides, who knows when he'll be home?" She leaned close to me as we boarded the elevator and whispered, "He keeps odd hours, so you might be waiting until midnight."

Martin lived on the sixth floor and his place was at the very, very end of a long hallway. Mae made chitchat the entire time and, to be honest, I had no idea what she was talking about. Staying with Martin when I was tired, hungry, and stranded seemed like a reasonable alternative to catching trains daily back and forth between New York and New Haven.

Now, faced with the reality of Martin's apartment, I was beginning to question my judgment. I wondered if I should add a new life rule: never stay at an ex-boyfriend's place.

Mae unfastened the lock and opened the door, practically pushing me inside when I loitered a little too long at the entrance. However, she did not enter the apartment. I took a few stumbling steps into the space and greedily absorbed the surroundings.

The first thing I noticed was that Martin's apartment was not ostentatious, at all. Other than its size, the impressive view of Central Park, and the fact he had an actual patio with chairs and a table—currently covered in snow—everything else was rather modest. And cozy. And homey.

The visible walls were plain white, but mostly the room was lined with honey-colored wooden bookshelves, all of which were full of books. He had a worn-looking, dark brown leather sofa in the center of the living room, two matching club chairs in the same leather, a Shaker-style coffee table, and an antique looking drafting table in the corner; it was covered in papers with sketches tacked to a corkboard to one side.

He also had a stone fireplace; the hearth was free of decoration, but a large painting of an eight-person crew boat done in a Norman Rockwell style hung above the mantel. It was the only art or picture I could see. The living room looked like a comfy library.

"Okey dokey. You're all set." Peripherally I heard Mae call to me just before the apartment door clicked shut. I turned around and found that she'd gone, leaving me alone in Martin's home.

My back twinged and I was reminded of the heavy backpack I'd been carrying for the last few hours. Sighing, I placed my sleeping bag on the couch and relieved myself of my luggage, letting it fall to the sofa as well. Then I realized I needed to relieve myself of...other things.

I decided I wasn't going to feel weird about invading Martin's space since I'd been invited, and set off to find the bathroom. The first door I opened was to a very tidy, very large bedroom. The walls were white and within was a bed with no headboard or footboard. The comforter was sky blue. The side table and dresser were a distressed, Shaker style. If I didn't recognize the craftsmanship of the woodwork, I would've assumed they'd been purchased at a garage sale. Both were completely bare of stuff. This was obviously a guest bedroom.

The next door was to a closet with sheets, blankets, pillows, and towels, or as I would call them later in order to tease Martin, linens. I checked to see if his towels were monogrammed. They were. I smirked.

The next door was to a bathroom. I flipped on the light and sucked in a surprised and delighted breath. The bathroom was very vintage and very cool. The tilework was checked black and white, a pedestal sink stood to one side, and the nobs appeared to be antique porcelain.

The shower was a stall with a glass door and the toilet looked old and new at the same time. Perhaps it was a reproduction of antique-style toilets. I had to pull a chain hanging from a ceramic box in order to flush it, which I honestly thought was exciting.

I would have to make a special effort to keep from flushing the toilet for no reason.

But like the bedroom, it was entirely free of clutter. The only items in the bathroom other than the fixtures were two white towels, toilet paper, a soap dispenser, and an empty trashcan.

I walked back to the living room and decided to send him a text, let him know I made it.

KAITLYN: *I am texting from inside your apartment.*
Martin: *Are you going through my things?*
Kaitlyn: *Yes. And I've soiled all your linens.*
Martin: *Just stay away from my fancy watches.*

HIS LAST MESSAGE made me laugh, and then I caught myself. Texting back and forth with Martin was fun. It made me remember conversations we'd had during spring break, the quick exchanges, the teasing. The messages reminded me of how easy and right it had felt between us.

My phone vibrated again and I had to blink several times to bring the screen into focus.

MARTIN: *I'm almost home and I have pizza. Your room is the first left down the hall. Get comfortable.*

MY HEART SPED at the thought of seeing him so soon and I told it to calm the frack down.

We were friends now. If I was going to be seeing him I was going to have to learn to control my body's reaction. I was going to have to learn how to become indifferent. That meant no more celebratory jigs and no more heart races.

Lugging my backpack from the couch to the sparsely decorated room I'd spied earlier, I unpacked. While hanging my tuxedo in the empty closet—which was strange to see, who has empty closets?—I walked by a mirror and caught my reflection. My hair was in two thick, long braids on either side of my head. I was wearing an extra-large men's concert T-shirt, a very baggy pair of cargo pants, and Converse. This outfit was great for travel because it was comfortable and I didn't care if it became dirty.

But it was undoubtedly frumpy. I did not like how I looked in it.

I decided to change into one of the outfits I'd bought earlier: a dark pair of (women's) jeans, a fitted long-sleeved, red and white rugby-style shirt with Avogadro's number on the back. I thought this was hilarious.

The lady at the store didn't know what Avogadro's number was, but she told me I wasn't supposed to button the placket at the collar because it was meant to be a deep V-neck; she said that leaving it open would highlight my cleavage, that it was sexy.

I glanced down at my chest, saw that just the edge of my black bra was visible. I decided leaving it unbuttoned was, indeed, sexy. However, I also decided that buttoning just one button would make me more comfortable, so I did. Glancing in the mirror I assessed myself. I was comfortable, but I was not frumpy; I also felt good about how I looked instead of merely ambivalent. I liked that I could incorporate my inherent nerdiness into my new style. I liked it all.

I'd just started pulling my hair out of the braids when I heard the front door open.

My heart wanted to race like a contestant at the Kentucky Derby, but I yanked it back, taking several deep breaths. All of the floors in the apartment were wood and creaked, so I could hear Martin's steps as he moved through the apartment. Satisfied I wasn't going to act like a spazz, I walked calmly into the living room while I pulled my fingers through my hair.

"Hey," I called, searching for him, "what kind of pizza did you get?"

"Who are you?"

I turned toward the sound of the voice—a British female voice—and found a beautiful woman dressed in an expensive black skirt suit, black high-heeled boots, and long wheat-colored hair, glowering at me.

"Oh, hi. I'm Kaitlyn. You must be Emma. We spoke on the phone earlier." I reached my hand out to shake hers.

She glanced at my fingers like she was a vegan and they were greasy pork sausages. She didn't shake my hand.

"How did you get in here?" Her irritation was obvious, and not just because she wouldn't shake my hand. It dripped off her...she was leaking ire.

I let my hand drop and shrugged. "Through the front door."

She gnashed her teeth. "Who let you in? Why are you here?" She was practically snarling.

"Whoa, just, calm down for a moment. There's no reason to be upset."

"I'm not upset!" She yelled this.

I widened my eyes and took a step back, holding my hands up between us. "Okay, my bad. You're not upset. You always walk into other people's apartments and yell at their guests. This must be a normal Tuesday for you."

Her eyes narrowed and her lip curled into something like a snarl. "You are a dimwitted—"

And, thankfully, Martin chose that moment to walk in the door. "Emma? What the hell?"

We both turned our faces to him as he swept into the living room and deposited a large pizza box and a plastic bag on a table behind the sofa, then quickly crossed to stand next to me.

As usual, he was more than just a tall good-looking guy. He was a presence. A swirling, atmosphere changing force, a magnetized center of attention—or at least he was to me. I felt my heart do a few jumping jacks and I told it to sit still.

Emma took a step back as he approached. She swallowed, looking just a tad worried, and crossed her arms over her chest. I noted she was good at masking her nerves as she lifted her chin in a stubborn tilt.

"Really, Martin? Really? You think this is a good idea?"

"Emma." He shook his head, his jaw set, and his eyes flashed a warning. "It's none of your business."

"Your business is my business, and *she* is bad for my business." Emma indicated to me with a furious wave of her hand.

Well, this was awkward. I thought about slowly backing away. To that end, I furtively glanced behind me to see how successful I might be sneaking out of the room without either of them noticing.

"You're going, now. And leave the key." Martin's tone was low, monotone. Yes, he appeared to be angry; more than that he appeared to be disappointed.

"If I don't have a key, how am I supposed to pick up your planning documents for the foundation? How about your *sketches*?"

She said sketches like most people say poop. I surmised she was not a fan of his sketches.

"We're not talking about this now because you're leaving."

Her brow pulled low and she hesitated for a bit, searching his face before asking, "Does she even know what you did for her? What you gave up? Did you tell her? Is that why she's here?"

I turned my attention back to the argument, and again my eyes widened. I stared at Emma, really looked at her, and I realized she wasn't jealous, not in a love interest, girl longing for a guy kind of way. Rather, she was extremely frustrated—and definitely jealous—but for a different reason.

Martin drew himself straighter, his face stone and his eyes unyielding icicles. "You need to leave before I sever our partnership, because we've already had this discussion, you're too fucking stubborn to listen, and now you're really pissing me off." He was furious and his voice was beginning to lift. I remembered facing his temper and I could see he was close to losing it now.

Emma coolly studied him for a long moment. "Fine. I'll leave." She reached into the satchel slung over her shoulder and pulled out a ring of two keys. "Here is your key." She held it to him and he took it out of her hand.

Her eyes slid to mine and her gaze narrowed as she spat, "You are selfish. But worse, you are naïve and ignorant and stupidly obstinate—just like your mother."

I opened my mouth to say something, but it didn't matter because she'd already turned on her heel and marched out of the apartment, slamming the door behind her.

Martin and I stood perfectly still for several seconds. I was trying to wrap my mind around everything that had just happened and the odd verbal exchange I'd witnessed. I arranged my questions in order from most pressing to simple curiosities, and turned to Martin to gauge his mood.

His mouth was curved into a decisive frown and he was staring at the spot where Emma had just been standing.

I gathered a deep breath, preparing to pose the first of my questions, when he turned toward me. His eyes, how they moved over me, made my breath and words catch in my throat.

"You look different," Martin said, his attention on my hips, moving to my thighs then back up to my stomach, breasts, neck, lips, then hair. If I wasn't mistaken, he looked appreciative of the changes in my wardrobe. "What's different about you?" This question was softly spoken and teasing.

I shrugged, pretending I didn't know what he was talking about. "I don't know. I'm using a different moisturizer for my face now."

His gaze met mine and narrowed. "That's not it."

"I switched from Crest to Colgate." I showed him my teeth.

"No." He smirked.

"My hair is longer."

"Maybe..."

I lifted an eyebrow at him and wondered if he were stalling, trying to distract me from the issues at hand—such as Emma's mention of me being the reason Martin had given up...something big.

"Why don't you tell me what your business partner meant when she said—"

Martin turned away, drawing his heavy coat from his shoulders. "Can we not talk about that tonight? Can we just..." I heard him sigh, "can we just hang out?"

"I don't think so. I won't be able to focus on anything else until you tell me what's going on."

My eyes moved over him as he walked to the entryway closet and hung up his coat. This left him in an exceptionally well-tailored, dark gray, three-piece suit. His tie was cobalt blue and matched his current eye color.

"Kaitlyn," Martin paused, facing me, loosening his tie and unbuttoning the top two buttons of his crisp business shirt, "I've been looking forward to seeing you all day."

This admission made my insides flood with warmth and I marveled at how open he was with his thoughts, how fearless. I surmised our friendship would be similar to our previous courtship; I'd never have to wonder what he was thinking or feeling about me. He would be direct and honest.

In truth, I admired this about him. I wasn't nearly as fearless. By comparison, and especially with him, I was a feelings and thoughts hoarder.

"I don't want to talk about Emma or her constant nagging. I want to sit on the couch, drink a beer, eat pizza, and talk about shit that doesn't matter—and laugh."

He looked older than his twenty-one years; his suit was partially to blame. However, he also just looked tired—really, really tired. Upon further study I saw that his color was off, paler than before; his eyes were rimmed red, the dark circles beneath giving his face a drawn appearance. As well he was sporting a stubbly, late-afternoon beard.

I studied him, his obvious exhaustion, and felt like a compromise was in order. "Okay, fine. We don't have to talk about it right now."

He gave me a grateful, and tired, half smile. "Good."

I held up a finger and pointed it at him. "But once you've recovered from your day, and you've had your beer and eaten your pizza, and we've talked about things that don't matter, we will discuss the meaning of the ominous and mysterious conversation with your partner."

He'd removed his suit jacket and vest, and was now unbuttoning his cuffs. "Fine."

"Fine. I'll get plates."

"And beer."

"And napkins."

He nodded once and stumbled toward the hallway. On his way he stopped directly in front of me, paused for a moment, then scooped me up in his arms and gave me a tight hug.

"I'm so glad you're here."

I hesitated as I my chest had grown tight, confusing emotion momentarily choking me. I wasn't expecting us to be *hugging friends*. But then I returned his embrace because…Martin.

And also because his arms around me were like chocolate chip cookies for my soul. He felt strong, sturdy, warm, snuggly, good, right —delicious.

Yet my heart ached for him, he sounded so weary.

"Are you okay? Is something going on?" I soothed my hand up then down his back.

"No, not the way you mean. Nothing serious. I just…" I felt him exhale and relax a bit more into my arms. "I just missed you."

Gah! Right in the feels.

"**THAT'S IT. I'M** going to make a list of all the TV shows you need to watch." I was sitting cross-legged on his couch, facing him and resting my head on the back of the overstuffed sofa. Martin was sprawled on the other side, holding his beer on his stomach and fighting to keep his eyes open.

"I own the Sherlock Holmes books."

"The BBC show is awesome. Have you read the books yet?"

"No."

"Maybe try reading them."

"I will. Didn't I read The Lord of the Rings?"

"Yes. But Sherlock has maybe the best sidekick in the history of forever." I glanced behind him and found the clock on the wall. It was almost 10:30 p.m.

This conversation—about books, movies, pop culture, international current events, Internet memes, and music—was entering its third hour, although it felt like we'd just started talking, like no time had passed.

"I liked Sam, Frodo's sidekick," he said, stretching his legs. He was dressed in pajama pants and a gray T-shirt. I tried not to notice how delicious he looked. I tried and failed. His deliciousness paired with our easy conversation was somewhat intoxicating. I was feeling giddy.

"If you like sidekicks, then you have to watch Doctor Who." I sipped my tea and studied the tea bag. "The Doctor has several companions, which is unusual but really works for the series."

"I think you're a sidekick person."

"You think I'm a sidekick?" I glanced at him over the rim of my cup.

He peered at me. "No. I think you like sidekicks and side characters, maybe better than main characters."

I thought about this for a moment before nodding. "Yeah. I can see that. I feel like sidekicks aren't as well developed as the main character in a story, but they're essential in defining that main character. And the protagonist needs the sidekick more than the sidekick needs the protagonist. Sometimes the villain is just as important."

He lifted his beer toward me and said before taking a sip, "But every sidekick and villain is the main character in his or her own story. Everyone is the main character in their own story. Even if the person is an asshole."

This made me laugh. "Are you thinking of a person in particular?"

"No." His eyes narrowed on me. I watched him take a deep breath, then amend, "Actually, yes."

"Really? Who?"

"Do you remember Ben?"

I searched my memory and quickly registered the name. "Ben Salsmar, the drugging rapist," I supplied. "Yes. Unfortunately, I do remember him. He's responsible for the figurative potato sack of guilt I carry around."

"What do you mean?"

"I mean, I should have gone to the police when we got back from the Island. Instead I… didn't."

"Kaitlyn, there is nothing you could have done about Ben. You need to free the potatoes."

"I overheard at the end of last year that he was arrested for sexually assaulting a minor, and I might have done something before he had a chance to—"

"Well, that's not exactly true. He didn't sexually assault her because he was stopped before he could do anything beyond drugging her and dropping his pants."

I felt an immediate warm relief spread through my veins.

Martin studied me before continuing, "Just know that you couldn't have stopped him. It would have been your word against his, and you had no evidence. But did you hear anything else?"

"Just that there was video proof."

"Yes, there is a video. Actually, there were a few videos, from several different vantage points. He was arrested for the drugging, assault, and attempted rape. He was also expelled once the video was shared with university administration."

I hesitated for a moment, then asked, "Was he convicted?"

"He will be. A few of the guys on the team will testify. Plus there's the videos. His dad tried to delay the proceedings and, because of the delay, a few other girls have come forward. As of now it looks like he'll be facing more than one rape charge."

I felt sickened by this news—that several girls had been abused —but also heartened they had come forward. "Well, that's good, right?"

"Yes. That's good."

"Well…good. I'm glad he was stopped."

"Me, too." Martin stared at me for a long moment and I knew he wanted to say something more. I was just about to prompt him when he said, "I don't think I ever thanked you for that night, when you came to the fraternity house and told me what he was planning."

I gave him a half smile. "It's no problem. Did you ever find out who the girl was?"

"No... but thank you," he said solemnly. Then, he added just as solemnly, "I promised you I'd take care of him, and I wanted you to know I kept my promise."

My left eyebrow lifted of its own accord. "*You* took care of him?"

His expression grew cagey. "Technically, he did it to himself. I just installed the cameras..."

I studied him, guessing he'd likely been more involved than just installing cameras.

Martin heaved a heavy sigh, settling deeper into the cushions of the couch. "Like I said, everyone is the main character in their own story. Even villains."

I shook my head. "I don't know... Not necessarily. I mean, sometimes the story is bigger than the characters, like Jurassic Park. The Park was really the central focus of the story, and all the characters were secondary to the Park. Their only purpose was to react to the Park."

Martin yawned, set his now empty beer on the coffee table, and closed his eyes. "That's because dinosaurs are awesome. We're all sidekicks to dinosaurs."

"Or dinner."

"Or dinner," he slurred, issuing me a sloppy nod.

I watched the rise and fall of his chest, noted he appeared to be completely relaxed. If I was very quiet I knew he'd be asleep in less than sixty seconds.

But the conversation—or confrontation—with his business partner earlier was still nagging at me. If he fell asleep I'd have to wait another day to get my questions answered.

"Sandeke," I whispered. "Why does Emma dislike me so much?"

He shifted, his head lolling to the side, and heaved a sigh. "She doesn't know you."

"That's why she doesn't like me?"

"Yeah...if she knew...you...she'd...really like you."

Aaaand he was asleep.

I studied him for a long moment, but knew I didn't have the heart to wake him. He'd been so tired. As we talked I saw the tension ease from his shoulders. He needed a night off from whatever genius high-stakes shenanigans he'd been up to.

I set my tea on the coffee table, then remembered the blankets in the linen closet. I tiptoed to the hallway and grabbed one, laying it gently on his sleeping form and tucking it between his hip and the sofa cushions so it wouldn't slip off. Standing back, I surveyed Martin. Unable to help myself, I threaded my fingers through the hair at his forehead and pushed it gently to one side.

He turned his head toward my hand, pressing against my lingering touch. The simple action, the way he instinctively sought affection and warmth made me smile sadly. I'd forgotten how lost Martin was, how completely used and abandoned he'd been by his family. In my own grief surrounding the breakup, I'd forgotten he didn't have many friends, and trusted very few.

This made my heart hurt in a new way, one focused outward instead of inward, and I felt the weight of my childish selfishness.

He needed a friend, someone who truly cared about him.

I still cared about him a great deal. I was maybe (definitely) in love with him. So shouldn't that mean I wanted what was best for him? Shouldn't I want to see him happy? Even if we didn't find happiness with each other?

I let my palm press against his cheek for a few more seconds before drawing slowly away, and I made a decision. I was going to give our friendship a real chance, and not just use it as a way to get over Martin Sandeke. He deserved better than that. He deserved human kindness and consideration.

I was going to shelve my persistent feelings of romantic attraction and be a good friend to him. I was going to be his safe place, the friend he needed.

[9]
PERIODIC PROPERTIES OF THE ELEMENTS

MY PHONE ALARM announced the end of happiness (sleep). It was obscenely early in the morning. For a moment I was confused by my surroundings, but then I remembered whose apartment I was in and the happenings of the last twenty-four hours. This served to wake me up quite effectively.

It was still dark outside. My first show for the day was at a fancy tree-trimming party in a penthouse not far from where Martin lived. It would be just Fitzy and me, and for that I was grateful. I wasn't ready to discuss rebound guys with Abram, or heroin as a viable life choice with Janet.

Tossing the covers to one side and grabbing my clothes, I planned to tiptoe to the bathroom as quietly as I could, not wanting to wake Martin at this ungodly hour.

As it turned out, I didn't need to worry about waking him because he was already up and leaving his room just as I exited mine. But he was dressed in workout clothes whereas I was still in pajamas. He didn't see me at first because his attention was on his phone.

"Martin," I whispered—as I was prone to do early in the morning when regular speaking volume is blasphemous—wanting to get his attention before we collided in the hall.

He lifted his eyes, frowning as though he were confused by my presence, and took a step back. "What are you doing up so early? Did I wake you?"

"I have a show." I indicated with my chin to where I held my tuxedo.

"Ah." His gaze skimmed over me, probably taking in my sleepy and rumpled appearance.

I decided then and there that something about the way he looked at me would always make me feel awkward. It wasn't his fault. It was just him being Martin: the shade and intensity of his eye color paired with the brilliance and acumen behind his gaze; the sharpness of his bone structure; his towering height; the graceful line of his form and movements—he couldn't help causing my self-consciousness any more than I could help the reaction.

I made a decision to just accept it rather than fight it. Maybe if I accepted that my body would respond to him no matter what my head and heart might prefer, then I would be able to move beyond the sensations until they felt commonplace.

"You're off to work out?" I asked unnecessarily, still whispering.

"Yeah. I meet a few guys at the Hudson boathouse and we try to get in a few thousand meters before breakfast. The river isn't frozen yet, so we still have a few weeks. Why are you whispering?"

I cleared my throat, managed to lift my voice slightly, though it was still low and sandpapery from sleep. "I don't know. I just always do this early in the morning. It's like my ears aren't ready for sound yet."

This made his mouth curve into a small smile. He walked slowly forward until he was standing between me and the bathroom. Martin leaned against the hallway wall and peered down at me.

"I know what you mean." His answering voice was soft, low, rumbly, and delicious. Again, I allowed the sensations of being close to him in a dark, small space and speaking with him in low, intimate tones wash over me. Accelerated heart rate, warming cheeks, fluttery stomach. No use fighting it.

I tried to redirect the conversation back to him and his morning routine. "So, you're still rowing? That's great."

He nodded, his eyes on mine, but he appeared to be distracted, torn. "I could…I mean, I could cancel if you want company this morning."

"But if you cancel how will they row the boat? Doesn't every seat need to be filled?"

"Technically they need an even number of rowers. So, most of them—six plus the coxswain—would be able to go, but someone might have to sit out."

"Then go row your boat. Don't worry about me. I have to leave soon anyway."

Martin glanced at his phone again. "I can stick around for another ten minutes. Come out here." He motioned for me to follow as he pushed away from the wall and walked past me. "I'll make you coffee and I have muffins."

I watched his back while I considered this offer, and followed him into the kitchen. I deposited my clothes on the couch as we passed. He was being awfully solicitous, maybe he wanted to talk about the Emma situation.

"Is ten minutes enough time for me to ask you my questions about yesterday? What happened with your business partner?"

He shook his head, giving me his profile as he fiddled with the coffee machine. "No. No—I do want to talk to you about all that—but we don't have enough time this morning. I don't," he paused, apparently struggling over his word choice, "I don't want to be rushed. A lot has happened and ten minutes isn't enough time to explain everything. What's your schedule today? Could we have lunch?"

"Not unless your office is in Harlem. I have a gig up there all afternoon. Dinner?"

"No." He frowned, turning to face me while he leaned against the counter, the coffee machine coming to life. "I have a dinner meeting tonight until late."

"Well, I'll be here all week. I'm sure we'll have a chance to catch up at some point."

He appeared to be a tad frustrated; it was plain irritation at the situation, not irritation with me.

"Thanks for the break last night. But I want to know what's been going on with you. What have you been up to? What have you been doing? Any big changes?"

I gave him a half smile. "You mean any big changes I can adequately summarize in eight minutes or less?"

"Yeah. Good point." His grin was surprising because it was somewhat self-deprecating. Self-deprecating at 5:05 a.m. looked really adorable on Martin Sandeke.

But then, that was the crux of my problem. To me, *every* smile looked good on Martin Sandeke. Every expression, anytime, anyplace. I simply adored his face because—despite our history and his past assholery—I still adored *him*.

"Well, I'll give you the Cliffs Notes version then we can discuss in greater detail later, sound good?"

He nodded. "Sounds good."

"Okay, let's see." I sorted through the last nine months, filtering out the epic sob-fests, chronic melodramatic closet visits, and angry acoustic guitar music. "Sam and I moved off campus at the beginning of the summer. I auditioned for the band in July. I decided to change my major around the same time and take a semester—the fall semester—off school so I could audition for the music program."

For some reason, the fact I'd switched majors felt like a really momentous proclamation, especially saying it out loud to Martin. I slid my eyes to the side to gage his reaction and I found him grinning at me.

"That's," he started, stopped, looking a tad overwhelmed. He leaned away from the counter and crossed to stand in front of me. "That's fucking awesome news!"

I laughed, partly as a release of nervous energy and partly because his voice was much louder and he sounded so excited for me. Really, he sounded ecstatic.

"Thank you." I dipped my head to the side, feeling a bit too pleased by his reaction.

"Really, this is great." He was beaming with happiness, his smile now enormous. Obviously unable to help himself, Martin grabbed me from where I loitered at the entrance to the kitchen and pulled me into a tight hug.

I laughed at his effusive display of excitement and wrapped my arms around his waist. "Yeah, well, I know I want to play music and I know I love to compose, but I'm not sure what I want to do exactly."

He leaned away, his hands shifting to grip my arms above the elbows, seemingly wanting to see my face as I relayed the rest of my thoughts.

"Do I want to teach? Write for record labels? Score soundtracks? I have no idea." My stomach twisted with unease; my mother would be asking me about performing at her fundraiser and benefit again as soon as the holidays were over. Eventually I would have to make a decision.

Martin mistook my grimace of anxiety for nerves about switching my major, and said, "But you'll make a lot of good contacts in the school of music, people who can help you figure out what to do next. Don't hesitate to exploit them for their knowledge."

"Yes. Exactly. I like the idea of expert unbiased input."

His smile widened again as his gaze skated over my face, his eyes were positively glittering. "That's a very Kaitlyn Parker thing to say."

Of course I returned his smile, his happiness for me was heady and infectious. "So you mean it was an awesome thing to say?"

"Exactly."

His coffee maker beeped or chimed or made some odd musical notation to announce that my coffee was ready. The sound was very official. Martin didn't release me immediately and for a second I thought he might pull me back into another hug. Instead he sighed—a happy sounding sigh—and let go, moving to a cabinet and grabbing a coffee cup.

"You know, we should go out and celebrate."

"Celebrate my switch in majors?"

"Yes. And hopefully other things, too."

"Like what other things?"

97

He placed the cup on the counter in front of me, looking a bit distracted, pensive.

He hesitated before answering, but when he did his eyes were sharp and sober, and his tone told me he was a smidge frustrated. "It might speed things up if you read some of the interviews I've given over the past few months. Then when we have time this week to talk you'll know...everything."

"Sure. Fine. That makes sense." I nodded, sipped my coffee.

This seemed to both relax him and stress him out. I watched him gather a deep, bracing breath. "Good," he said, sounding like maybe me reading the interviews was both good and bad. Abruptly he pulled out his phone and frowned. "I'm late. I have to go."

"Okay." I gave him a reassuring smile because he seemed to need it. "I'll see you later."

Martin loitered, just looking at me, his expression unreadable. Again I experienced an involuntary reaction to his *looking*. And again I just accepted my body's flutterings and warmings as one of life's truths.

Then Martin nodded once, turned, and left.

He just...left, the sound of the apartment door shutting punctuating his abrupt departure.

I stood in the kitchen for a full minute staring at the doorway where he'd disappeared so unceremoniously. He hadn't said goodbye.

The longer I stared the more the early morning silence felt harsh and loud, so I gave myself a mental shake—deciding he must've been in a hurry—and crossed to the counter where I spied the aforementioned box of muffins.

Grabbing one—and my coffee—I decided that now was a good time to start reading the interviews he'd mentioned. Now that I had food and caffeine, I didn't need the extra time I'd allotted to secure both before my gig nearby. I left my breakfast on the kitchen table and returned with my laptop, figuring I had a good twenty minutes of reading before I absolutely had to take my shower.

I bit into my delicious banana nut muffin, pulled up my Internet browser, and typed *Martin Sandeke interview* into the search field.

What popped up made the delicious muffin in my mouth taste like sand.

Picture after picture of Martin and a redheaded woman wallpapered the results page—a very pretty, petite, smiling redheaded girl about my age or a little older. She was always smiling, either at him or the camera. The photos dated as far back as August and as recently as three weeks ago.

They looked so pretty, the two of them, so young and vibrant and *suited*.

My heart thundered between my ears and I forcefully shut my laptop, blinking rapidly at nothing in particular. This wasn't like seeing him briefly with the brunette at my show last week. This was very different. All those feelings I'd been trying to avoid for the past nine months, the fear of irrefutable evidence that he'd moved on, seeing Martin with someone else, were finally realized and made my chest feel vice-grip-tight.

And yet, as I sat there, having my freak out, calming my breathing, and staring at nothing, a little voice reminded me that he'd texted me the day before and stated he didn't have a girlfriend. He wouldn't have lied to me, not when it would be so easy for me to discover the truth. And besides, Martin hadn't ever knowingly lied to me before, he wasn't a liar.

Perhaps she was a friend. A really good friend. A friend who he'd been photographed with a lot, since August. A friend he saw all the time.

Then another little voice asked me why it mattered, because he and I were over. And that little voice made me immeasurably sad.

I briefly contemplated opening the laptop and continuing my search. But instead, I decided I didn't have time to contemplate Martin, the pretty redhead, and my jumbled feelings on the matter and still make it to work on time. I could always go back to the search later if I was feeling brave enough.

I gulped my coffee and threw the muffin away, then grabbed my laptop and clothes from where I'd discarded them earlier. I had all morning to consider my next course of action. There was no need to make myself late.

* * *

THE TREE-TRIMMING PARTY WAS FINE.

I spent the entirety of the three sets obsessing about the pictures of Martin and the redheaded girl. But the time obsessing was ultimately productive as I came to the conclusion that I was definitely not ready to read his interviews or see the pictures. I knew my limitations, and seeing Martin happy with someone else—even if he didn't have a girl-friend now and they weren't together anymore—was not in my wheel-house. Not yet.

I had no desire to read about his relationship status via the Internet.

I decided that my questions about his business partner and her insinuations, as well as my new questions about the girl in the pictures, would just have to wait until Martin and I found the time to talk. I felt good about this decision. Less ragey—*ragey* because I couldn't think of an equivalent real word to describe what I was feeling—and flus-tered. More in control of my mental state.

The show in Harlem with the entire band was also fine.

Although things between Janet and me were still frosty. Willis called us on it and wanted to know what happened. I think she expected me to air her dirty laundry—telling him about the drugs and her druggie friends—but I didn't.

Instead I told Willis that she and I were having a disagreement about whether Jimi Hendrix or Jimmy Page was the most influential guitarist of the modern rock era.

He said he understood, as we both had good points, but that we needed to work through our differences like a knife cutting peanut butter...or mayonnaise...or something else that didn't make any sense. He really had the nuttiest analogies.

Once he walked off, Janet turned her glower back to me, but it wasn't quite as hostile. "Why didn't you tell him?"

"Tell him what?"

"You know what."

"Why would I? It's none of my business. You want to ruin yourself, that's your business. But I don't have to watch you do it."

Her glower softened into a suspicious glare. "Why are you so weird about this stuff? Did something happen to you?"

"No. But the fact you think I'm being weird because I have no tolerance for heroin is a bit distressing. The truth is, I have very little patience for people who choose to waste their potential and destroy themselves in the process."

"Hmm…" The glare melted away, leaving only an uncomfortable frown. "See now, I completely disagree. Heroin helps me see the world differently, it opens up my mind. It makes me feel free. It doesn't destroy me, it improves me."

I shrugged noncommittally, because her words sounded crazy. I'd never done drugs, so I couldn't comment with any authority on her personal experience. Plus we had fifteen minutes until show time; now was not the time to point out all the extensive research that proved heroin destroyed peoples' lives. Plus, you know, it kills people.

Instead I pulled my bowtie from my bag, excusing myself to the ladies' room. I could have affixed my bow tie in the backstage area, but Abram had just entered and I found his presence highly distracting. And agitating. I was avoiding him.

He liked me. I knew that. His suggestions I get a rebound guy notwithstanding, I wasn't so clueless that I could miss the giant neon sign he'd dropped on my head last Saturday. According to Abram, he'd been waiting for me to see him, to notice him.

The more I thought about his words, the more they reminded me of similar sentiments expressed by Martin in the past.

It occurred to me that perhaps I'd been so busy hiding, trying to keep myself from being seen, that I hadn't been paying adequate atten-tion to the world around me. I was the one who wasn't seeing others clearly. Maybe I needed to stop focusing inward and start paying atten-tion to what was in front of my face, starting with Abram.

I was never going to be a jump-in-feet-first, flash-the-Mardi-Gras-crowd-for-beads kind of girl. I knew it would take me some time to actually *do* anything about Abram. But I was now willing to entertain the possibility.

* * *

YES, I WAS spending the week with Martin on an island. But that was basically where the similarities to our spring break week ended.

After our pre-dawn chat Wednesday, I saw him zero times over the next few days. When I woke up in the morning, Martin had already left. By the time I came home, Martin was either already asleep or not yet home. I hadn't talked to him other than a daily exchange of hand-written notes.

This started on Thursday morning, when I woke up and found a simple note on the kitchen counter,

BREAKFAST STUFF *in the fridge if you're hungry. I'll be home late. –Martin*

ACTUALLY THE FRIDGE was stocked with every good thing. Because I had the time, I made myself eggs benedict and bacon, with a raspberry and banana fruit salad. I also baked chocolate pecan cookies, and was sure to clean up all my mess. Admittedly, I might have been stress baking. My drama-prone side wondered if Martin would be home late because of his redheaded friend. But my pragmatic sided quickly assaulted my drama-prone side and gagged her.

I left the cookies in a sealed plastic container on the same spot where I found his note with a message that read,

EAT ME. *–Cookies*

WHEN I ARRIVED BACK to Martin's apartment that night, I found his suit jacket on the arm of the couch and the door to his room closed. I surmised he was already asleep; but he'd left me a note on the counter that read,

I'LL EAT anything you tell me to eat. –Martin
P.S. Did you read the interviews yet?

I NOTED that the plastic cookie container was empty. He'd eaten all the cookies.

Not allowing myself to get caught up in a marinade of uncertainty (where the ingredients were: my lingering feelings and resultant confusion, the unknown nature of his relationship with the pretty redhead, and his business partner's mysterious insinuations) I jotted down a quick response,

MARTIN,
I have no time for reading interviews when cookies need to be made. Instead I've decided to wait until we have time to talk/discuss. I'd like to hear everything from you rather than the Internet.
-Kaitlyn

AND SO THE next several days passed, and our note exchange proceeded as follows:

Friday morning

PARKER,
Make me more cookies.
–Martin

MARTIN,

> Here are more cookies.
> –Kaitlyn

Friday evening

KAITLYN,

> What's in these cookies? Magic?
> –Martin

MARTIN,

> No, not magic. But I do use unicorn blood to make them chewy.
> –Kaitlyn

Saturday morning

KAITLYN,

> Unicorn blood? You can find that in Manhattan?
> –Martin
> P.S Make me more bloody cookies.

MARTIN,

> You can find everything in Manhattan…except affordable rent.
> –Kaitlyn
> P.S. Here are your bloody cookies.

Saturday evening

PARKER,

> Move in with me. I'll accept unicorn cookies as rent payment.

—Martin

SANDEKE,

I haven't seen you in so long I'm beginning to think you're a figment of my imagination, except that you keep eating my cookies. Are you avoiding me because I smell like denture cream?
—Kaitlyn

Sunday morning

KAITLYN,

Merry Christmas Eve. Do you have to work tonight? I thought I might take the afternoon/evening off if you're off. Do you want to hang out? If you can't today then how about tomorrow?
—Martin
P.S. I didn't want to say anything about the denture cream, but yes. The smell is why I'm avoiding you.

MARTIN,

Merry Christmas Eve to you as well. I have shows today from 2 p.m. until 1 a.m. But, miracle of miracles, I have nothing on Christmas except for a short late afternoon gig that's over at 4 p.m. We should hang out tomorrow morning. Also, know that I have burning questions you haven't yet answered. We could make food, then eat it...since we have no tree maybe I could pick up a Yule log?
—Parker
P.S. I will stop using the denture cream, but then you will have to chew my food for me...

I WAS ACTUALLY grateful Martin and I hadn't seen each other for several days. The notes allowed us to settle into our friendship without all the looking at each other getting in the way and making things tense. He was still so completely and brain-meltingly *lookable*, as my pants liked to remind me whenever we shared the same space.

As well, it gave me time to contemplate and accept the very real possibility that the girl in the pictures had been his girlfriend. I decided I should feel happy for him, that he'd been able to move on so completely. I *decided* this, but I didn't *feel* it. So I worked on feeling it, I worked on moving on as he'd obviously moved on.

Therefore, I stopped avoiding Abram.

And once I stopped avoiding Abram, he and I actually had a fantastic time together. We hung out backstage and discussed mostly music and our childhoods.

We ate meals together between shows and sets, and I learned about all his (visible) tattoos, what they meant and why he'd had them done.

After gigs I played a few of my compositions for him and he played a few of his for me. We were talking and enjoying each other's company and it felt so very, very good to let myself like someone. Almost liberating.

As the week drew to a close I was feeling like things were moving in the right direction. Martin was my friend. Abram was my maybe future more-than-friend. Though I still had bucketfuls of residual feelings for Martin, all-in-all it had been a good week.

The plan was to head back to New Haven on Monday. I'd found a good price on the train ticket; tickets on December twenty-six were almost three times as expensive as they were on Christmas day.

Christmas Eve morning was actually my first and only chance to explore the city. I made a list of places I wanted to check out and crossed my fingers they'd be open. On the way I called my parents and wished them a Merry Christmas. It was a nice conversation, as they both sounded happy and relaxed.

My first stop was an independent record store in Greenwich Village that also served beer. Since it was only 10:13 a.m. when I arrived, I abstained from the beer, but I dug into the vintage collection of vinyl.

I found a few treasures to add to my record collection. As I was checking out, a discounted cover caught my attention. It was an original edition of Stevie Wonder's album *In Square Circle*, dated 1985. I checked the song list on the back and was gratified to see *Overjoyed*.

Not wanting to overthink the gift, I added it to my purchases then left the shop. My next stop was a book store, also in the Village, that was supposed to have antique medical textbooks. I'd already sent my dad his Christmas gifts, but he was always looking for wall hangings for his office.

Again, after finding something for my dad, I stumbled across something for Martin. Actually, it was a signed edition of *The Princess Bride,* one of my favorite books and movies of all time. I was caught up in the desire to share my book joy with him and since the hardcover wasn't a first edition I could actually afford it.

Then I went to a candy store famous for saltwater taffy. I bought more than I needed, deciding to wrap the extras up for Martin.

On my way back to his apartment, I passed a craft store and maker's space that had handmade Christmas stockings in the window. Again on a whim, I ran in and purchased a stocking with a crew boat and eight oars on the front in a very unusual black graphic design on red cotton. They also sold ceramics; I grabbed him a Hobbit soap dispenser for his guest bathroom that looked like a garden gnome with big feet.

Then spotted an awesome, handmade coffee mug with the picture of a bass guitar that read, *All about that bass*. It made me chuckle so I picked it up for Abram.

Before checking out I found some cool stationery; the desk set that immediately called to me had a fishing pole in the right corner and read at the bottom, *I'm not lazy, I just like to eat fish.* So, of course it was perfect for Martin. So, of course I grabbed that, too.

I maybe spent more money than was prudent, but I figured Martin had let me stay in his home for free; the least I could do was pick him up a few cool things for his apartment. Plus, I felt strongly compelled to buy him these items. I saw them and I felt an undeniable compulsion to give them to Martin.

I was juggling my bags and trying to fish out the key to his place while navigating the lobby of the apartment building, when I heard a familiar voice call to me from behind.

"Kaitlyn, may I speak with you?"

I stopped and tensed, waiting a beat before turning and glancing over my shoulder. The voice belonged to Emma Cromwell and—good news—she wasn't looking at me like I was responsible for Ebola.

But she did look determined.

[10]

ATOMS, MOLECULES, AND IONS

I FACED HER, feeling caught and a little confused regarding what I ought to do next. "Um, hello, Emma."

I'd always been raised to say, *Nice to see you.* But in this case I didn't feel like it was appropriate because I didn't want to lie. She crossed to me, her eyes moving over me and to the bags in my hands. She smirked. It wasn't a nice smirk.

"Spending Martin's money already?"

I sighed, because she was already being distasteful. "No. I don't spend other people's money."

Her eyes narrowed as her attention moved back to my face. "Not even your parents' money?"

"That's a terribly rude question, Emma. Why do you feel like you have the right to be rude to me?" I asked this calmly because I was calm. She hadn't upset me, but I was curious as to why she felt like attacking me constantly. As far as I knew I hadn't salted the earth around her house or erased her DVR.

Her eyebrows notched upward and her lips parted. I'd obviously surprised her with my direct question.

"I...I..." She struggled for a few seconds, then finally her expression lost its hard edge. "I'm sorry. You're right. That was rude."

"You're forgiven. Do you want to come up for tea? I can't figure out his coffee maker, it has too many buttons. I feel like I might launch it into outer space."

I didn't wait for her to respond, instead I turned and walked toward the elevator. This was mostly because I was losing circulation in my fingers due to the heaviness of my bags. I knew she was following because her heels clicked on the lobby's marble floor.

Once inside the elevator I waited until she boarded before pressing the button for his floor. A few other passengers also filtered in, so we remained quiet for the duration of the ride. As well, we walked in silence down the hall, and she stood silently as I used my key to unlock the door.

She grabbed two of my bags and helped me carry them into the living room. I didn't miss how she peeked inside as she set them on the table behind the couch.

"Tea first or talking?" I asked, unburdening myself of my winter coat.

"Talking. I don't want tea."

"Fine." I shrugged, tossing my coat to the couch and claiming a leather club chair. "What's your mind?"

She didn't sit. I noted she was bursting with restless energy. "Aren't you even a little bit sorry? A little ashamed?"

"Sorry about what?"

She huffed, like I was being purposefully irritating. "About Martin? About what he's done for you?"

I studied her, cocking my head to one side. "Here's the thing, Emma. I have no idea what you're talking about."

She snorted and crossed her arms. "Yeah, I find that hard to believe."

"I don't. I haven't been keeping up with Martin, I haven't been searching out news stories about him. In fact, I've been avoiding them."

"But you read the news, right? You keep up with current events?"

I shook my head. "Nope. I've been spending the last nine months avoiding the world, outside of music and work. I haven't read a newspaper or a headline in almost a year."

Something behind her glare loosened as I spoke and she blinked at me several times, like she was seeing me with new eyes. Her arms uncrossed and fell to her sides. Emma slowly sat down on the couch, her gaze growing introspective.

"You don't know about…anything that's happened?"

I shook my head.

"And Martin, didn't you ask him?"

"I haven't seen him since Wednesday morning, and he didn't want to talk about it then, so I didn't push."

"You haven't seen him since Wednesday?"

"Nope."

"But aren't you two back together?"

"Of course not."

"Why of course not?"

Now I huffed. "Would you please tell me what's got your piano out of tune? Because I need to leave for a gig in about a half hour."

She studied me for a beat, her eyes narrowing, but with thoughtfulness, not suspicion. At last she said, "Do you know about the houses?"

I shifted in my seat; this topic was a bit of a sore spot for me. "You mean the houses Martin was to gain as part of the trust his father set up?"

"He did, he got them. And then he sold them for approximately one hundred twenty million dollars."

This wasn't a surprise, given what I'd seen of the house in the Caribbean. "And then his father…? Did something happen?"

She shook her head. "He could do nothing about it. By the time he found out, the houses were sold and the money was offshore. Though he tried to file an injunction, a petition to sue for the proceeds, it was thrown out."

"How nice." I gave her a flat smile and she issued me a questioning look; I clarified, "How nice for Martin, that he got his revenge."

"His revenge? Hardly." She rolled her eyes, scoffing at me.

"What do you mean? He sold the houses, didn't he? He launched his fancy satellites?"

"He sold the houses, sure. But, so what? What's a measly one hundred twenty million to a man worth billions? Nothing. Denver's injunction was half-assed at best. Honestly, I think Denver had been looking for a reason to cut Martin off. As of right now, Martin is Denver's only child. He stood to inherit over twenty billion if he'd just been patient and quiet."

"Twenty...billion?" My mind had trouble comprehending that much money. It might as well have been a googolplex of pirate gold.

"Yeah." She nodded once, then added with an impressive amount of derision, "The money was invested into the satellite project, but instead of using these first satellites to drive Sandeke Telecom out of business—which was the whole purpose of his involvement and investment—he's proposed to the board that the satellites focus on delivering Internet to areas with the most need."

"He what?"

"Nothing about selling the houses has gone according to the original plan," she said, mostly to herself. "He gave the money away!"

I tried not to show my interest, but I was interested. Martin's plan and his unwillingness to deviate from it had been—at least in my mind—why we'd broken up.

"Gave the money away? What do you mean?" I picked a piece of lint off the knee of my jeans.

"He donated the sixty million." She said this like the words tasted sour.

I stared at her for a very, very long time, and she stared back. Her eyes were greenish and she was watching me with avid interest, as though keenly interested in my reaction to this news.

Certain I'd misheard her or misunderstood, I finally asked, "I'm sorry, what? He donated sixty million dollars? To whom?"

"To a non-profit foundation, one which he established early last summer. It provides funding for startups that focus on training rural educators, both domestically and internationally in the use of the latest classroom technology and web interfaces."

"I don't understand. He sold the houses for, what? A hundred and twenty million?"

"More or less, yes."

"And he donated half, and then invested the other half into the satellite project?"

"No. The donation and the investment are the same sixty million. He still has the other half—or thereabouts—in some offshore bank-account."

"I'm confused. You just said that he invested in the satellite project."

"No. *He* didn't invest in anything. The foundation he established owns what would have been his share of the 'satellite project'. He forfeited his profits. All the profits go to the foundation and will be used to purchase equipment for schools and students, and will fund initiatives to train teachers."

I sucked in a slow breath, trying to wrap my mind around this story she was telling me. "So, he…what? He gave away sixty million dollars to a foundation he founded?"

"Yes."

"So, the satellites will still be launched?"

"Yes."

"But the foundation owns his share?"

"Yes."

"And he'll…receive no profits?"

"He'll receive no profits. He's given up billions of dollars and probably his only chance to get revenge on his father."

I shook my head because I felt muddled. "Why would he do that? Why would he give it away?"

She smirked. I recognized it as her not-nice smirk. "Why do you think?"

I kept shaking my head. "I have no idea. It doesn't make any sense."

"For you. He did it for you."

I stopped shaking my head; instead I made a very unflattering scoffing noise that sounded a bit like a gurgle. "What? No. No…did he say that? Did he tell you he was giving away sixty million dollars because of me?"

Her smirk fell away and she looked suddenly tired, older. "No. But he didn't have to. We'd been planning this for three years. Then he meets you and everything changes. Of course you're the reason."

"No. That doesn't make sense. We're not together."

"He wanted you back. That's why he did it."

"Did he *say* that he—"

"No. We never talk about shit like that. We're not gal pals, we're business partners. But I have a working brain and I saw him after you broke his heart. Then suddenly all his plans changed and he's giving up his future because Joss Parker's daughter filled his head with bullshit altruistic nonsense? Yeah…he wanted you back, at least he did then."

I only half heard her tirade because I was lost in my own head. I started speaking, but honestly I'd forgotten she was in the room.

"We haven't been together since March, and then it was only for a week. He never called me, never tried to contact me. Not until a week and a half ago, and he didn't say anything about it. He hadn't said anything to me about this. Nothing. If he did this for me, then he would have called or tried to get in touch." My attention drifted back to Emma and I appealed to her simply because she was the only other person in the room. "Right? He would have called me and told me, if he wanted to get back together. He wouldn't have waited for months. That's not how Martin does things, that makes no sense…"

She shrugged, pursing her lips. "Well, I have no idea what he wants now. I mean, I believe he was seeing that intern from RER, Rural Educational Reform—that do-gooder think tank in Washington—another bleeding heart martyr type. But now I don't know, since you're here."

I involuntarily winced at this news, confirming my suspicions he'd been seeing someone else. I felt like all the air had been sucked out of the room and my heart was being stabbed with a fork. I rubbed my chest, the spot over my heart.

"He's…he's seeing someone?" I had trouble not choking on the words.

"Yes. I don't know how you missed it, they've been all over page six since August. They can't cross the street in each other's company without getting photographed. The problem is that they're just so pretty together. Her family is like yours. You know, lots of impressive ancestors with impressively good deeds." Emma's eyes moved up then down my form before she added, "You don't look anything like her, but he definitely has a type."

"What does she look like?" I asked, my question spewed forth unchecked.

Emma rolled her eyes. "I don't know, petite, *really* pretty, red hair, delicate. Who cares?"

It was the girl I'd seen earlier in the week in the pictures, when I'd made the mistake of googling Martin so I could read the interviews he and Sam kept talking about.

"Forgive me if I have no tolerance for gossiping and giving relationship advice to the person who stole my profits."

"Your profits?" I asked lamely.

"Yes. My profits. I was to receive a percentage of his share. And so now you see it's all gone. Instead he offers me a position at the goody-two-shoes foundation and a share of his third world broadcast rights."

"His what what what? Broadcast rights?" I forced myself to re-focus on the conversation, the real issue, not who Martin had been dating...or had recently dated. Honestly, I was only able to re-center myself because Martin had point-blank texted me he didn't have a girl-friend and I trusted him to tell me the truth.

Of course, that just meant he didn't have one right now. But it didn't mean he'd been celibate since we split. This thought made me queasy, more fork stabbing to the heart, so I pushed it from my mind.

Emma released a derisive snort. "Some crazy idea he has, and invested three million of his remaining monies." She waved her hand through the air like his idea was a gnat and she was trying to swat it. "He purchased broadcast rights for basically all of the third world. He has a virtual monopoly on Internet streaming of syndicated shows for the next fifty years, as well as the big sites, like Netflix, Amazon, etcetera." Then she added under her breath, "A lot of good it will do him since no one in those areas owns a computer and they can't get Internet."

I stared at a spot over her head as a picture arranged itself in my brain; unthinkingly, I spoke my stream of consciousness out loud. "Broadcast rights for the third world will never yield a profit...unless underserved areas can get cheap access to Internet. Or free access."

"And are given computers," she added unnecessarily.

My gaze flickered to hers, held it, and my mouth dropped open because Martin was a genius.

"You mean, if they are given computers by a goody-two-shoes foundation? And trained to use them, by the same foundation? A goody-two-shoes foundation that receives funds from the profits of satellites delivering cheap or free Internet to underserved areas?"

Her frown turned thoughtful, then startled, then amazed. "Oh my God."

I nodded, grinning at his cleverness. "Hasn't he discussed this with you? Don't the two of you talk about anything?"

"No. I wouldn't...I was so angry, I didn't want to talk about it."

"And you didn't figure it out?"

"No." She laughed a little, shook her head disbelievingly. "Martin always said you were smart, and he was right. I mean now that you point it out, everything is so obvious. I guess I was just so angry that he didn't follow through with the original plan, plus that stupid foundation... Oh my God. We're not going to make anything close to what we would have made if he'd directly invested in the satellite venture, and he'll never be anywhere near as rich as his father, but wow. We might break a billion. Maybe two."

"It might take a bit, but yeah. In about ten years, once the foundation does its thing and the satellites are buzzing around up there, giving people in rural Africa and the rainforests of Brazil high-speed Internet service, he'll be the only one making money off streaming video in what used to be the third world."

She looked at me and smiled. It was the first time I'd seen her smile since meeting her. Her eyes were bright with excitement and every bit of bitterness had melted away. It was almost a nice moment.

But then she had to ruin it by sighing happily and saying, "God, I love that man."

* * *

EMMA DID STAY FOR TEA, and she was chatty. She also had a habit of tossing her long, perfect, wheat-colored hair over her shoulder in excess. It wouldn't have irritated me so much if she weren't so suddenly effusive about how much she admired Martin.

Really, he was all she talked about: how smart he was, how intelligent, how he was going to change the world. How he was Steve Jobs and Bill Gates and Mark Zuckerberg, except being born into wealth, and therefore able to make a substantial difference earlier in his life, not having to wait for pesky things like investors.

"You know Mark Zuckerberg created Facebook when he was nineteen? And Steve Jobs founded Apple at twenty-one?"

"Hmm." I did know this. I think everyone in my generation knew this information—or at least every person with any geek persuasions. Except I also knew that Steve Jobs was just a smart enough and pushy guy who exploited his friend (Steve Wozniak), pilfered his ideas, and passed them off as his own.

"There's no one like Martin, though. No one who thinks about strategy like he does, who sees the whole picture. He's completely brilliant." Her eyes scanned me, up and down, like she was expecting me to do a cheer for Martin, maybe suggest that we dedicate a fan site to him, and was irritated I didn't seem to share her enthusiasm.

I couldn't decide whether I liked Emma or not. Furthermore, I couldn't decide if it mattered. Perhaps it was the naïve do-gooder in me, but I was disappointed she saw no merit in Martin's foundation until after I pointed out his plan and the foundation would ultimately bring her millions. I also didn't like that her loyalty seemed to hinge on how much money she could make off him.

Plus, I couldn't stop thinking about the very pretty redhead he'd allegedly dated and with whom he'd been photographed countless times. I reasserted the prudence of my decision to never search for any news story or interview related to Martin until I was completely over him. Just thinking about him with someone else made me want to throw a month-long drama parade.

"Did you know I used to work for Martin's dad?" Emma asked apropos of nothing.

I shook my head, surprised. "No. I didn't know that. What happened?"

"Have you met Denver Sandeke?"

"Yes...unfortunately."

"Exactly. He's a complete ass. He's brilliant, but he's an ass and that means he's arrogant. And he's known for sexually harassing his female staff. Once you get used to it, it's...bearable. Mostly I just ignored that part of my job. But my work with Denver is how I met Martin. He was a junior in high school and I was arranging a corporate event at Denver's house in Santa Monica. Martin definitely didn't look like a seventeen-year-old. I knew who he was so I tried to be nice. He started asking me all these questions about what I did for his father, and I thought to myself, *This kid is brighter than his dad. He's going places!* It also helped that he was completely disinterested in me other than my knowledge. Unlike his father, he seemed more interested in what I had to say than my cup size."

"So how did you become Martin's business partner?"

"Well, I had access to information Martin did not. So Martin pulled me aside at one of the parties and asked me how I liked working for his father. I was careful at first, but eventually I saw that he had a plan. And, honestly, I liked the idea of screwing over Denver Sandeke—he is so awful. I agreed to stay on with his dad and pass Martin any information that might be useful. I figured once Martin trusted me enough, he would share his plans with me. He did and the rest is history."

"Hmm..." I studied her. "You placed a lot of faith in a teenager." Not to mention she'd just admitted to corporate espionage like it was no big deal.

"I did," she admitted soberly. "But there's just something about Martin, right? Do you know what I mean? He inspires confidence. People *want* to follow him. I thought about my position with his father and knew—other than gaining work experience—I had no growth potential at Sandeke Telecom. Denver runs it like a good-old boy's club. I was doing the work of an executive and being treated like a 1950s secretary."

"That does sound awful."

"I trusted Martin and he never made me feel like he was interested in anything from me other than my brain. I can't tell you how refreshing that was."

"I bet." I nodded, studying her and finding her to be sincere. Emma may have been a corporate shark, but she was a well-reasoned, capable corporate shark. I understood better why Martin had singled her out.

"What do you think of this place?" She indicated to Martin's apartment and sipped her tea, changing the subject and issuing me a friendly smile.

"I like it. It's very Martin." I hadn't thought about it until she asked, but it was very Martin. It was no fuss, but not sterile. Comfortable. It felt like a home.

I don't think she heard me, because she followed her question with, "I keep telling him he needs to move into a better space. We can't have dinner parties here. This apartment is…okay. But he should be in a penthouse. Did you know he picked out all the furniture himself? I tried to get him to use a decorator." She shook her head, like he was a silly child. "Sometimes I forget how young he is, how much he still needs to learn about the corporate environment. Eventually he'll see things my way."

I opened my mouth to ask why he couldn't have dinner parties in this apartment—it seemed fine to me—but then she started talking again.

"Maybe you could help me. Together we could get him to see reason. I'm sure you have a good perspective, with your parents being who they are. You're probably even better suited to persuade him than I am." She giggled meaningfully.

I tried to keep the abject horror I was feeling from painting itself on my face. I decided it was time for her to go.

She left when I mentioned I needed to get ready for work. Of note, she was diligently nice to me as she departed, asking if she could take me to lunch the next time I was in the city.

"I think it would be really great for Martin if you and I became friends," she said, then added as though to clarify, "that way he won't feel torn about his loyalty to either of us."

I gave her a noncommittal smile and nod, but felt like she was communicating in a different language. I didn't know how to speak corporate politics and networking.

Once Emma left, I made quick work of wrapping Martin's presents, stuffing as many as would fit into his stocking, hiding everything under my bed, then leaving for my gig.

I tried not to let myself get caught up in the idea that Martin had established the foundation and made sweeping, philanthropic changes to his grand plan as some sort of gesture to win me back, as Emma had suggested originally. If he wanted me, the Martin I'd known would have just shown up on my doorstep and demanded we reconcile.

No. There was more to the story of the foundation. I was sure of it. Maybe it had something to do with the pretty redhead he'd been dating...

Again, this thought made me queasy and was accompanied by forks piercing my heart, so I pushed it from my mind.

I decided I would wait to draw any conclusions until after I had all the facts, after I questioned Martin.

[11]
CHEMISTRY OF THE NONMETALS

C HRISTMAS IN NEW YORK is magical.

It's also a time for drunken holiday party hookups, engaging in yelling matches with co-workers after imbibing too much holiday cheer, and sloppy make-out sessions behind fourteen-foot plastic Douglas fir trees.

By the third set of the night I felt like the audience was much more entertaining than our band. We were playing a Christmas Eve party for some huge conglomerate at a skyscraper downtown. Willis told me they were originally supposed to have *a real band*, but then that real band backed out two weeks ago. A real band meaning recording musicians who wrote and sold their own compositions.

And so they were stuck with us and we were stuck with them and that set a very surly, rebellious tone for the evening. Willis decided we would end our third set with *I Wanna Be Sedated* by The Ramones.

When we walked off stage it was the first time they had applauded, and I even heard a few whistles of appreciation.

"We're playing punk, loud, and defiant for the rest of the night," Janet said as she fished a cigarette out of her bag.

Abram pulled out his own pack of cigarettes and his voice was tight and angry when he spoke. "Those fuckers out there are pissing me off."

"Agreed." Willis marched over to Janet and put his hand out for a cigarette. I'd never seen him smoke before; in fact, I was pretty sure he'd quit several years ago.

"Katy, you want to go take a walk?" Fitzy gave me a hopeful smile. He really was cute, handsome, nice. And yet he did nothing for my pants.

I was beginning to suspect that my pants were actually my brain.

Before I could respond, Willis laughed at Fitzy's suggestion. "Where are you going to go for a walk? On the roof? You'd be pacing a small square and shivering your nuts off. We have to be back out there in fifteen minutes, bucko."

"No thanks, I think I need to find the ladies' room," I tossed over my shoulder and didn't wait for anyone to respond. Rather, I exited the backstage area through a giant steel door in a rush because I actually really needed to use the facilities.

I walked through a window-lined hallway, the sounds of recorded music from the party following me most of the way. I stopped when I encountered elevators and a fork in the path. Shrugging, I decided to go left into a new hallway. One side was glass, looking down on an atrium several floors below. The other side was lined with offices.

Soon I found I'd gone in a circle and was back where I started. This was bad news as my bladder was sending up the yellow emergency flag and I was doing the pee-jig to keep myself together. Thankfully, I encountered a pair of intoxicated women who appeared to be on a mission. On a hunch, I followed them and sent a silent thank you to the heavens as they stumbled into a nondescript—and unmarked—women's bathroom with several stalls.

At this point I was cutting it close, so after my business was finished I jogged back to the backstage area and rushed through the door just in time to hear Fitzy say, "She's not even with you! Katy is none of your business—"

I halted, my eyes flickering over the scene before me. Abram was smirking at Fitzy, leaning his shoulder against the brick wall. Fitzy was standing in the middle of the room and appeared to be quite riled up. Willis was between them, apparently keeping them apart. And Janet was nowhere to be seen.

All eyes turned to me as I entered; I didn't know quite what to do. The only person who didn't appear to be upset was Abram. In fact, he looked positively pleased.

At a loss, I stared wide-eyed at the trio and gave the room a little wave. "Hey, guys... What's up?"

* * *

ABRAM DIDN'T STOP CASTING SINISTERLY pleased looks in my direction through most of the fourth set. I assumed this had everything to do with getting under Fitzy's shirt collar, so I ignored his antics.

But then abruptly, his expression sobered during the last song and turned irritated, his eyes narrowing on me as we wrapped up the last stanza. No sooner was I off the stage, I felt his hand on my upper arm leading me out the steel door I'd used earlier on my hunt for the bathroom.

"Where are you going? We have one more set!" Willis called after us.

"Just for a quick walk," Abram called over his shoulder, practically pulling me behind him.

Once the door closed behind us, I demanded, "Let go of my arm, this is a very uncomfortable way to walk."

He didn't turn, but his hand slid down to mine. Abram threaded our fingers together and continued leading me forward.

We came to the fork in the path and I volunteered, "It's a circle. No matter which way you go we'll end up back here." I was honestly too tired to give his strange behavior much consideration.

He pulled me to the right and finally spoke. "Your boyfriend is here."

"My boyfriend?"

"The stockbroker." His eyes slid to mine, his big jaw working, his brown eyes dark and unhappy.

I stumbled, forcing Abram to stop. "Martin? Martin's here? Where? I didn't see him."

"He showed up at the end of the last set."

"He did?"

"Yeah. Now, why would he be here? I thought you two were over."

I tugged my hand from Abram's and crossed my arms over my chest. My heart was racing now.

"We are over. But we're...we're friends. I'm staying with him."

"You're staying with him?"

"This week. I've been staying at his place in Manhattan for the week."

Abram's hands moved to his hips and he released a frustrated sigh. "If you needed a place to stay, you could have called me. You don't have to stay with your douchebag ex."

I scrunched my face, not liking that Abram was calling Martin a douchebag. I knew this reaction was silly as he'd done it before and I didn't object. But things between Martin and I had changed. I'd always cared about him, yes. And now that I'd let go of my anger about our breakup I didn't want people calling him names.

"Listen, he's not a douchebag. Like I said, we're friends. It's no big deal."

"And nothing's happened?"

I grew very still, but felt compelled to ask, "Why is that any business of yours?"

He grit his teeth, his eyes abruptly dimming. "I guess it's not. It's none of my business."

We stared at each other for a long moment in silence and I could see him building a virtual wall between us. He was making his mind up, having a conversation in his head, while I stood here and waited for him to give me a real response.

But he didn't. He closed himself off, burying his thoughts and feelings, and I realized Abram and I were extremely similar.

He wasn't fearless. We were both feelings hoarders.

He may have suggested a few weeks ago that I sleep with Fitzy, or use him as my rebound guy and whatever that entailed, because I wasn't in any danger of falling for Fitzy. And then Abram wouldn't be my rebound guy. He wanted to be with me, but wanted everything to be just right, just perfect, and all sorted before really putting himself out there.

I briefly wondered if the scene I'd walked in on earlier was Abram trying to push Fitzy in that direction.

I felt a smile of ironic understanding claim my features and I exhaled a small laugh, realizing that if I wanted bravery and honesty, it was going to have to come from me.

"Look, I think I like you. And I think you like me, too. I don't need a rebound guy. In fact, I don't *need* any guy. But I would *like* a partner. I would like to be part of a team."

Abram's cold expression didn't change but I did see something pass behind his eyes, a flicker of acceptance, of understanding.

He cleared his throat, his gaze moving to the carpet then back to mine. "It's none of my business, I know. But we've had, at least I've had, a really good time with you this week. So, what are we doing here? Are you back with your ex?"

I shook my head. "No."

"Are you over him?"

I hesitated, my attention moving to a spot behind Abram as I thought about the question, how to answer it honestly. "I don't know. He was my first everything. I'm starting to think it's not possible to ever truly get over that person, the first person who made you feel like… But maybe it is possible to move on."

He was silent for a beat, then acknowledged quietly, "I get that. I know what you mean."

We gave each other quick, commiserating glances and flat smiles. I twisted my fingers while he stuffed his hands in his pockets.

"Katy…do you want to be over him? Do you want to be with me?"

My eyes collided with Abram's and I saw it cost him something to ask the question. As much as I wanted to respond, *Yes, I want to be over Martin. Yes, I want to be with you*, I couldn't. Because my feelings were so much messier than a yes or a no.

He nodded, just a subtle movement at first, as though I had spoken, as though I'd already given my answer and he was processing it.

Before he got too far ahead of me I rushed to clarify, "I don't like feeling this way. I don't like being stuck in limbo and wanting two completely different things. Yes, I want to be over Martin. I know he's moved on, as he's had a girlfriend since we broke up—at least one that I know about. And, honestly, I don't trust him not to hurt me again. But part of me feels like things aren't finished."

"That's just you wishing." He didn't look upset, he looked resigned. "But I get it. I do. Because I didn't feel like things were finished with me and my ex. I hadn't moved on and I kept wishing things could be different."

"Did you tell her?"

"No. I was a coward." He uttered this with no bitterness, just a matter-of-fact assessment of himself.

"When did you stop? When did you feel like things were finished?"

"Not 'til recently. Not until I met you."

I sighed. His words, made with his powerful and deep voice, his soulful brown eyes, caused my heart to ache.

"Abram—"

"Does he know?"

"Know what?"

"That you're still wishing?"

I didn't answer. I didn't need to. Abram gave me a sardonic smirk and shook his head, his eyes teasing but also a little sad, like he felt sorry for me.

"You and I are a lot alike, Katy."

I returned his smirk and shrugged at my weakness. "I don't know how to tell him. I feel so paralyzed. I don't want to ruin our friendship."

Abram closed the distance between us and threw his arm over my shoulder, tucking me close to his broad chest and steering us back for our last set.

"If he hasn't moved on and he's wishing too, then you need to put him out of his misery and tell him what's going on in your head. Be brave."

"Ha! Says Abram. Self-professed coward."

He continued as though I hadn't spoken. "But if he has moved on, you need to know for sure. Because then you can move on, too."

* * *

MARTIN WAS IN THE AUDIENCE. He was standing by the bar and was surrounded by people. I spotted him almost immediately when we took the stage; I explained away this phenomenon to myself, reasoning that he was several inches taller than everyone else.

But really, I found him so fast because he was Martin. I think my blood chemistry had changed when we were together, because locating him in the crowd had been exceptionally easy.

His eyes lifted and found mine, and he held them until I looked away. I felt his gaze on me for the duration of the set. At first it was distracting. But then I settled into it, accepted it, and it began to feel oddly comforting.

When we finished the last song I think we were all surprised at the round of applause we received. The night had not started well, but Janet's idea of punk and rebellion seemed to do the trick. I lifted my attention to the audience, again my eyes immediately finding Martin. He lifted his cell and gestured to it. I interpreted this to mean, *check your phone.*

Backstage, Fitzy was waiting and jumped between my bag and me. "Hey, so, you want to grab a drink?"

I walked around him. "No thanks. I'm really tired."

"And she's got someone waiting for her," Abram chimed in, pulling on his heavy coat.

Fitzy glanced between us. "Who? You?"

"Nope." Abram's eyes met mine and I was impressed by all the different sentiments I saw there: humor, regret, acceptance, exhaustion, and a subversive pleasure in giving Fitzy a hard time.

I checked my phone, saw that Martin had sent me two messages; the first provided directions on where to meet him. The second read,

MARTIN: *Don't go out with the band, I'm driving you back to my place. I haven't seen or talked to you all week.*

I FROWNED at this second note, felt like it was an unnecessary addition. The more I studied the text, the more it looked like a command. I rolled my eyes. Typical Martin. I quickly typed out a response.

KAITLYN: *You're not the boss of me.*
Martin: *I know. But sometimes I act like I am.*
Kaitlyn: *Why?*
Martin: *Because you like it.*

I STARED at his last message; it set my heart off at a gallop. I did like it. I liked arguing with Martin, challenging him, bucking under his attempts to boss me around. Or, I had liked it when we were together.

Abram was right. I was still wishing. And yet, there were still so many things unsettled between us. Even if I told him I still had feelings for him and he returned them, would it matter? All of the reasons we split before seemed to have evaporated except for the biggest one: he'd chosen his revenge over us...or maybe he hadn't.

The way Emma described the situation, it sounded like Martin hadn't put his revenge plan into action. And yet, he'd let me walk away in the spring. GAH! I was confused. I didn't *know* if I could trust him.

Nevertheless, there was the girl in the pictures. Even if he'd ultimately abandoned his revenge, he'd still been able to move on with someone else and I hadn't.

Absentmindedly, I gathered my things and left the backstage area, only peripherally aware that Fitzy and Abram were still talking and that it might have something to do with me. I easily found the elevators, the sounds of the remaining party fading the farther I walked from the event space.

But then I became aware that someone was behind me and I turned, finding Willis. He looked grim.

I gave him a questioning look, stopping and facing him. "What's up?"

"I thought we talked about this."

"About what?"

"You and Abram. You and Fitzy."

I breathed my relief. "Nothing is going on with Abram. He and I are friends."

"What about Fitzy? He's looking at you lately like a sushi roll with no tuna."

"Nothing is going on with Fitzy and me either, at least not on my side."

He crossed his arms. "Don't shit on my leg and tell me it's frosting."

The elevator dinged, announcing its arrival.

Meanwhile, I did an admirable job of not laughing at the mental image of me defecating on Willis's leg then trying to pass it off as chocolate frosting.

"Again, nothing is going on."

"I told you before, I don't want you going on any mattress tours. This stuff between you and the boys needs to stop."

"Willis, I have no part in their boy-angst. Whatever they're arguing about is between them."

Willis nodded thoughtfully, but then his attention snagged on something behind me. I twisted to see what it was and found Martin standing just inside the elevator, his eyes narrowed and focused on Willis.

"Oh...oh!" I turned completely around, feeling my cheeks flood with warmth while I wondered how much of that conversation Martin had overheard.

"Do you want something?" I heard Willis ask.

"Yeah. Her." Martin lifted his chin toward me as he leaned forward, grabbed my arm, and pulled me into the elevator.

Willis snorted. "Take a fucking number."

"Hey!" I objected.

Martin ignored me, moving me behind him, obviously misunderstanding Willis's meaning. "You don't talk about her that way."

I heard Willis sputter, "I'll do whatever the fuck I want, *son.*"

Uh oh... Of all the things Willis could have called Martin, son was probably the worst.

"Those are big words coming from a little man who's all washed up. So listen, grandpa, you treat her with respect or I'll—"

"You'll do nothing. He'll do nothing." I jumped in front of Martin, covered Martin's mouth with one hand and pushed the close-door button with the other. "Bye, Willis. See you tomorrow," I squeaked as the doors slid shut.

When the elevator finally started its descent, I let my hand drop from his mouth and leaned heavily against the wall behind me, letting my head fall back with a *thud.*

"That guy is an asshole," he said. No, actually he growled it.

I sighed, closing my eyes, "Martin..."

"What?"

"That guy is my boss."

"You need a new boss."

"Can you try being a little nicer?"

"What did I do?"

"You weren't very nice to Willis."

I heard Martin move, the rustle of his coat. "He deserved it."

"You misinterpreted the conversation."

"Really? I misinterpreted, 'Take a fucking number'?" He sounded really angry.

I sighed again, opening my eyes and sliding them to the side, peering at him. "Yes. Willis can be crass. But he wasn't insulting me. I promise."

"Doesn't matter. I don't like that guy."

"Just because you don't like people doesn't mean you can go around treating them like crap. What is so hard about being nice?"

"It's time-consuming." He said this completely deadpan and of course it made me laugh.

"Oh, Martin…" I wiped tears from my eyes. I was laughing so hard I was crying, but also I was just completely exhausted.

After a minute of watching me laugh at him, he reluctantly smiled and shook his head. "Besides, I'm nice to you."

"Is that supposed to make me feel special? That you deem me worthy of kindness?"

"Yes."

The doors opened and Martin grabbed my bag, hoisting it to his shoulder and leading me out of the lift with a hand on my lower back.

"Well, it doesn't," I said tiredly. "My self-worth does not rise and set based on your treatment or opinion of me. I want no special treatment, I insist you treat me like you treat everyone else."

"That's not going to happen."

"Why not?"

He didn't answer at first. In fact, he didn't speak for so long I started to think he wasn't going to respond. He guided me out of the building's main entrance to where his car was waiting. A man stood next to it, like a valet or a guard and had been waiting for us. Martin opened the passenger door for me, took my hand, and helped me inside.

But right before the door closed I heard him say, "Because you're Kaitlyn."

[12]

LIQUIDS AND INTERMOLECULAR FORCES

W E DIDN'T TALK in the car, mostly because I fell asleep during the quick ride. I woke up briefly when Martin lifted me from the car and into his arms. I curled into him because I was drowsy and he smelled like Martin. On the short walk to the elevator I fell back asleep, but this time I dreamt.

We were back on the boat. The sun was setting. The air was hot and salty. Martin carried me down the steps to our cabin. His hands were loving, caressing, amorous, as were his looks. We were both dressed in almost nothing, scraps of bathing suits, the feel of his skin against mine, and our combined warmth was intoxicating. He laid me on the bed, climbed over my body. He slipped his callused hand into my bikini. He touched me. I sighed. I trusted him. His oceanic eyes captured mine. He leaned down to kiss me...

I woke with a start in the present as he laid me on the bed in my room in his apartment and moved to take off my shoes. My body was humming and confused. My mind was still preoccupied with my dream, of us together, and all the ways I desperately wanted him.

"I've got it." My voice was unsteady as I bent my legs and sat up a bit, pushing my hair out of my face, needing him to leave before he saw my disorienting desire and embarrassment.

"Go back to sleep." He grabbed my right foot and took off my shoe.

"No, I got it." I wiggled my leg, trying to break free from his grip.

"Kaitlyn," his hand slipped into my pants leg, caressed my calf, making me freeze but also sending a lava flow of *Yes, please* to my center, "go back to sleep. I'm just taking off your shoes."

I couldn't respond. His hand on the bare skin of my leg meant I was rendered speechless. His eyes were visible even in the inky darkness and I couldn't look away. How pathetic was I? Martin inadvertently touches my leg, looks at me in the eye, and I'm mentally begging him to take off his pants. *Then my pants. Then our underwear. Then...*

But he doesn't. He holds my gaze as he takes off my shoes. He sets them on the floor at the foot of my bed. He turns. He leaves. And I experience a sensation I imagine is akin to falling off a very tall building.

As soon as I heard the soft click of the door, I lay back in the bed and stared at the ceiling, restless and overwrought, my center throbbing, aching. I tried to bring my breathing under control as well as the intensity and sharpness of my longing.

And the strangest thought occurred to me.

Really, it wasn't that strange. I'd touched myself in the past, but not since being with Martin. Before, it had basically been an experiment, an exploration of sorts, born out of detached curiosity. I'd wanted to make myself orgasm at the time because I wanted to know what it felt like, what all the fuss was about. My experiment had never yielded anything, just me feeling immeasurably silly.

But now—the specter of my dream and his lingering scent filling the room—the idea didn't feel silly at all. In fact, I could still smell him on me, expensive soap and aftershave. My desire, my craving for him felt abruptly overwhelming; I couldn't breathe. I was suffocating with it.

I knew he was in the apartment. I could hear him moving around. I closed my eyes and pictured him. I unbuttoned my shirt, unhooked my bra at the front, then let my other hand drift down my stomach to my pants, under the waistband, into my panties. I was on autopilot, my movements compulsory.

I was already wet. And when I touched myself I was shocked at how sensitive I was, how responsive. I glanced down—my fingers on my bare breast, my smooth stomach illuminated only by the city lights, my wrist disappearing into the waistband of my tuxedo—and imagined Martin watching me, seeing what I was seeing.

Maybe he was sitting on the edge of the bed, telling me to do this. Instructing me, giving me praise and loving—yet dirty—words of encouragement. Just the thought of him seeing me this way and liking it made my breath become ragged, and I felt myself edge closer to release.

Impatient, I unzipped my pants and spread my legs. This time I imagined he was in the chair at the end of the bed; he could see me, all of me, and he was silently watching. Maybe he was dressed in his suit, his pants unzipped and open, stroking himself…

Aaaand, that did it. I came. And I had to turn my head into my pillow to keep from crying out. Though I continued the fantasy, envisioning that imaginary Martin had also reached his release and was holding my gaze as we came together.

I sobered relatively quickly, the experience leaving me spent but unsatisfied. I removed my hands from my body and turned away from the door. I pulled my shirt closed, tucked my knees to my chest and stared out the window overlooking Central Park, at the tall buildings with their twinkling lights in the distance.

A cold lump of nothing settled in my stomach. I finally understood why Abram had been trying to get me to consider a rebound guy.

A warm body. A soft touch. A gentle kiss and whisper. It would have made a difference. True, they wouldn't have filled the void, but they would have softened the fall.

My chin wobbled and I tried to breathe normally. My eyes stung. I fought the urge to cry by biting my bottom lip fiercely, focusing on the voluntary pain I was inflicting with my teeth rather than the gaping hole in my chest that never showed signs of healing.

But then I started and tensed, because I heard the unmistakable sound of my bedroom door opening. I held my breath and squeezed my eyes shut, thankful I now faced the window.

"Kaitlyn?" he whispered. Goosebumps raced over my skin at the sound of his voice, but I couldn't speak.

Heck, I couldn't breathe. I didn't want him to see me. I felt certain if he saw my face, the front of my clothes, he'd know what I'd been doing. I didn't want him to know. If he looked into my eyes he'd know I was still crazy for him. And if there was even a chance he'd look at me with pity, I didn't want to see it.

So I said nothing.

I felt him move closer. He hovered at the edge of the bed. Martin set something on the side table...it sounded like a glass. My heart was hammering between my ears and I fixated on it, ignoring the urge to turn toward him and make a fool of myself, to tell him I didn't care if he'd ever loved me. I loved him. I wanted him. I needed...

I was concentrating so hard that I flinched my surprise when I felt a blanket fall gently over my shoulders. My lids opened automatically, startled, and I found Martin standing in front of me, covering me with a duvet from the closet.

"Go back to sleep." Again, he whispered this, his attention following the line of the blanket, perhaps to make sure I was completely covered.

But then his eyes moved to mine and our gazes collided, or at least it felt that way to me, like a head-on collision. His movements stalled then stilled. He looked surprised.

"What," he started, stopped, then stared at me. He seemed confused by what he saw. "Are you still angry with me about Willis?"

I shook my head. "No. Just tired." My voice was rough, uneven.

He frowned, lifted his chin slightly, and I could tell he didn't believe me. His eyes moved over my body where it was now covered by the blanket and narrowed with obvious suspicion.

"What were you doing—"

I cleared my throat, interrupting him. "I'm tired. Goodnight, Martin."

I turned my head into the pillow, my hair providing a concealing curtain. Especially right now, looking at him made everything harder, more painful.

He didn't leave immediately. Several seconds ticked passed, my heart rising higher in my throat with each passing moment. But then I heard him leave—his feet on the wooden floor, the soft click of the door.

And for the first time in several months, I cried.

* * *

I WAITED UNTIL I heard Martin's bedroom door close. After another ten minutes, I wrapped myself in a towel and tiptoed to the bathroom. My face was red and splotchy, and my eyes were itchy from my odd bout of tears. Standing under the hot spray of the shower did wonders for my peace of mind. I took my time washing my hair and soaping my body, feeling warm, soothed, and much calmer when I finally turned off the water.

Back in my bedroom I quickly dressed in yoga pants pajamas, one of my Death Cab for Cutie concert T-shirts that had been regulated to sleepwear, and my Abraham Lincoln socks. Just as I was climbing back into the bed my foot connected with something beneath it. I turned on the light and bent to peer under the mattress.

It was Martin's stocking and presents. I'd completely forgotten about them in my sleepy—then aroused, then depressed—haze. I pulled them from their hiding place and flipped off the light switch. Clutching the gifts to my chest, I held my breath and listened for any sounds of movement coming from elsewhere in the apartment. As far as I could discern all was quiet.

Again, I tiptoed out of my room, this time intent on the fireplace. I figured I could hang his stocking somehow then put the rest of the presents on the hearth. But when I entered the living room I stopped short and my mouth fell open in surprise.

Martin had procured a tree.

It was a small, Charlie Brown type of tree, no larger than four feet tall. The baby tree was in a tin bucket draped in white lights, yet held no other ornamentation, not even a star at the top.

However, the tree wasn't responsible for my paralysis. The reason why I was standing just beyond the hallway, still clutching Martin's gifts, with an expression of shock and awe, was because of what the tree sat upon.

His unfussy Christmas tree rested on top of an antique Steinway upright piano. The piano had a huge red ribbon and a bow wrapped around it. I couldn't move. It was the prettiest picture I'd ever seen. The little minimalistic tree, the classic piano with a big red bow, both sitting next to Martin's gray stone fireplace in his warm, cozy, bookish living room. Windows on the other side of the fireplace showcased a snow-covered New York City beyond.

I felt like I was looking at an image in a magazine. If I'd seen this image in a magazine I would have paused on the page, maybe even ripped it out and filed it under *my ideal life*. I couldn't move because I didn't want to move. I wanted to stay in this picture forever.

"What are you doing up?"

I yelped, jumped, and ungracefully twisted toward the sound of Martin's voice, gulping in a large, shocked breath. I struggled to keep hold of the packages in my arms, having momentarily flailed and loosened my grip. Martin rushed forward, seeing I was just about to drop a box, and caught it with one hand while steadying me with the other.

"Oh my God, you scared me." I closed my eyes, my heart hammering in my throat as the rush of adrenaline subsided.

His hand slipped from my waist to my shoulder, squeezing. "I thought you were tired."

"I was. I mean, I am. But I was waiting for you to go to sleep."

"I heard you take a shower so I couldn't sleep."

"You couldn't sleep because I was taking a shower?"

He ignored my question and asked me instead, "Are you okay?"

I nodded, laughing a little, and peeked at him through one eye. "You just missed Santa Claus. He dropped this stuff off for you, but left in a huff when he found no cookies."

He shrugged, giving me a brilliant smile. "Those bloody cookies are mine. Fat man needs a diet."

This made me laugh harder, and we both ended up laughing together for several minutes. As the hilarity and enjoyment of our own jokes subsided, I caught Martin eyeing the presents in my hands.

"What's all this?"

"Just some stuff I saw that I thought you might like."

His gaze lifted, his smile growing softer as his eyes searched my face. He asked in wonder, "These are all for me?"

"Yes. But you weren't supposed to know about them until morning. Congratulations, you've ruined Christmas."

Martin pressed his lips together and gave me a look reminiscent of our time on the boat last spring, like I was perfect and strange. "Technically, it's already morning."

"Oh, well, in that case," I stepped forward and dumped the cornucopia of wrapped presents into his arms, "Merry Christmas, Martin."

He accepted them gingerly, shifting to the side to make sure none of them fell. "Jesus, Kaitlyn!"

"That's right, Jesus." I nodded. "Jesus is the reason for the season."

This only made him laugh again while he struggled to keep his grip. "I mean—help me carry all this stuff to the couch."

Grinning at him, I took the boxes most precariously perched and turned for the couch, stumbling a little when I caught sight of the piano and tree again. A rush of uncertain happiness spread from my stomach to my extremities.

"Do you like it?" he asked from behind me, obviously noticing where my attention had snagged.

"Is it for me?" I asked, a rush of emotion — confusion, hope, hopeful confusion — making my throat tight.

I heard him deposit his stuff on the couch and felt the heat of his body directly at my back just before his arms wrapped around my shoulders, his cheek brushing against my temple.

"Of course it's for you." His voice was a rumble above a whisper.

I placed my hands on his forearms and squeezed, glad he couldn't see my face because I was overwhelmed. My hopes and my questions were assembling themselves, trying to partner up so I could begin to understand what this gift meant. I had to clear my throat before speaking.

"I...I don't understand."

"What's to understand? It's a piano. The guy tuned it yesterday and it's all ready for you. You should play something."

"Now?"

"Yes. Now."

I couldn't do that. I didn't want to touch it. If I touched it then I'd want to keep it and nothing in this apartment was mine to keep. And when the time came for us to part, which felt inevitable, I would lose something.

No. The piano wasn't mine any more than Martin was mine.

So I shook my head, clearing it of these maudlin thoughts, and decided to tease him instead. "You got me a piano for your apartment."

"Yes."

"So I have to visit in order to play it."

"That's the idea."

"So it's blackmail."

"It's an incentive."

I let my head fall back on his shoulder and looked up at him. "It's bribery at best."

He grinned down at me. "It's an enticement."

"Don't try to out-synonym me. Let's settle on enticing extortion."

"I'm fine with that."

"But you don't have to buy me a piano in order to ensure I'll visit. Friends visit each other. If you want me to visit, just ask me."

His arms tightened then let me go. I felt him draw away, heard him sigh quietly. "Do you want something to drink?"

"Are we going to finish this conversation?" I turned to watch him disappear.

"Yes. But I need some scotch to finish this conversation," he called from the kitchen.

"Scotch? Are you drinking scotch?"

"Yeah. It's good. You'd like it."

"Monogrammed towels, business cards, fancy watches, corner office, and now scotch. It's like I don't even know you anymore. Are you golfing now, too? Pretty soon you're going to retire and move to Miami."

He barked a laugh and reappeared with two glasses and two bottles of unlabeled red liquid.

"Fine. No scotch. How about sangria?"

"Oh! I'll take sangria."

I moved all of his presents to the center cushion of the couch and claimed one end while he poured us both a glass and settled on the other side. The sangria was really, really good. It didn't even taste like it had alcohol in it, except maybe a little red wine.

I sipped mine.

Meanwhile, Martin gulped his then refilled his glass.

"So…" I peered at him while he studied his loot. "Like I said, just ask me to visit."

"I will."

"You don't need to buy a piano."

He took another gulp of his sangria then set it to the side. Selecting a box, he tore through the wrapping, and said offhandedly, "I know I don't *need* to buy you a piano, but I like hearing you play—and more than that stuff you play in the band. I want to hear your music, the stuff you compose."

He grinned as he discovered what was inside the wrapping paper and held it up. "I like this. I'm going to use this when I send you letters."

It was the lazy fisherman desk set. My chest filled with warmth, the kind caused by giving someone a gift and seeing that they love it. Plus… letters from Martin.

"Open the rest." I bounced in my seat, caught up in the excitement of opening presents, and tossed him the hobbit soap dispenser—but I surreptitiously held back the Stevie Wonder vinyl. I felt a little weird about the record. When he'd played *Overjoyed* for me on the boat, it felt like he'd been trying to communicate with me. But this record was just a record, right? Or maybe it wasn't.

I pushed my anxiety away and took a large gulp of the sangria.

He dutifully opened his gifts, smiling and laughing and just generally having a fantastic time. I soaked it all up—the wonderful feelings and his expressions of happiness—storing it for later, hoarding it for when I would need the memory. I also drank two glasses of sangria, and began to suspect it contained quite a lot more alcohol than just red wine.

"The Princess Bride?" He opened the first few pages of the book, his eyebrow lifting in question.

"You're going to love it. It's full of awesome sidekicks and side characters, like a giant who rhymes, and man who is hunting another man who killed his father and has six fingers, and—"

"Isn't this a movie?"

"Yes. They're both great, but you should see the movie after you read the book. And look," I leaned forward, flipping the pages back to the beginning and pointing to the swirling signature, "it's signed by the author."

I gave him a satisfied grin, which he returned. As I sat back in my seat I was feeling warm and a little dizzy, the sangria and lack of sleep was going to my head.

"Thank you," he said softly. "I'll read this next. Then you'll come over for pizza and we'll watch the movie."

"Sounds good." For some reason this thought made me melancholy, a future that involved me visiting him in a few weeks to watch The Princess Bride.

With a silent sigh, I handed him his last present, feeling unaccountably nervous about the record, and grateful he'd suggested drinks before presents and conversation.

Part of me hoped that when he opened the gift he would see it merely as a record of a musician he liked. Another part of me hoped he would read more into it and tell me that he'd been wishing, too—but I wasn't holding my breath. Martin wasn't the wishing type. When he wanted something, he took it; or at least he was vocal about it.

If he wanted me still, then he would have done something, said something already. Therefore... not holding my breath.

He pulled back the paper, his big grin in place. Then his eyes moved over the front of the album and his grin fell away. He blinked at it. My blood pumped hot and thick through my veins and I fought the urge to cover my face with my hands. I didn't hide though. Instead I braced myself, deciding I would take whatever came next like an adult.

He seemed to stare at the front of the record for an eternity, and when he did look at me, he lifted just his eyes. Something raw but also detached made his stare feel like a brand. He examined me. The air in the apartment shifted, became heavier, hotter.

"Do you regret it?" he asked, glancing away, his voice cool and calm. He set the record on the coffee table along with the other gifts.

I swallowed thickly and managed to croak, "What?"

"Do you regret what we did?" His gaze swung back to me, held mine as he pushed, "That I was your first? The first guy you—"

"Engaged in gland to gland contact with?"

His grimace told me he didn't like my word choice. But the phrase had slipped out in a poor attempt at protecting my heart, some instinctual need to keep the conversation from becoming too serious.

Martin corrected, "Made love with."

I stared at him, giving my aching heart a moment to settle, wondering if I should be flippant or honest. In the end I decided on being flippantly honest, because sangria made me brave, but not brave enough to risk everything.

"No. No, not at all. I don't regret it at all. First, you are quite handsome, you know. Hot even. I'll never regret getting me some of all that." I pointed at him then moved my index finger in a circle, making him laugh lightly and roll his eyes.

Reluctant, slightly embarrassed laughter looked damn good on Martin Sandeke.

"And secondly, you really seemed to know what you were doing, how to make things easier, better for me. Since I was going to lose my virginity at some point, of course I wanted to lose it to an expert."

He stopped smiling then, the merriment in his eyes waned, and his mouth curved into something that wasn't quite a frown.

"And lastly..." I started, stopped, then decided to abandon being flippant and just be completely honest—however I kept my eyes fastened to my yoga pants.

"Lastly, I was in love with you. I wanted you—and not because of all that," again I pointed to him with my index finger, moving it in a wagging circle, "but because I wanted *you*, Martin, and all that you were, and how you made me feel, and how I hoped I made you feel."

I paused, gathered a breath for courage then met his gaze again, adding, "I wanted you."

"I was in love with you, too."

His words made me feel like someone had deflated all my birthday balloons. I gave him a flat smile, my eyes flickering away from his, but I said nothing, because I knew he'd never actually loved me. This knowledge was now bone-deep.

If he'd loved me then he would have chosen us over revenge.

If he'd loved me as I'd loved him, then he wouldn't be feeling platonic indifference toward me now; he wouldn't be able to settle for being my friend. He would be struggling as I was struggling.

If he'd loved me as I'd loved him, then a Martin Sandeke google search wouldn't have yielded pictures of him and a pretty redhead, who I was now convinced—after speaking with Emma—was his last girlfriend.

I glanced at my glass. It was empty again.

"What?"

"What, what?"

"Why did you give me that look?"

"Because I'm out of sangria."

"No. Before you looked at your glass." His eyes narrowed with suspicion. "You don't believe me." He stated this as though the thought had just occurred to him.

I gave a non-committal shrug and reached for the bottle at my left, intent on pouring a larger glass so it wouldn't run out quite as fast.

"You don't believe that I loved you." He stated this as fact and I felt the mood in the room shift from friendly to antagonistic.

"Meh…" I shrugged again. "What does it matter? It's in the past."

"It matters." His rising anger was tangible.

I felt a spike of furious indignation and tried to distance myself from my feelings on the subject, because, if I didn't, he was going to end up with a face full of sangria.

Instead I attempted to be pragmatically truthful. "Well, if it makes you feel any better, I'm certain you liked me a lot. And it was obvious you made a valiant—but failed—effort to feel more."

"Wow." He breathed, then exhaled again, like I'd knocked the wind out of him. "That's a really shitty thing to say."

Yep. He was super-duper mad.

But I couldn't feel sorry about what I'd said—a little twinge of guilt perhaps, but not sorry. He was the king of blunt (and sharp) honesty. He *never* pulled his punches. If he didn't like or couldn't handle my honesty then that was just too damn bad.

Regardless of the certainty of my own righteousness, discomfort and disquiet made a camp in my chest. I forced myself to look at him. "Listen, twisty britches, listen to the facts—"

"Fuck your facts." His eyes burned like an inferno, but his voice was surprising low and quiet.

"Well, see, here we go." I gestured to him with my refilled glass but averted my gaze. "This is an example. Your language. You see no problem talking to me like that, you never did. That's not how you speak to people you love."

"It is when you're passionate about them."

"No. It's not okay. It's disrespectful."

"We can't all be frigid robots."

I ignored this statement, obviously made with the intent to wound, in favor of pointing out the other facts. "And then you chose revenge on your father over us."

"And you chose your mother's career over us."

I nodded. "Yes. Yes I did. Because it was the right thing to do."

"And God forbid you do anything for yourself. God forbid you be selfish for one single, fucking second and give into your passion, take what you want." This was said through clenched teeth; I could tell his temper was rising and he was struggling to keep his voice from rising with it.

"At the expense of good, innocent people? That's not love, Martin. Love is supposed to make you a better person, love is supposed to... to..." I moved my hands in a circle, some of the wine dripping on his leather couch. I wiped at it with the bottom of my shirt as I searched for the right words. "It's supposed to improve your character, not demolish it. If you loved me—if you wanted what was best for me— then you wouldn't have wanted me to destroy my mother's career due to my own selfishness."

"I wanted you to choose me." He wasn't yelling, but I could tell he was barely controlling his impulse to intimidate with volume.

I responded quietly, "And I wanted you to choose me."

He looked away, the muscle at his temple ticking, the lines of his jaw and lips severe.

I shrugged. "So I chose reason, and you chose passion, and nary the twain shall meet."

"I chose passion?"

"Yes. Revenge against your father."

He nodded slowly. "Yes. I was passionate about that." His words a reluctant confession as his eyes focused over my shoulder.

"It's the love of your life." The words slipped out before I could catch them and I wished them back immediately. It was one thing to be honest, it was another thing entirely to bare my bitterness. Martin winced like I'd struck him.

I hadn't meant it to be mean, but it was mean. My heart constricted with a sharp ache—because I saw my blurted statement caused Martin pain. I didn't want to hurt him. That was the opposite of what I wanted.

"Barnacles," I said, shaking my head, trying to figure out how to apologize without sounding even more like a wicked witch. "I'm sorry, Martin. I'm sorry. I shouldn't have said that."

"That's right. That's who you see, and that's who I am." His tone was frosty, laden with animosity and sarcasm. "You still think I'm an arrogant asshole, and that's all I'll ever be to you." This last part sounded as though he were talking to himself.

I grimaced. "I don't want to hurt you."

"Waaaay too late." This statement was paired with a sardonic chuckle.

Another piercing stab nailed me through the heart and I felt cold and a little nauseous. "Okay, well then I'm officially the asshole. I accept the title and all the death stares that accompany it." Again, I couldn't meet his eyes; I busied myself by draining my glass.

"Parker." He sighed, obviously frustrated, rubbing his hands over his face. "Can we move past this?"

I nodded, still swallowing, and eventually was able to answer in earnest—but perhaps a little too loudly and with slurred speech. "Yes! Yes, let us never speak of the past again."

"That's not what I mean."

"Sandeke," I leaned forward, depositing my glass on the table and tucking my legs under me on the center cushion, kneeling directly in front of him, "despite my awfulness, I really do want us to be frie—"

"Are you drunk, Kaitlyn?" He cut me off, his eyes glinting with a dangerous mixture of exasperation and barely contained fury.

"No. Just tipsy enough to say what's on my mind without over-thinking it."

"What were you doing earlier, in your room, before I walked in?"

I held very still and stared at him, a shock of flustering embarrass-ment crashing through me. His question was unexpected and made me chase my breath. I'm sure I looked guilty because I felt guilty. He was staring at me with contemptuous certainty, like he already knew the answer, like he thought I was a coward.

I felt caught.

Even so, I would never tell him the truth. "I…I was—"

He didn't give me a chance to lie. "If I kissed you right now, would you remember tomorrow?"

"Why would you…why would you kiss me?" I couldn't keep up with this conversation.

"Because you're beautiful. Because I want to." His gaze was on my mouth and he sounded completely belligerent; meanwhile, my heart was in my throat.

"Do you? Do you really? Or are you just tipsy enough to be feeling nostalgic?"

"No. I'm just tipsy enough to say what I want without overthinking it." He mimicked my earlier words through clenched teeth.

I couldn't help my next question because I needed to know, "Would it mean anything?"

"Kissing you always means something to me. Would it mean anything to you?" Despite his anger, he appeared to be choosing his words carefully.

"I guess it would confuse me. Are we...would we still be friends? After? If we kissed?" I couldn't choose my words carefully; they tumbled out of my mouth in a mass of disoriented chaos.

He shrugged, like he didn't care, but his gaze had turned sharp, menacing. "If you wanted to be."

I felt his response like a punch to my stomach, because I didn't want to be his friend, not really. I wanted him to love me. I wanted him to still wish like I wished. Yet I did want to be his friend, because it was the right thing to do. Because I cared for him. Because I wanted him to know he had a safe place.

This exchange hurt, and the rush of dismay bubbling to the surface of my psyche made my throat feel tight. And yet I couldn't help the desperate desire twisting in my lower belly at the idea of just one kiss, just one more time. I wanted him so badly.

Martin leaned forward, his eyes capturing mine, though they were sullen, verging on hostile. He placed his hand on my thigh as he advanced, his thumb rubbing back and forth drawing all my awareness to the heat of his palm.

"What if we kissed, and I touched you? What if we fucked? Would you remember tomorrow?"

"Yes, I would remember. But I don't understand why you're doing this." A hint of pleading had entered my voice and my eyes stung. Martin paused his forward momentum, now just ten inches separating us, his eyes searching mine.

"Would it mean anything to you?" he questioned softly, then his voice grew a bit rough as he asked, "or would it be sex between friends? No strings? Could we just make each other feel good for one night?" Martin's hand inched higher on my thigh, taking the heat of his fingers closer to my center. It was obvious he was very angry with me, as his touch felt vindictive, punishing in its gentleness.

I shook my head, though my body—and especially the vicinity of my pants—was on fire for him, for his touch, for his attention. The ache was physical, and made forming words difficult.

"I'm not built that way," I admitted clumsily, my voice unsteady as I balled my hands into fists because they were beginning to shake. "I think one more night together, just for the purpose of making each other feel good, would be the end of our relationship."

By the time I finished speaking my whole body was trembling with the effort to hold myself away from him.

I read hunger in his eyes, but I also saw resentment and malice. His fingers on my upper thigh drew away, and I captured his hand before he could retreat completely. I cradled it in both of mine and he let me.

My voice was wobbly, and my vision blurred as I gathered my remaining courage and said, "Martin, I am sorry for what I said. I can see you're mad at me and I hurt you and I'm sorry. But I don't want to lose you completely. Not again."

The rancor in his glare softened, but didn't quite disappear. He nodded and ground his jaw, his eyes falling away.

He used my grip on him to tug me forward but I resisted, feeling raw. I didn't trust him, and I certainly didn't trust myself to resist him.

His gaze lifted back to mine at my reluctance. He studied my face, likely saw my confusion, hurt, and apprehension, because his eyes filled at once with what looked like a rush of remorse.

"I'm sorry, Kaitlyn. I'm…God, I'm such a fucking asshole. I'm sorry." As he said this, Martin raised the hand not holding mine and wiped two tumbling tears away from my cheeks with his thumb, his palm moving back to my jaw and cradling my face.

"Come here." He swallowed, and I saw he did so with effort. He tugged on my hand again and this time I let him bring me to his chest. He moved both of us down the couch until he was laying horizontal and I was half on top of him, snuggled between his body and the couch.

I was so confused.

"I'm sorry," he said again. "I'm sorry."

I sniffled. "Me too. I'm sorry too. I wasn't trying to hurt you."

His arm squeezed me. "You're forgiven and obviously you were right, I'm still an asshole."

Something about the way he said, *I'm still an asshole* made me laugh lightly, but uncertainty and the lingering ache in my chest kept me from relaxing against the length of him. His suggestion that we use each other's bodies felt like an assault, like an affront against the sacredness of what we'd shared—at least on my side—and the tentative friendship and trust we'd been building.

And yet...

I felt him stroke my hair lovingly, his other hand held mine and he toyed with it. He lifted my fingers to his mouth and brushed feathery, cherishing kisses on the tips and knuckles. Eventually I forced myself to relax, and turmoil gave away to melancholy, and finally to exhaustion.

My cheek rested against his chest where his heart beat, and I listened to it slow then even, lulling me to sleep.

[13]
CHEMICAL EQUILIBRIUM

I WOKE UP in my bed with a Martin mattress.

Meaning, we were in my bed and I was sprawled on top of Martin. I frowned, searching my memory, getting ready to stone myself if we'd had wild monkey sex and I'd blacked out in the middle of it. But then I remembered everything from last night/early morning, and I sighed—both in lusty disappointment and levelheaded relief. He must've carried me into my room and decided to stay with me until I woke up; and I'd been so exhausted I didn't wake up.

A very Martin-esque move. He was smart, so he knew—after last night's awkwardness—I would avoid him this morning. But I couldn't avoid a Martin in my bed.

"Are you awake?"

I nodded against my pillow, turning my face toward his. I cracked open my eyes and studied him. It was obvious he'd been up for a while. I took stock of where my hands were, where his hands were, etc. None of our touching was technically friend-inappropriate, but I took the opportunity to stretch and shift my leg so it wasn't quite as insinuated between his.

"Yes. But barely," I mumbled, yawning.

"Good. I'm starving."

He lightly pinched my rib, making me jump and squeak. Taking advantage of my involuntary spasm, he rolled above me, planking, and captured my gaze with his, reminding me of the moment right before I'd lost my virginity nine months ago. My throat was Sahara desert dry. I blushed scarlet, but couldn't look away.

He was sexy. Epic, unlawful levels of sexy. I was suddenly very awake and quite incapable of moving.

"Parker, what happened earlier this morning—and I'm not talking about the Hobbit soap dispenser—it doesn't change anything." His tone was stern, as though he were commanding me to not feel awkward. "I was a jerk-face and I am really sorry. You made it clear that you don't want to risk our friendship and I'm going to try to respect that."

I blinked at him and nodded, giving him my best brave smile.

"Me too," I croaked.

A momentary frown pinched his features, and he faltered, studying me, his gaze straying to my lips. But then he gathered a large inhale, rolled off and away, and then strolled out of the room.

He called over his shoulder, his voice tight, "You make music, I'll make breakfast."

* * *

BREAKFAST WAS SOME sort of delicious egg casserole with onions, bacon, spinach, and more bacon. The smell of it cooking filled the apartment causing my mouth to water.

While he was in the kitchen I eyeballed the piano, found myself caught in its gravitational pull. It was so pretty, so magnificently alluring. The keys were real ivory—which meant the antique upright was over fifty years old—and were warm to the touch. I pressed middle C and found the sound rich, full, and beautiful.

"Play it."

I glanced at him.

He must've visited the muffin man and the danish man yesterday, because he brought me a very fresh-looking cherry and cheese danish, a banana nut muffin, as well as a lovely cup of black coffee. Martin placed his offerings on a table beside the piano then straightened, giving me a stern look, but his words were gentle.

"Please, play it."

I saw it meant something to him, so I sat, gathered a breath for courage, and teased out a tentative melody. Meanwhile Martin hesitated next to the bench. Then, as though abruptly making up his mind, he bent down and kissed my cheek, his morning stubble scratching my face and leaving a warm mark on my skin.

"You need to visit me all the time." He lifted his voice as he disappeared back into the kitchen, "Think about moving in. I was serious about accepting cookies as payment."

I smirked reflexively, my tune becoming light and silly, and thought about becoming Martin's roommate. As long as we both dated no one else, were celibate, and never drank sangria around each other, it sounded like a winning idea.

I allowed myself to get lost in an improvisation, though it was mostly based on a song I'd written over the summer after drinking a Red Bull and being unable to sleep for forty-eight hours. The composition was originally manic, but I slowed it down, added a few bass clef-only stanzas, and closed my eyes.

When it felt finished, I released the keys, pressing down on the sustain pedal with my last chord, allowing the notes to go on and on until they faded and reverberated like the memory of an echo. It really was a magnificent instrument.

When I opened my eyes I realized Martin was sitting in one of the nearby club chairs, his elbow on the arm rest, his thumb brushing back and forth against his bottom lip, and his eyes watching me intently.

I straightened, blinking at him and the room as I came out of my daze. "Sorry...how long was I playing?"

He didn't respond right away and I noticed he was also lost in a bit of a daydream.

"Martin?"

He shook himself, his gaze focusing sharply on me. "Yes?"

"How long was I playing?"

His eyes flickered to a spot behind me on the wall. I turned and followed his gaze, found a wall clock that told me I'd been at it for over forty-five minutes.

"Gah! Is the casserole ready?" I reached for my coffee, found the tumbler tepid and I pouted. "Cold coffee."

"Don't worry, I have more coffee." His voice was stiff as he plucked the cup from my grip and disappeared into the kitchen. "And breakfast is ready."

I followed him, loitered at the entrance, and appreciated the sight of a fine man moving around the kitchen like he knew what he was doing.

"How and where did you learn to cook?" I asked, as he opened the oven set to warm and withdrew a casserole dish.

"Mother had a cook. Her name was Esmerelda. She taught me."

"Hmm…" I grabbed my coffee cup from where he'd left it on the counter and dumped the cold coffee into the sink. "Can we play forty questions while we eat breakfast?"

"Forty questions?"

"Yes." I rinsed the cup then moved to refill it with fresh coffee. "Emma stopped by yesterday, and—"

"Emma was here yesterday?" His tone told me he wasn't happy.

"Yes, no big deal." I sipped the hot beverage, placed it on the small kitchen table, then turned to the cabinets to seek out dishes for breakfast. "We talked. It's all good. But she deposited a lot of information in my brain and I think it's going to take at least forty questions for me to gain the answers I seek."

"What kind of information did she deposit?" In my peripheral vision I saw he was grabbing knives and forks.

"Well now, you can play forty questions too. I ask you a question, you ask me a question. There's no need to keep tally of how many, it's just that I'd like to clear up as many unknowns as possible before heading home this evening."

He was quiet for a beat as we set the table, then said, "That's right. I forgot you're leaving today."

I took stock of our progress, found everything to be satisfactory, and sat next to him as he served the casserole.

154

"I'll start—I'll answer your question about what kind of information Emma shared."

He nodded, glanced at me warily, then grabbed a muffin and tore it in half. By the time I was finished relating the story of Emma's visit the day before, he'd eaten three servings of casserole, two danishes, and a muffin. As well, he was on his second cup of coffee and third glass of orange juice.

I stripped the conversation of all my emotions, tried to relate just facts, but he interrupted me a few times and asked for clarifications, making my tale longer. I decided to leave out the part where Emma and I discussed his last girlfriend as I felt like her existence wasn't really pertinent to the issue at hand.

At last I was able to question him. "So my question is, why did you set up a foundation as the controlling shareholder in the venture capitalist company instead of keeping the profits for yourself?"

He shifted in his seat and I saw he was considering how best to answer this question.

"You can tell me the truth, Martin, whatever that might be."

"I know." He drank some more coffee, examining me over the rim of his cup. "There were actually several reasons."

"Okay, what was the biggest reason?"

"How about I start with the most important business reason?"

"Fine."

He cleared his throat and set the coffee cup on the table, leaning forward. "After what my father did—with your mother, trying to use us to control her—I realized that if I invested directly into SAT Systems, the venture capitalist company launching the satellites, then there was a small chance—but a chance nevertheless—that he'd be able to take legal action against my investment. So I established the foundation. Its non-profit status cleaned the money, basically, and meant he had no claim to it. I didn't want to put the project in jeopardy."

"But you gave up sixty million dollars and subsequently billions of dollars in revenue."

"But that didn't matter to me as much as following through with SAT Systems. I mean, I'm the head of the foundation. I have the same voting power at SAT Systems that I had before. Only the profit doesn't come to me, it comes to the foundation."

"So," I tried to understand his motivations, "launching the satellites was more important than the money part of your revenge plan? Sorry to use the term, but I thought the main ambition of your revenge against your father was to eventually ruin him and make yourself three times as wealthy in the process."

He stared at me, gritting his teeth, his jaw ticking for a long moment, as though debating with himself. But then abruptly stated, "When you walked out, the *revenge plan,* as you call it, didn't hold much meaning anymore. It took me a while, but I figured that out by June, three weeks before my birthday, before I had access to the trust. You were right. Focusing my energy on fucking over Denver Sandeke was a waste. And you would have known all this if you'd read any of my interviews."

I sat up straighter, surprised, feeling like I'd been slapped—but not in a violent way, more so in a reprimanding, wake-the-fuck-up kind of way.

Before I could stop myself—riding a rising wave of resentment—I said, "Listen, I would have read the interviews, but when I did a google search all that came up were pictures of you with your girlfriend—or ex-girlfriend."

Martin frowned at me, his face scrunching in a way that told me he had no idea what I was talking about; in fact, he said, "I have no idea what you're talking about."

"Red hair? Petite? Pretty? Ring any bells? Emma also mentioned that you two were dating."

His lips parted and he blinked at me as though seeing me in a completely new light.

I couldn't hold his gaze any longer because I felt an abrupt spike of fear that his eyes would soon be clouded with pity. Instead I stabbed at my casserole and tried to fight the swelling distress that I'd just exposed myself.

I mumbled, "Like I told you last week when you came to the coffee shop, I avoided news about you for a reason."

He didn't respond right away, but I felt his eyes on me, considering me. Peripherally I was aware that he'd placed his fork on his plate and was leaning his elbows on the table.

"I'm considering Dr. Patterson as my replacement at the foundation for operations. Rose Patterson, the girl in the pictures, is his daughter." His voice and words sounded careful.

I took a bite of the delicious casserole that no longer tasted delicious, careful to keep my eyes averted. "Oh?"

"Yes."

"Okay." I was determined not to cry. I would not be that stupid girl who cries when she talks to her ex-boyfriend about his current exploits. Therefore—to ensure that I did not cry—I distanced myself from him, his words, and my feelings.

He was silent for a beat, still watching me. "I told you last week, I'm not dating anyone."

I shrugged. "It's really none of my business."

"Rose was a way to meet Dr. Patterson."

I nodded, cleared my throat, found that I really, really didn't want to talk about this. After ensuring that the buttresses around my heart were completely fortified, I lifted my eyes back to his and tried to bring the conversation back to its original focus.

"So, you were saying about the interviews?"

"Kaitlyn—"

"You decided revenge wasn't worth it?"

"Damnit, just listen for a second."

"Fine. I'm listening." I leaned back in my chair and crossed my arms over my chest, giving him absolutely nothing.

"I wasn't ever really with Rose. I needed to meet her father. She was..." Martin looked frustrated and seemed to be searching the kitchen table for the right way to explain.

Watching him struggle I suddenly understood the situation, and I supplied for him. "She was a means to an end? You used her because of who her father is?"

For some reason this thought made me feel both better and worse.

Martin gritted his teeth. "Maybe it will make more sense once I explain more about the foundation."

"Okay, tell me about the foundation."

I watched his chest expand with a large breath and his eyes settle back on mine; but now they looked as guarded as I felt.

"The actual plan—alternate source of Internet delivery for rural areas—still made sense, even without the ultimate goal of revenge on my father. So rather than focus my energy on Denver Sandeke, I turned my attention to how I could work with the team I'd assembled to make this venture meaningful and profitable. We're not doing this to drive my father out of business—although that may eventually happen, and at the very least, Sandeke Telecom and the rest of the big monopolies will have to cut their prices drastically—we're doing this because it makes sense. It's a unique opportunity, and, yes, it will make a difference."

His mouth was a flat, stern line, and he was glaring at me.

"I see," I said, because I did see. As Emma had suggested, Martin had truly given up revenge. I thought about telling him I was proud of him, but couldn't quite bring myself to do so.

Sighing, Martin glanced at his plate and shook his head. "I sold the houses—with Emma's help. She made that happen before Denver found out. I sent half the profits offshore and I donated the rest to the foundation. The foundation invested the money in SAT Systems. Emma explained to you what the foundation does, right?"

I nodded.

"Well, Dr. Patterson currently leads a think tank in Washington called Rural Education Reform. He's dedicated his life to trying to equalize the opportunities for children in underserved areas. I know I'm not the best person to lead the operations of this foundation if I truly want it to succeed—and I do, I need it to succeed. He is a content expert and he's passionate about the subject. I think he might be the best guy for the job."

"So you met him through his daughter?"

"Yes. I befriended her because I wanted to meet him." This admission held no note of an apology.

"So, you're friends?"

I noted that Martin's gaze was veiled before it fell away. He studied his plate, but I knew he didn't really see it.

Finally he said, "I used Rose to get to her father. It worked. He's probably going to take the position."

I felt my heart sink. I thought about asking him to clarify the extent of his relationship with Rose, but ultimately I decided against it. If he wanted to tell me, he would tell me. And he wasn't my boyfriend; we weren't involved. It wasn't my place to ask.

His eyes lifted back to mine; they held a new edge, like he was bracing himself for my reaction.

I shrugged, feeling frustrated but resigned to my place. "So, the foundation. You need it to succeed?"

He sighed and I couldn't tell if he was relieved or disappointed I didn't press the Rose issue.

Nevertheless, he answered my question. "Yes. Although the mission of the foundation is noble, ultimately I'm leveraging the work they do to make money for myself. Lots and lots of money."

I nodded again. "I figured that out when Emma told me you'd purchased the broadcast and streaming rights for the next fifty years in underserved areas."

"Good. I'm glad you understand that. Because, I'm never going to become a person who is selfless. If I see an idea to exploit, I'm going to exploit it." His tone was harsh, like he was trying to communicate something of great importance to me, like he *needed* me to see that though he'd let go of his plans of revenge, he hadn't suddenly become a philanthropist.

"Well then, I'll cancel the application for sainthood I filed on your behalf." I gave him a wry smile that didn't quite meet my eyes, hoping he'd see I never expected him to be a saint.

But he didn't.

"Kaitlyn..." He looked discontent, pushed his plate to the side, and rested his forearms on the table. His frown was pensive and severe. "I'm never going to be a person who thinks about honor before personal gain; it's not second nature to me, like it is to you. I

159

might do things in the future that you don't agree with. But I hope that—"

I stopped him by covering his hand with mine. "Stop, listen for a second. I know you're not perfect. No one is perfect. I know that how you were raised means you're a survivor. You needed to be. I understand that. But revenge was a choice, protecting yourself is instinct."

His eyes were solemn, yet I saw he understood my meaning. I squeezed his hand then continued, "You said to me a few weeks ago at The Bluesy Bean that you had plenty of logic, or reason, or something like that. But you also said that you wouldn't mind having my self-sacrificing, martyring bullshit input either."

"Did I say that?" he deadpanned, fighting a smile.

"Basically. More or less. My point is, this friendship is good for both of us. I make lots of mistakes. So do you. And maybe we can get to a place where we trust each other enough to be a mirror for the other person. I'll let you know when you need more saintliness in your life. You let me know when I'm being a self-sacrificing martyr. How does that sound?"

His mouth crooked to the side as his gaze wandered over my face. "That sounds good."

"Also, I'll tell you when you're crossing the line between hot young executive, and an uptight corporate sell-out."

"Are we talking about my towels again?"

"You mean your *monogrammed linens*? If so, yes."

He huffed a laugh. "They were a house-warming present from Emma."

"I'm burning them."

"That's fine."

"And I'm replacing them with Lord of the Rings beach towels."

"That's fine too. I don't give a fuck about my towels as long as they dry me off."

"Good to hear. Then I'll also be adding some My Little Pony ones as well."

We shared a small smile and I released his hand, taking the pause in conversation as an opportunity to steal a chocolate chip muffin. As I did so, I noticed Martin fingering his calluses, rubbing the pad of his thumb over the tough patches of skin.

I guessed he had more to say, so I prompted, "Anything else I should know? Did you get a tattoo over the last few months?"

"No. Did you?" His eyes shot to mine.

"Yes. It's a centaur mounting a unicorn on a rainbow." I took a bite of my muffin and smiled.

He looked horrified. "Really?"

"Maybe."

His eyebrows jumped and his eyes automatically moved down my body, as though he could see the hideous hypothetical tattoo through my clothes.

Suddenly, catching himself, he closed his eyes, pressed the base of his palms against his forehead, and shook his head. "Actually, there is something else you should know. There's another reason I set up the foundation instead of taking the profits directly, and that has to do with your mother."

"My mom?"

He opened his eyes again, giving me a very direct and pointed look. "Yeah. The activities of SAT Systems fall under the jurisdiction of her senate committee. But my broadcast and streaming rights do not, especially since most are for international areas. The foundation is non-profit, and isn't regulated as one would regulate a for-profit corporation. Different rules apply."

"Okay..."

"Meaning," he paused, watching me intently, "meaning that you and I can have this...friendship, and your mother can't be accused—with any legitimacy—of having a conflict of interest or bias."

* * *

"YOU DON'T HAVE TO COME."

"I want to."

"You want to spend your Christmas afternoon at a senior center in Queens?"

Martin shrugged, switching gears. His car went *vroooom*.

Meanwhile I was still mulling over the information he'd detonated during breakfast. I was still wondering what the exact nature of his relationship with Rose Patterson had been. Plus I couldn't stop thinking about the fact he'd purposefully structured his involvement with the satellite project, and established the foundation so our *friendship* wouldn't compromise my mother.

I didn't want to read too much into the action, but it seemed like this meant he'd been thinking about me, and some future relationship with me, several months ago when he'd established the foundation. And this simmering thought process twisted me up into a ball of confusion.

Because I didn't know what his actions months ago meant for us *now*.

In fact, I opened my mouth to ask this question when Martin broke the silence with his own question.

"Why are you leaving tonight? Stay an extra day." He glanced at me briefly, his question and slightly demanding statement pulling me from my thoughts. He returned his attention to the road. "I'll take the day off tomorrow, show you around the city."

"That's nice of you, but train tickets tomorrow are really expensive. But I did want to ask you about—"

"I'll drive you home."

"No." I scrunched my face at him, shook my head. "Don't be ridiculous. That would be four hours of driving for you. Plus I promised Sam I'd be home tonight so we can have dinner together. She's been alone all day, and we have a plan."

"A plan?"

"Yes. We're going to exchange gifts, drink wine from a box, and binge watch the last season of Doctor Who."

He nodded and I noted that the corner of his mouth was curved downward into a frown. I could tell he was lost in thought. Meanwhile I was re-gathering my courage to ask him about the foundation.

Suddenly he asked, "When are you in New York next? When's your next show?"

"Oh, well." I cleared my throat, flexing my fingers over my knees. "Not until the end of January, as far as I know. Plus, with school starting up again next semester and all the new departmental requirements, I might have to cut back with the band."

"You seem…happier." Martin's eyes flickered to me, his gaze sweeping over my face.

His words and how he watched me as he said them, like he respected and valued me, made my chest feel airy and light. I recognized he was trying to be a good friend. I glanced down at my hands, feeling self-conscious beneath his steady and apprizing scrutiny.

"I am happy." I nodded at this assertion.

I was happy.

Even without Martin I would be happy and this realization caused a burst of gratefulness to warm me from my head to my toes—for him, for our week on the island, *and* for our odd Christmas in New York.

Because I wanted him to know he'd helped me and that I would always be grateful, I continued unprompted, "I love music, I love playing it and composing it. You were right to push me. You made a difference in my life and I don't think I've thanked you for that yet. So," I glanced up, found him watching me with avid interest, "thank you, Martin. Thank you for finding me in that chemistry closet and seeing me in the first place. Thank you for helping me see myself."

We were at a light and Martin studied me for a long moment. His jaw ticked pensively and he seemed to be working through a problem of some importance. I allowed him time and silence to ponder.

At last he said, "I'm sorry."

Or, at least I thought that's what he said. But the chances of Martin Sandeke saying *I'm sorry* out of the blue felt really slim. More likely he'd said, *I'm starry* or, *I'm a Ferrari.*

I sought to clarify. "What? What did you say?"

"I'm sorry," he repeated, his eyes moving over my face while his lips curved into a small smile, possibly because I looked so entirely incredulous.

The light turned green and we were off. As he spoke his eyes never strayed from the road.

"I let you down, and you'd trusted me. I thought...after spring break, I thought I could wait you out. I kept expecting you to change your mind, kept thinking you were bluffing, that eventually you'd agree to see me in secret—that way we'd both get what we wanted. But when I chased you down in the student union and you told me I was ruining you...I saw that you were right and how fucking stupid I'd been to wait. It didn't occur to me that we were over until you asked me to walk away. And when you did, I realized I was too late."

The sobriety that accompanied an unpleasant memory and serious matters chased away my smidge of warm fuzzies, and replaced them with a simmering discontented heat and a renewed flush of discomfort. I remembered that day with vivid starkness, like it had just happened. I remembered how well he'd looked at the time, how unchanged, until I'd practically begged him to leave me alone.

And then he'd looked destroyed. His agony a tangible thing, and a mirror of mine.

I stared at his profile, really looked at him. He was the same Martin, but different. We were both so different. I wasn't hiding in closets and he wasn't losing his temper.

"You deserved better," he said quietly. He sounded like he was talking to himself.

Martin pulled into the senior center and parked the car. His movements were jerky, like he was irritated with himself, or regretting his words, or the memory. Whatever it was, he was agitated and distracted as he exited the car. Meanwhile I felt incapacitated by the puzzle pieces arranging themselves in my mind.

He'd looked fine that day at the student union because he hadn't thought we were over. And this realization made me feel hollow, because I'd misjudged him.

And *he'd* deserved better.

[14]

MOLECULAR SHAPES

MARTIN STAYED FOR the show, but things were tense.

Willis glared at Martin.

Fitzy glared at Abram.

Janet glared at the senior citizens. I surmised she wasn't a fan.

And Abram…well, he played his guitar and ignored the ire.

Luckily the show was only two sets of classic Christmas hits. When it was over, most of the band went their separate ways in record time and with no pleasantries. I hoped the weighty tension was due to spending a week together almost non-stop, and we'd get our groove back after a break.

Abram lingered, taking his time packing up his bass. Once we were alone, he walked over to where I was stuffing my tie and jacket into my bag and stopped just in front of me.

"Hey," he said, his smile small and genuine, but as always with a hint of smirkiness.

"Hey." I peered at him through one eye. "You look like you're up to no good."

"Me? Never." His grin spread as he reached for my hand and pulled it face up between us. Then he placed a small bunch of greenery tied with a white ribbon in the center of my palm.

"What's this?" I split my attention between him and the little package.

"It's mistletoe." His smile became lopsided and his dark eyes danced merrily. "For granting wishes."

I laughed, though I'm sure it was shaded with dejection, and I sighed. "You're good people, Abram Fletcher."

"So are you, Katy Parker."

I stared up at him and he stared down at me. I knew he perceived my melancholy because his crooked smile became a questioning frown.

"Hey…everything okay?"

I didn't know how to answer, but in the end I didn't have to, because Martin picked that moment to walk into the room. Both Abram and I turned our heads at the interruption. Martin's gaze narrowed as he assessed the scene before him, his eyes settling on where Abram still held my hand between us.

Before he could slip a mask over his features, I saw a range of emotions flicker behind his eyes, but none were permanent. In the end it was just an unreadable jumble.

Eventually, he straightened, standing taller, and his gaze meandered back to me, cool and aloof.

"Are you ready? I don't want you to miss your train." His tone was as flat as the line of his mouth.

"Yeah, almost." I turned to my bag and placed the mistletoe gently in the front pocket then retrieved the gift I'd purchased for Abram and handed it to him. "Here, this is for you."

His eyebrows lifted into sharp arches and his small, genuine smile was back. "For me?"

"Yep. You don't have to open it now. Put it under your tree and save it for when you need a mug."

He laughed and rolled his eyes. "Well, thanks for ruining the surprise."

"You're welcome. And thanks for the…other thing."

"You're welcome." Abram gave me a gracious nod then lifted his chin toward the door where Martin waited, his eyes never leaving mine. "Now go. I don't want you to miss your train."

* * *

MARTIN CARRIED MY bag to the car, which was silly because it weighed almost nothing. But I let him because I got the distinct impression that carrying my one-pound bag meant more to him than it did to me.

Plus, he was scowling.

My suspicions regarding his mood were confirmed as soon as he pulled into traffic. He was driving really fast, and aggressively, *and* impatiently. I checked the security of my seatbelt.

It was one of those situations where I felt like, had we been meant for each other, then I would know the right thing to say. But I wasn't sure whether he was upset about his sudden confession on the drive to the senior center, or if he were irritated about something else.

Regardless, I felt compelled to break the silence and *say something.* I wasn't okay with stunted communication between us.

"So, my mother wants me to perform at a fundraiser she's having." I allowed my eyes to flicker to him, watched as the hard lines of his profile didn't exactly soften, but almost.

"Your mother wants you to perform? So she's okay with the change from chemical engineering to music?"

"I didn't really give her a choice to be honest. I just decided, then told them about my decision. I then started working two jobs to make sure I could cover myself financially."

"Because you thought they might cut you off?"

I shook my head before he finished asking the question. "No. I wasn't ever concerned about them cutting me off. It's just, it was important to me to prove I could support myself financially, that music was my career and not a hobby funded by my parents."

He nodded and I noted that most of the tension had eased from his shoulders. Maybe distraction had been the right approach.

"I can understand that. I mean, if you think about it, you're more self-made than I am. All of my money, all the money I've invested, has come from my father, even though he didn't willingly give it to me."

"Does that bother you?" I tried to keep my voice low and gentle so he didn't think I was judging him, because I wasn't.

He shrugged but said, "Honestly? Yes. He used me. I used him. I'm so fucking tired of being used and using people. I'm..." he paused, his chest rising and falling with the silent breath, "I'm just tired of it."

"So, stop using people," I said before I thought better of it.

Martin glanced at me then back to the road, his expression a cross between incredulous and amused. "Just stop using people?"

"Yes. And don't let them use you."

I watched the corner of his mouth reluctantly curve upward as he gave an almost imperceptible head shake. "Okay... Maybe I'll try that."

His easy acceptance of my suggestion made me feel brave, so I pushed, "Maybe even apologize to the people you've used."

I watched as his eyebrows lifted and his smile faltered. "You want me to apologize to my father?"

"Oh, *hell no*! Not him, never him. But maybe...Rose?"

Martin's smile completely fell away. We were quiet for a moment and I could tell he was giving my suggestion serious consideration. Again I left him to his thoughts.

Then abruptly—and I suspected mostly to himself—he said, "We weren't involved, but she was a friend and I did use her. She wanted to be more than friends, but I wasn't...I didn't. At least I was honest about that from the beginning."

I bit my top lip because, inexplicably, I felt like smiling. It was likely the vain, selfish part of me; the part that did jigs in Grand Central Station. I was relieved, so very relieved, that he and Rose had never been involved. Because, obviously on some fundamental level, I was a selfish harpy and never wanted Martin to find happiness if I wasn't the source of it.

But instead of giving into the smile, I suggested, "Then tell her you're sorry and make an effort to not be that guy. Be a good friend."

His smile was back as he watched the road, but this time it was softer. "I think I will."

"Good."

It was a nice *friend* moment for us. It felt...pleasant, meaningful. We fell into a companionable silence, the earlier strain between us seemed entirely forgotten.

Martin's eyes darted to mine then away, and I watched his hands tighten on the steering wheel. "I'm so glad you changed your major."

I gave him a mock suspicious stare. "Why? Because I sucked at chemistry?"

"No, no. You excel at chemistry. Plus you excel at sucking..." Martin's smile turned sly and he glanced at me. Then he winked.

The villain was flirting with me...!

FLIRTING!

WITH ME!

AFTER OUR FRIEND MOMENT!!

Hot outrage flooded my system with an unexpected violence. I couldn't believe he was bringing up friends with benefits again after our conversation last night, after how much it had hurt me. I couldn't do that with him. Before I could catch myself, I reached over and pinched the inside of his thigh, just above his knee.

"You're a dirty, shameless flirt!" I spat.

"Ow!"

"That didn't hurt, flirt."

"I'm driving. Are you trying to kill us?" His words had no effect since he was smiling and trying not to laugh.

"No more flirting." I crossed my arms over my chest and scooched lower in the seat, tucking my chin to my chest, seething.

I felt him eyeball me before he demanded, "Why?"

"Because it—" I caught myself, gulped a large breath of air, and glanced out the window.

The silence was not companionable. It was tense and unwieldy. I fought my desire to reach over and pinch him harder.

"Why?" he asked again, this time his tone was softer, curious.

I heaved a heavy sigh and tried to release some of the potentially irrational anger that had built a home in my chest.

"I loved you, Martin. You were my..." I had to pause again, clear my throat before I could finish. "You were my first in every way that matters, and losing what we had was a big deal for me. That month, after we broke up, I lost twenty pounds. I felt no joy. I didn't even like cookies. Things didn't improve and I didn't start moving on at all until August."

Silence stretched again. He downshifted, turned on his blinker. The car decelerated. We stopped at a light. I heard him gather a breath like he was about to speak.

Still staring out the window, I cut him off before he could. "I don't think I'm ready for you to flirt with me. It...hurts. I need us to be one thing or the other. In between stuff just confuses me. So don't flirt with me. And don't suggest that we have no-strings sex."

"Kaitlyn, I'm doing this all wrong—"

"Then stop. Just," I glanced at him, allowed a hint of pleading to enter my voice, "stop confusing me. Be a good friend."

He nodded solemnly, his jaw working, and returned his attention to the road. Once again, tension hovered and surrounded us, permeating the inside of the car.

I tried to push the melancholy from my mind. I tried and failed. Therefore I felt remorseful relief when we pulled up to Grand Central five minutes later.

He opened my car door and helped me affix the large backpack in place. He remarked on the size of the backpack. We loitered for a few moments at the trunk of his car, continuing our benign discussion until uncomfortable conversation gave way to uncomfortable silence.

I stared at my shoes for five seconds then forced myself to look at him in the eye.

"Well," I said louder than necessary, nodding for no reason, "I guess I'll see you later."

His jaw ticked as his eyes moved between mine, searching. "Yeah..."

I stuck out my hand, gathering a bracing breath and feeling some

170

unknown emotion rise in my chest, making it tight. He hesitated, then fit his hand in mine. Neither of us shook our combined hands. We just stood there, our hands suspended between us, sharing a strange stare.

"When will I see you?" he asked.

"I'll call you when I have the dates for our next show in the city. Maybe we can grab pizza."

He nodded, not exactly frowning. "We could watch The Princess Bride."

"Yeah, that sounds good."

"And you can visit your piano."

I gave him a half smile and moved to withdraw, but he tightened his grip, halting my progress. I glanced at our hands then back at him.

"I have to go."

"Right." He nodded again, again not exactly frowning; he let my fingers slip away, took a step back, and repeated, "Right."

"Goodbye, Martin." I reached into his trunk for my sleeping bag, my gaze flickering to his once more. He wasn't looking at me. His hands were in his pockets and his attention was on his shoes. I waited for a beat.

When he said nothing, I turned and walked toward the station. But this time, because I felt oddly and irresistibly compelled, I looked back.

He was still there, right where I'd left him, and he was watching me walk away. So I waved. He waved back, stuffed his hands in his pockets, but he made no move to leave.

After a long moment, I tore my gaze from his and entered the building.

[15]
THE ATOMIC THEORY OF MATTER

A FTER NO CONTACT for a week, during which I tried my best to ignore all non-friend feelings for Martin, I received a very nice text message from him on New Year's at exactly midnight. It read,

MARTIN: *I wish you were here so we could start this New Year together.*

IT WAS PAINFULLY SWEET.

And confusing.

I didn't reply right away because I didn't know what to say. Was that a friend message?

My heart was scrambled and tangled in my chest, and I had difficulty sleeping because I was obsessing about his text. I waited until the next morning to respond. In the clear light of day I read his message again. Pragmatic and sober Kaitlyn decided I'd inferred way too much from the simple message of well wishes, and I opted to tap out a benign and friendly reply.

KAITLYN: *Happy New Year! I wish you'd been here so I could show you your new towels. Look for "An Unexpected Party" to arrive this week.*

I STARED at my screen afterward, but then set my phone aside when he hadn't replied after ten minutes. Really, it was the perfect friend response. I couldn't figure out why it made me feel so lame.

I didn't know how to navigate these waters with Martin. Yes, I was doing this blindly. But I realized late in the afternoon on January first —after reading his text message at least twenty times—that I was not following my heart. Eventually I meandered to my keyboard and tried to arrange music as a conduit for my chaotic feelings.

A thought began to form, that felt suspiciously like the beginning of a plan, which I assumed was the start of a decision. I was going to have to come clean with Martin. I was going to have to put it all out there, all my messy and disorganized wishes, and be brave. I was in the limbo of uncertainty and I was tired of it.

"I'm giving you my copy of Cosmo. Can you put it in the kitchen when you're finished?"

I blinked at Sam's sudden appearance in my room then at the copy of *Cosmopolitan* she'd just tossed on my bed.

"You're giving me your copy of Cosmo?"

"Yes. To borrow. There's a stupid quiz I want you to take on whether you and your best friend are compatible."

"If it's stupid then why do you want me to take it?"

"So we can make fun of it later. Also, remember my friend Kara? The one we went dancing with? The one who needs a place to stay?"

"Ah, yes. The potential new roommate."

"That's the one. Let me know what night next week we can all get together so you can interview her and share your chore checklist. We need to make a decision soon."

I studied Sam for a bit as she thumbed through our mail. "Sam...do you like the chore checklist?"

She shrugged, not looking up. "It doesn't bother me. I know you like it, but you're a lot tidier than I am. Dirty dishes don't give me hives."

With that statement she meandered out of my room.

My eyes drifted back to the magazine on my bed; a heavily photo-shopped and airbrushed model graced the cover—more a manufactured pixilation than an actual person. I twisted my lips in distaste at her unrealistically long legs and the unnatural curve of her waist and boobs.

Basically, magazines wanted Jessica Rabbit—the animated character—not real women. Heck, even supermodels weren't good enough anymore. Real women didn't sell magazines. Unrealistic and unhealthy images of female beauty sold magazines. And in this men were not to blame, because the female readership dictated and perpetuated the cycle of dysfunction, not men. Women.

In many ways, women were the enemy of realistic representations of beauty. We sabotaged our own self-interests…and that was sad. I sighed at the model and flipped open the magazine, scanning the contents, noticing with no interest that there was an interview with *America's Next Top Model's* latest winner.

And then I remembered.

I remembered I'd been derelict in reading Martin's *Men's Health* interview from over the summer. Now that his relationship status with Rose Patterson had been clarified for me, I felt no trepidation at the thought of being faced with images of them together.

Sucking in an anxious breath, I jumped from my bed, and in my haste to scramble for my computer, tripped over a chair. It took a bit of browsing through smiling pictures of Rose, but I finally managed to locate the magazine article.

It had been given a month before his birthday and published the month after. His wasn't the feature story. In fact, the interview was rather short and toward the back of the magazine. There were several pictures of him—shirtless of course, and in spandex of course—looking pensive and muscular, staring out over the water with a blue sky behind him.

The first half was about him being the youngest team captain in the

American Collegiate Rowing Association. But, as Sam had warned, the second half was about me.

Interviewer: We have to ask you about your love life now, as a service to all our female readers. Any special girl in the picture?

Martin: No. Not anymore.

Interviewer: Not anymore?

Martin: Nope.

Interviewer: Care to elaborate?

Martin: Nope.

Interviewer: You were at one time romantically linked with Kaitlyn Parker, Senator Joss Parker's daughter. Any credibility to that rumor?

Martin: Yes.

Interviewer: But you two split up?

Martin: Yes.

Interviewer: Did it have anything to do with Senator Parker's politics?

Martin: No. It had to do with me being an a__hole.

Interviewer: Whoa! Should we take this to mean Kaitlyn Parker is *The One That Got Away*?

Martin: If you want, but I prefer to think of her as simply *The One*.

Interviewer: Okay then. You should know you've just broken a lot of hearts with that statement, but let's move on. So what's next for Martin Sandeke?

THE FIRST TIME I read it I didn't absorb half of what it said. The second through hundredth time, I paused at the part where Martin said, *If you want, but I prefer to think of her as simply The One,* and my chest constricted.

If I thought I'd been obsessing about Martin before, then I hadn't known the true meaning of the word. I tried to remember every look, every conversation we'd had over the last few weeks. Basically, I chased my tail in a racetrack of circular logic, ala:

IF I WAS THE ONE, as Martin had said, then why didn't he try to contact me before December?

Because you told him to leave you alone, that's why. So he left you alone.

But now he's, what? He's over me? He wants to be friends? Then that means I was never The One.

That's right. You're not The One.

Then why did he say that in the interview?

Maybe you were The One over the summer but he changed his mind, or maybe you are The One, but he's waiting for you to give him a sign.

A sign? Like what? Ye Martin of Old would have just told me how he feels! What am I supposed to do?

I don't know! Ask him!! I HAVE NO ANSWERS FOR YOU BECAUSE I AM YOU!!

Stop yelling at me…

Going to sleep that night I was still epically muddled.

However, I was also experiencing a growing sense of responsibility for the current state of my relationship (or non-relationship) with Martin.

* * *

JANUARY SECOND ROLLED AROUND, and I was very happy to be back at the Bluesy Bean making coffee and going through the motions, though—admittedly—still obsessing about Martin Sandeke. But instead of obsessing about *what ifs*, I'd moved on to obsessing about my plan to confront him.

I was going to do it.

I was going to arrange to meet him in a neutral spot and point blank ask him about the interview and the text message on New

177

Year's. I was going to put on my bad-ass-girl trucker hat and "adult" like an adult.

That's why, when Martin Sandeke walked into The Bluesy Bean that afternoon, an immobilizing shock coursed through my body and I dropped the glass measuring cup I was holding. It shattered on the floor, making a really obnoxious *crash*.

Chelsea sucked in a sharp breath and jumped back from my inadvertent mess, possibly because she was wearing brand new, soft-soled leather slip-ons and didn't want shards of glass near her feet.

"You startled me!" She pressed her hand to her chest, fluttering her eyelashes like she might faint.

The male customer who was at the counter (and with whom she'd been flirting for the last ten minutes) gave me a harsh glower and reached forward, gripping her upper arm.

"Are you all right? Do you need to sit down?"

"Yes. Yes, I think so." She nodded and gave him a grateful smile.

She turned to face me so she could sit on the counter. Just before she swung her legs over, Chelsea gave me a conspiratorial wink, then turned into the waiting arms of the man. He was a Brad Pitt. Or, at least that's the label she'd given him when he'd walked in.

Luckily the place was empty except for Chelsea, the Brad Pitt, Martin, and me.

Martin didn't walk to the counter. He took a beeline to where I was standing behind the machines, his eyes moving over me as though searching for injury.

"Are you okay?"

I nodded, releasing a weary laugh. "Yes. Just...clumsy."

He gave me a half smile. "Let me help you clean this up."

"It's okay, I can get it."

But he was already walking into the back closet and returned quickly with a broom. "I'll clean, you make me an Americano."

"Martin—"

"Don't argue with me, just once. Just once, please."

I pressed my lips together, showing him I was displeased.

He mimicked my expression, but it looked ridiculous on him. Then

178

he made the strangest face. His eyes crossed and he bared his front teeth as though he were a rabbit.

I blinked at him. "What are you doing?"

"Making a funny face in an effort to make you stop staring at me like I murdered your beloved goldfish. What are you doing?"

Of course, this made me laugh.

The problem was, I couldn't stop laughing once I started. It was absurd that he was reminding me of our time on the island, using my own lines and strategy against me so he could clean the floor. But it worked. It distracted me from the mess and it also distracted me from my Martin Sandeke obsession. It felt good to laugh, a necessary release. I had to hold on to the counter because I was laughing so hard. Basically, I had laugh-paralysis.

He chuckled and squinted his eyes at my inability to control the hysterics, but took advantage of my arrested state to sweep the glass and deposit it in the trash.

As soon as I could breathe again, yet still wiping tears, I turned from him and grabbed a paper cup to make his Americano. I figured I couldn't be trusted with anything breakable at this point.

When he finished, he replaced the broom and dustpan then moved back to the other side of the machines, waiting for me to finish.

"Feel better?" he asked.

I nodded.

"Can you take a break?"

My gaze flickered to his then around the shop. No one new had entered.

"Yes." I sighed and paired it with a nod. "But just until we get a customer."

"Good. I'll be over there." He indicated with his head to the table we'd used the last time he was here, then added, "And grab some cookies."

* * *

I BROUGHT ENOUGH cookies to share plus a muffin with butter, his coffee, and a cup of strong coffee for me. Really, I needed hard liquor, because I was going to do it. I was going to confront Martin Sandeke. I was going to demand answers.

However, no sooner had I sat down, he asked, "Now that we're friends, can I ask you for advice?"

I sputtered for a moment, then finally managed, "You want to ask me for advice?"

"Yes."

"Uh…sure. If I don't know the answer I'll look it up on consumer reports."

"Consumer reports?"

"I have an online account. I bought a mattress based on their recommendation, sight unseen until the delivery day, and it was the best decision of my entire life."

"Really?" He was smiling, his eyes shimmering at me with happy amusement, and he wasn't even trying to hide it. "The best of your entire life?"

"Yes. Of my entire life. It's so comfortable, and when I'm at home I'm basically in bed the entire time. I'm going to marry it and we're going to have twin beds together."

"When we were together we were in bed most of the time, too." He uttered this with no intonation in his voice, and his eyes were free of mischief, as though he was just making innocent conversation.

"Yes, well." I had to clear my throat, feeling off kilter, not knowing how to segue this conversation into the discussion I was determined to have. As well, my pants never let me forget how much they liked that time in bed with Martin, so I was feeling a bit hot and distracted. "We weren't sleeping much that week. In my new bed all I want to do is sleep."

"I think I hate your bed. If we ever get back together, you'll need to get rid of it." Again, his tone was conversational.

I tripped over my words, my heart in my throat, thumping wildly. The time was now, this was my chance to confront him and decide things between us.

However, before I could form the pointed question that would serve as the key to unlocking our conversation, he said, "So, let's say I like this girl…"

My mouth dropped open and I felt like I'd been tackled from behind, my breath leaving me with a *whoosh*. I blinked at him. The room tilted.

"Kaitlyn?"

"Yes?" I managed to breathe, though the room continued to dip precariously. I realized I was gripping the table and forced myself to release it, my hands falling to my lap.

"Are you…" his eyes narrowed on me, "are you all right?"

Just because you don't feel calm, doesn't mean you can't be calm.

I nodded. "Yes. Fine. So you like a girl." I sounded like a robot.

"Yeah. And I need your advice about her."

"You need my advice about her." I was careful to keep my expression unruffled and unconcerned, even though my brain was abruptly on fire. I noted there was a butter knife on the table and I briefly imagined stabbing him with it.

Really? Two days after that text message, he was going to ask me advice about another girl? Really?

Wow.

WOW!

Boys are stupid. I needed to explore becoming a lesbian. I needed to add this to my to-do list and bump it up to the top.

How had the male gender managed to survive millions of years? Given that Martin, as a sample of his gender, thought asking me—his ex-girlfriend, the one who he'd spent Christmas with, snuggling on the couch, the one he'd bought a piano for—about another girl was a good idea, the male portion of the human species should have been extinct by now.

Of course, I knew he was going to date someone else eventually, and I wanted him to be happy, but…

JERK-FACE!

Did he have to ask *me* for advice? Where was Emma? Where were Eric and Ray? Couldn't he pay someone to do this?

And yet…though my heart felt like it had suffered a new fracture, I couldn't help think I'd just narrowly escaped a brand new broken heart. I'd been on the precipice of being brave, and nothing can make a person more foolish and vulnerable than bravery.

He was interested in someone else. He'd just provided me with the definitive answer to all my questions. Martin Sandeke was officially over Kaitlyn Parker. I had my answer because I was never *The One*, and now I could stop wishing.

"Kaitlyn?"

"Hmm?"

"What do you think?"

I blinked my confusion at him and shook my head. "I'm sorry, what did you say?"

I must've zoned out, what with the planning to become a lesbian and eradicating the world of men and whatnot. I allowed myself to feel the hollow hurt, but would be damned if I showed it.

His eyes narrowed and he gave me a look of intense suspicion. "What was the last thing you heard?"

"You were saying something about your…girl?" I was very proud I didn't end the sentence with, *and then I was about to stab you with my butter knife.*

"Yes, and then I asked you how I should go about informing this girl that I'm interested in her."

Now I issued him a look of intense suspicion. "Martin Sandeke, you can't be serious."

"About what?"

"You don't need advice from anyone on picking up girls." I cleared my throat after I said this because I didn't like how melancholy I sounded, how weak. I just needed to get through the next five minutes then I could finally close the book on our relationship. Now I definitely knew he wasn't wishing for me.

He was wishing for someone new.

"You're wrong, I do. When I'm interested in someone—actually interested—I'm terrible at it. I come on too strong, say the wrong thing, act like an asshole, push for too much too soon. I'm tired of fucking everything up. I want to do this right."

"Because women usually throw themselves at you and you've never had to work for it?" I was pleased I sounded more like myself.

He frowned, examining both me and my words, didn't commit one way or the other for a long moment, then shrugged. "Basically, yes."

I snorted. "You are so arrogant."

"Parker, both of us know why these girls throw themselves at me and it has nothing to do with my big head."

"Or your itty-bitty, microscopic heart."

He laughed, reluctantly at first, then just gave himself over to it. His eyes crinkling, the rumbly sound infectious and thrilling. I laughed too, shaking my head.

This felt weird, laughing with him now. It's hard to laugh with a person when your guard is raised. Laughing can be just as intimate as touching. Given the fact he was *definitely* moving on, I didn't want to be intimate with Martin ever again, so my merriment tapered off before his did. I searched for a way to let go of my jealousy and actually help him.

In the end I decided to fake and force my good intentions.

I was jealous of this hypothetical girl. I was *insanely* jealous. I had no way to get around my jealousy other than to pretend I wasn't jealous. And the thought of him trying to woo someone else didn't just make me murderous, it made me nauseous. I pushed away the cookies.

I tried not to show how flustered this conversation was making me and forced a steadiness into my voice I didn't feel. "Okay, so…you like this girl and you don't know what to do, how to let her know you're interested without coming on too strong, saying the wrong thing, and acting like an asshole."

"Yes. Exactly."

I peered at him, trying to approach this from a strictly problem-solving perspective and quell the ache in my heart. He stared back, his gaze intent and watchful, like the next words out of my mouth would solve all known mysteries of the universe.

I straightened in my seat, trying to distance myself from thoughts of Martin with someone else, because emotion was starting to clog my throat. "Pragmatically speaking, a lot of women like the whole caveman thing. You might be able get away with just being yourself, not changing your approach."

He looked disappointed, maybe a little frustrated. "Because I'm a caveman? That's how you see me?"

"No, no. Not at all," I said automatically, then sought to clarify, "I mean, we're…we are definitely friends now, things are different. Before, when you were interested in me, you were domineering and demanding."

"You liked that, I know you did."

"Sometimes I liked it…" I trailed off, thinking about how much I did like it when Martin would take charge when we touched and were intimate. I also liked debating with him, that he wasn't a pushover, so I added, "I liked that you challenged me and pushed me outside my comfort zone, pushed me to see that passion mattered. But I didn't like it when you were heavy-handed, or tried to manipulate me by yelling at me. No one likes being yelled at. I also didn't like how callous you were sometimes to my feelings. I appreciated your honesty, but it's important to be honest without being mean. Does that make sense?"

He nodded thoughtfully, his eyes losing focus. "That makes sense."

"Ultimately though, when I had a problem with how you were acting, I let you know. Like you said before, you aren't a mind reader. No one is a mind reader—Lord knows I'm still terrible at picking up on things even when they're staring me in the face. I think you changed that week, or tried to. But given the fact it was only one week, I really think both of us tried our best to hear each other and change for the better."

"That's what I'm talking about. Do you remember what you wished I would have done differently from the start? How do I approach this girl and not make the same mistakes I made before?"

I stared at him for a beat, wrestling with myself, my heart hurting with every beat. I wanted to lash out at him, scream at him for wanting to do things right with this girl and using me and our time together in order to make that happen; as such, I couldn't stop my acerbic remark.

"First, make sure her mother isn't a senator, so there's no external conflict of interest should you find an idea to exploit."

His jaw tightened as he ground his teeth and he focused his attention on the untouched cookies. There was a long pause, during which Martin looked like he wanted to say something but was remaining admirably quiet.

"I'm sorry, that was a stupid thing to say. I don't know what's wrong with me."

I tried to smile and make up for my regrettable sarcasm by adding earnestly, "Why don't you try asking her if she's busy over the weekend? Just ask, *Do you have any plans this weekend?* And if she says no, then ask her out for a movie or dinner. Not everything has to be flying to private islands for a week of dating boot camp."

"With us, it was too much too fast. I pushed you," he said with equal sincerity, his eyes ensnaring mine.

"Yes...and no. I mean, I doubt I would have given you much of a chance unless we'd been stranded on that island. But you're different now. You've changed." My words were honest because I was growing increasingly uncomfortable. I needed him to leave so I could process the end, *our* true end, without his tremendously brilliant eyes watching and assessing me.

"What do you mean?" He leaned and reached forward, pressed his palm to the surface of the table just two inches from where my hand rested next to my cup, but he didn't touch me.

"Well, you haven't yelled at me once since we've been friends. Even though I've said some incredibly moronic things—you've cussed, but you haven't yelled. You're...different. More mature, respectful. You seem calmer. Content."

"And that's good? You like the changes?"

"Yes, of course." I smiled because I couldn't help it, and even now, even when I knew our ship had sailed, I wanted to reassure him, because I cared about him. "Yes, I do. Contentment and self-control look good on you."

"Happiness and passion look good on you." Martin's hand inched closer to me, his knuckles brushing mine—like he was testing how receptive I'd be to his touch—before he captured my hand in his and entwined our fingers on the table.

185

I gulped in air and I let him, because HOLY CRAP it felt so good, like hot cocoa on a snowy day...with lots of Baileys. During Christmas we'd been in a bubble; hugging, lying together, and holding hands had felt natural. I'd missed his touch over the last week. I'd missed it so much. I hungered for it. And now, knowing this might be the last time we touched like this, the connection felt startling, necessary, and oddly provocative.

Maybe my body craved his body because I'd never been with anyone else. Maybe his touch intoxicated me and set my heart racing because he knew me so intimately. He touched me with an understanding of my strengths and weaknesses, of my desires, of who I became when I lost control.

I stared at our combined hands, pressed my lips together and rolled them between my teeth, because I thought I might whimper. This was bad. Very, very bad. We were just holding hands. How was I going to move on like he had if I couldn't even hold his hand?

And now he wanted to be with someone else.

He wanted me to help him, give him advice on how to woo another girl. If I continued to be his friend, this time I would be solely responsible for breaking my own heart, no assistance from Martin required.

I could feel myself starting to crack. My blood roared between my ears. Unable to maintain my calm under all the swirling and torrid emotions, I yanked my hand away and stood abruptly, my chair scraping against the wooden floor as I backed up two steps.

"I have to get back to work." I whispered this to the cookies because...self-preservation.

"What time do you get off?"

"Work?" I questioned dumbly, my eyes darting to his then away when they connected with his steady gaze.

But I did catch his smirk before he clarified, "Yes. Work."

"Not 'til late." I stepped forward to stack our cups and clear our dishes.

"What are your plans for the weekend?" he asked.

I shrugged, careful to not pick up the dishes from the table until they were pre-bussed so he wouldn't see my hands shake. "Um, I have shows Friday and Sunday at night. Mostly I just need to get stuff together for classes." I tucked the plates close to my chest and turned for the kitchen.

"Do you want to hang out on Saturday? Celebrate your change in major?" He stood as well, grabbing the last of the dishes and following me.

"Where? In the city?"

"No, I'll be here. We'll have dinner."

I thought about this for a split second, but then realized I needed more time to decide whether I could truly be friends—just friends—with Martin. I had no idea. Therefore, I decided that one dinner wouldn't hurt. At the very least it might give me an opportunity to truly say goodbye.

"Sure. Pizza?" My voice cracked.

"No. Something more formal. Wear a dress."

I dumped our empties into the sink, still feeling flustered and distracted.

"A dress?"

"Yeah, if you don't mind. I want to try something."

I turned and faced him, my hands on my hips, and gave him a questioning frown; I was a little breathless as I was trying to keep pace with our conversation and the dizzying thoughts in my head and the storm of emotions in my stomach. "Like an experiment?"

He nodded, his eyes trapping mine, pulling me further under his Martin Sandeke magic. "Yes. Exactly like an experiment. I'll even help you tabulate the findings after."

I exhaled a laugh that sounded more nervous than genuine. He needed to leave so I could figure out what to do without the dazzling interference of his presence.

I hurriedly agreed, "Sure. Fine. Saturday. I'll wear a dress. We'll experiment."

"Good. I'll pick you up at seven."

Before I comprehended his intent, he grabbed my upper arm to hold me in place, bent forward, and kissed me on the corner of my mouth. I was still paralyzed by shock—wondering if he'd meant for a cheek-kiss and had misaimed—when I caught his scent.

He smelled good. Really good.

Like a guy who showers with expensive, French-milled soap scented with sandalwood as well as something so completely him. It was the *him* part that hijacked my brain, because it took me back to a boat in the Caribbean where we'd laughed and fought and spooned... and forked.

It took me back to snuggling with him on the couch in his apartment, hugging him, and waking up with him Christmas morning. Liquid emotion stung my eyes and I felt overwhelmed by the fact he was unquestionably no longer mine. He wanted someone else.

Meanwhile Martin was in motion. He'd crossed to his chair, grabbed his coat, tossed a fifty on the table, and left without another word. The door chime alerted me to his exit. It broke me from my trance just in time to see him turn to the left and disappear from view.

He didn't look back.

[16]

THERMODYNAMIC QUANTITIES FOR SELECTED SUBSTANCES AT 298.15 K

"EXPLAIN TO ME what's happening with you and Martin, because...I don't understand."

"I told you, we're going out to dinner as friends." I mentally gave myself a high five because I sounded convincing and not at all brittle. And that was a miracle.

Despite the fact Martin had moved on, I had not. I could not be friends with Martin Sandeke.

I couldn't.

I wouldn't.

I wanted more, and I would likely always want more.

After a great deal of thinking since seeing him earlier in the week, I'd decided to go with my original plan of confronting him. I was going to adult like an adult and tell him I was still in love with him. Then I was going to ask Martin if, despite his interest in someone else, whether or not he still had feelings for me he wished to explore via a relationship.

After that, I had no concrete plan.

"As friends?" Sam sounded and appeared skeptical.

"Yes. As friends."

"*Riiiight.*"

"It's true. In fact, right before we made dinner plans, he asked me to give him advice about another girl." I shrugged. I was getting good at this, at *rising above.*

"Oh..." Sam's face fell, then to herself she said, "Well, that's kind of a shitty thing for him to do."

"It's fine. I'm fine."

I wasn't fine.

I was the opposite of fine.

But I would be fine...eventually.

Either he said yes, he still had feelings for me. In which case we would hammer out the details of our reconciliation and move forward.

Or he said no, that he'd moved on. In which case I would tell him I could not continue to be friends with him, but would wish him well.

At least I would know for certain. At least I would be moving forward one way or the other.

"I'm not fine, in case you were wondering," Sam announced, pulling me from my thoughts. "I'm not fine at all. Who is she? Is she smart? Pretty?"

"If the girl is who I think she is, his business partner Emma, then yes. She is very smart and pretty." I'd decided the hypothetical girl was either Emma or Rose, both of whom were most definitely beautiful.

And that was fine.

That was actually truthfully fine, not fake fine. I was completely at peace with being beautiful to myself rather than being pretty in comparison to someone else.

"I hate her."

I laughed at my friend. "There's no reason to hate her."

"Why are you being so okay about this? Martin was your first love. You *loved* him. You were in love with him. You cried for months after it was over in an uncharacteristic display of emotion."

"And why are you trying to make me not-okay with this?"

"I'm not. I'm just..." Her face scrunched up with pensive dissatisfaction. "I'm just worried about you."

"Don't be."

"I can't help it. I don't want you hiding in closets again."

I tried to give Sam a reassuring smile, noting that this—her worry —was precisely why I hadn't shared my plan with her. As far as she knew, Martin and I were platonic friends and I was over (or almost over) him. After what I'd put her through during the summer there was no reason to give her cause for anxiety now.

I turned my attention back to the mirror and frowned at my reflection.

"I can't wear this dress."

I liked the dress a lot in the store. It was a complicated dress. A beige silk sheath was beneath. Layered above was black, open-work lace crochet. The dress clung to my body—over my breasts, torso, and thighs—highlighting the smallness of my waist in comparison to my generous hips and bustline.

At the time, I also liked that it had a square cut neckline, and the fact it ended just below my knees. In my opinion, there weren't enough square cut necklines. Large boobs always looked nice in a square cut and it showed my collarbone and neck to best advantage.

In truth, I'd bought it just for this dinner with Martin. I felt good in it, confident. But now I was questioning the choice. I worried it was too sexy. I didn't want to come across as desperate or manipulative, not when I was planning to have a serious conversation with him about whether or not our future relationship was in the cards.

"Why? You look hot. It's sexy. I'd do you."

"Because it might be too sexy. And it's always catching on things." I moved my arm back and forth over the openwork lace and my bracelet caught. I stilled my movements so I wouldn't pull the thread and ruin the dress.

"See. My bracelet is caught."

"Of course, when you try to get your bracelet caught it's going to get caught." Sam rolled her eyes then crossed to me, helped me disentangle my arm, and removed the bracelet. "Just wear a different bracelet. Or no bracelet at all…" Then she added under her breath, "Less for him to take off when you both succumb to passion."

I flattened my lips into an unhappy line and affixed a scowl to my face. "I want him to be sensible, not succumb to passion."

Sam glanced up at me, her face said, *bitch, please.*

Then she said, "Bitch, please."

"It's true. I...I need to talk to him, get some things straight. And besides, like I said, he wants someone else."

"*Wanted* someone else, past tense, after he sees you in this dress."

I grew frustrated because Sam's sentiment was the opposite of what I wanted. I wanted Martin to want me, *want me.* Not want me because of the dress. I wanted him to think of me as *The One* because despite everything, he was still my *One.*

Gah! This is so confusing.

"That's it, I'm changing."

"No! There isn't time. He'll be here any minute. It's almost seven."

Oh. Shoot.

I stiffened, glanced at the clock next to my bed. "Oh shoot!"

"What?"

"I'll be right back." I scoured the room for my black shoes. "I'm going to run down to the cleaners and get my tuxedo before they close."

"What? Why?"

"I have that show tomorrow and I forgot to pick it up today. Shoot! They close in ten minutes and they're closed all day tomorrow."

I slipped on one of my flats, deciding the dress was just going to have to be okay.

"No! You can't wear those shoes!" Sam lunged for me, ripping the second shoe out of my hand. "It's a crime against fashion. I won't let you do it."

"Sam, I don't have time for this."

She turned hastily and marched out of the room—holding my shoe hostage—and returned seconds later carrying sexy, black silk stilettos. I was stuffing my black clutch with my wallet, Chapstick, and cell phone.

"Here. Wear these." She held them out to me.

"I can't wear those. They're too...too—"

"It's fine." She knelt down and picked up one foot, then the other, elevating me by three inches as she slipped the shoes on. "See, they fit. They're perfect."

I didn't check in the mirror. If I didn't hurry, the cleaners would be closed and I would have to wear my dirty tux instead. It smelled like sweat and barbeque sauce. I tucked my clutch under my arm and spun for the door.

"You want me to go? He'll be here any minute," she asked.

"No, it's fine. I'll just run across the street and do it really fast. I doubt he's taking me someplace that requires reservations or anything."

"I don't mind," she called after me as I sprinted down the hall to the front closet.

"I got it," I called back.

"Okay, fine. I have to drop a load anyway," she announced, and I heard the bathroom door shut.

I smirked as I stepped into the closet and felt for my formal coat. Of course mine was at the back. The last time I saw it was when I unpacked it two days after we moved into the apartment. I wasn't even sure it was in the closet.

I pulled the chord to turn on the hanging bulb above because the door had creaked shut behind me, cutting off my light source.

I shifted through the coats—all twenty plus of them—and reminded myself to ask Sam why she needed so many coats. There was one in each color of the rainbow plus four or five black ones that looked exactly the same.

"Weirdo," I said to the coats, shaking my head.

Then a knock sounded at the door and I stiffened, my brain shouting, *Oh barnacles! He's here!* I turned to abandon my coat search, my hands shaking a little, but found I couldn't move. I twisted, frowning down at myself, searching for the source of my immobilization.

The crochet dress was caught in at least three places on three different coats, by the buttons at the cuffs.

Blast!

"Coming!" I heard Sam call, the bathroom door opening and the sound of flushing toilet following her.

"Wait, Sam!" I whispered, reaching for the door, then realized my mistake too late. She couldn't hear me if I whispered behind a mostly closed door.

It was too late, because two seconds later I heard her open the front door and say, "Who the hell are you?"

I breathed a sigh of relief, glad it wasn't Martin after all, then turned to untangle myself from Sam's army of coats.

My relief was short-lived because, after a beat, Martin's voice responded, "I'm Martin. And you are?"

Ooooohhhh mmmmmyyyyy Gggggoooooodddd!!!!

I froze.

"Ha-ha, come in. Parker just left to run an errand, she'll be right back."

"An errand?"

"Yeah, she had to grab her dry cleaning from across the street. It should take her, like, literally less than ten minutes. They close in ten minutes, they're closed all day tomorrow, and she has a gig tomorrow night, so...you see how it is," Sam explained as she shut the door.

"Where's she playing tomorrow?"

"I don't know, some really fancy to-do. She has that tuxedo uniform for all the shows."

"Does Kaitlyn work every day? Does she ever get a day off?"

"Starving artist has to make a living somehow, you know?"

"Hmm..." His answer sounded non-committal, but also rang with frustration, like he was irritated I had to work every day. But I wanted to work, to prove I could support myself as a musician. It was important to me.

And I didn't know why I was obsessing about this since I was stuck in the closet and there was no way to exit gracefully. I glanced back at the coats holding me in place, deciding I was just going to call out and ask for help when Sam spoke again.

"Martin, are you still in love with Kaitlyn? Or are you just here to break her heart into a million tiny pieces again?"

I froze. My call for help stuck in my throat.

"Again?" His tone was dry. "I didn't know that happened. When did that happen?"

"Don't fuck around with me, hot stuff. I'm not impressed by your GQ good looks, your Scrooge McDuck money vault, or your genius brain."

"Then what impresses you?" I knew he was smiling...with his sharp teeth.

"Honesty," she said.

I could picture her face as she said it. Her eyebrows would be raised in challenge, like she didn't expect him to be honest, like she was daring him.

I opened my mouth again, but then stopped, squeezed my eyes shut, then turned to the coats. I couldn't call for help. It was too late. The only thing I could do was disentangle myself and try to sneak out undetected, praying Sam would lead him into the living room.

Instead I heard her press, "Why did you drop out of school? You didn't even try to contact her. That was kind of an asshole thing to do."

Then I heard Martin, who was by now, very close to the door, ask, "You want the truth?"

"No, Martin. Lie to me. I love it when boys do that." Sam's tone was flat and would have made me laugh if I hadn't been caught in the closet by her coats.

He did laugh, but it sounded forced. "Sure, fine, here's the truth. I left because if I hadn't, I wouldn't have been able to stay away from her."

"So you dropped out of school, out of college, abandoned your teammates, because you couldn't stay away from Kaitlyn?"

"Sure."

"And now? What are you really doing here?"

He didn't answer immediately and, stupid me, I was holding my breath, eavesdropping like a freak.

At last he said, "That's not really any of your business."

"But she is my business. If you have malicious intentions then that's my business. She's my BFF, do you know what that means? It means: Boy I will fuck up your face if you mess with my girl."

"Wouldn't that be BIWFUYFIYM...WMG?"

"No, nothing counts toward the BFF acronym except Boy, Fuck, and Face. It's a TLA."

"TLA?"

"A three letter acronym."

"Of course."

"Back to my original question, what are your intentions?"

"Sam..."

"Are you still in love with her?"

Silence.

"You are!" She sounded excited, like he'd answered, but I knew he hadn't. "You're in love with her! Of course you are. But is this some kind of revenge plot?"

Silence.

"It's not!" It sounded like she was jumping up and down. "Oh my God, you're in love with her and you...want her back?"

Silence.

"Hmm...you don't want her back. That's odd."

"I didn't say that."

"Ah ha!"

"I didn't say anything."

"You don't have to. I can read it all over your love-sick face."

"Shouldn't she be back by now?" His voice was tight, impatient.

"So, you're still in love with her, you want her back, but...what? Why haven't you just told her?"

Silence.

"Hmm...you're afraid."

Silence.

"No, no. That's not it. You're not afraid."

He sighed.

"You're with someone else. You've got another girl and—I can't believe I'm saying this out loud—you're too honorable to call things off with Emma."

"Emma? Did Kaitlyn mention Emma?"

I clenched my hands into fists, my heart jumping around my chest. I was going to kill Sam. She was going to die.

"Yes. She told me about adorable Emma. Kaitlyn thinks she's pretty and you two make a pretty couple."

"I'm not interested in Emma."

I covered my mouth with my hand to keep my gasp from being audible. I wasn't going to kill Sam. I was going to buy her a car.

"So you broke up?" Sam asked.

"No. We were never together."

"But you let Kaitlyn think you were together."

"No." He paused, then I heard his footsteps move away. When he spoke next he sounded frustrated. "I'm not discussing this with you, Sam. I need to make a phone call."

"Sure, sure. You can use Kaitlyn's room to make your call, it's at the end of the hall."

I heard his footsteps move farther away followed by the sound of my door closing. I stood, again frozen, for several seconds, making sure the coast was clear. I was about to turn back to the two coats still holding me hostage when Sam flung open the door to the closet.

"Oh my God!" she whispered, with feeling. "Did you get all that? He loves you! He's not with Emma!"

"Sam," I whispered back, scowling fiercely. "You knew I was in here the whole time."

"Yes. Of course, I didn't hear you leave so I figured you were hiding."

"No. I'm caught in the web of your superfluous coats and I was trapped."

She grinned, glancing down at where I was tangled in the cuff buttons of her garments.

"Ha-ha, that's funny. Here, let me help." She slipped in and quickly untangled me, then pushed me out of the closet.

Like a clothes ninja, she immediately found my formal black coat and yanked it off the hanger. She tossed it to me then pulled the string to turn off the light. As I frantically tugged on my jacket, she tiptoed to the front door.

She opened it.

She closed it.

She said loudly, "Oh. You're back."

I gave her a panicked look, untucking my hair from my collar, and whispered, "What are you doing?!"

"Were they already closed? You don't have your dry cleaning."

"Stop it," I whispered frantically. All my hope for bravado and planned bravery was scattered.

Meanwhile Sam smiled like a harpy.

The door to my room opened and I stiffened, my eyes closing briefly. I inhaled a steadying breath, repeating to myself, *Even though you don't feel calm, doesn't mean you can't be calm.*

Feeling only slightly more centered, I turned toward the hall and affixed a welcoming smile to my face. Martin's eyes collided with mine as he stalked toward me, making me take an instinctive half step back. It was the force of it, the force of him.

He was devastating, dressed in a black tailored suit, a slim black tie, a slate-blue shirt that hardened his eyes into steely blades. His heavy coat was folded over his arm. He must've just taken it off. I tried to get my heart to stop jumping on the bed of my lungs before I fell down and broke my head, but it wouldn't. It took a kamikaze leap in his direction, sending spreading warmth from my toes to my temples, making my knees weak.

Stupid kamikaze heart.

"Hey." My voice cracked, so I cleared my throat as he approached. "Sorry about that," I said, sounding a little more steady. I tossed my thumb over my shoulder. "My, uh, uniform is at the cleaners and I need it for tomorrow."

He didn't stop walking until he was almost on top of me, then he bent down and placed a soft kiss on my cheek, one of his hands coming to my upper arm to hold me in place. It was an echo of the kiss he'd given me earlier in the week, and again I was assaulted by his smell and closeness and warmth.

I thought I might swoon.

Once again, it was over before I completely comprehended what had happened. He took a step back, but didn't release my arm for two more seconds.

Once his hand fell to his side his gaze swept over my face then down to my closed coat. Then it traveled back to my eyes. They pierced me. "No problem, I just got here. You ready to go?"

I nodded. "Uh-huh." Even though I wasn't ready, because all my courage was still in the closet with Sam's jackets.

His mouth tugged slowly to the side as he looked at me and pulled on his coat.

Sam chimed in, "Well, have fun, you crazy kids. She has no curfew, Martin. But it would be nice if you bring her back *all in one piece*, if you catch my meaning."

His eyes slid to Sam and his expression darkened. "Goodbye, Sam," he said as he reached for the front door and held it open for me.

"Goodbye, Martin." She smiled at him, like a harpy.

* * *

I WAS WRONG.

The place he took me for dinner definitely needed reservations.

Despite my shaky start to the evening, once we got to his car things felt a bit more natural, easy. He asked me about work. Instead of talking about the band or The Bluesy Bean, I told him I'd abandoned my twenty or so venture capitalist projects in favor of investing heavily in science cabinet futures.

He laughed and the tension was mostly cut.

We talked on the way over about his Spotify playlist and what books we were reading. His handsomeness and brilliance felt less like a death ray aimed at my heart and more like *Oh...look, it's Martin.* I half convinced myself I could still move forward with my plan to settle things between us.

But now that we'd arrived at our destination and the restaurant was actually super swanky, I felt a renewed spike of discomfort. I was sure the dinner was going to cost more than half my paycheck. I couldn't afford it because I'd just spent my whole paycheck on the awesome dress I was wearing.

Distractedly, I let Martin take off my coat as my eyes moved over the setting. It was intimate. There were maybe six tables visible and all of them were mostly hidden behind privacy screens. The lighting was dim but not dark, cozy but not complacent. Everything screamed elegant boudoir—the plush red walls, the dark furniture, the heavy, striped, crimson velvet drapes. It was romantic.

Scratch that.

It wasn't romantic.

It was sexy.

And it looked very exclusive, like you needed a membership card to gain entrance. I swallowed thickly, pressing my lips together, and gripping my clutch.

Completely preoccupied by my distress, I surmised—based on the overt sensuality of the restaurant—that Martin had brought me here tonight in order to try the place before he took *her* here. Last week he'd said that tonight would be an experiment. Of course, he would want to test the restaurant before he brought his *real* date.

Dejectedly, I realized there was no way I would be able to confront Martin during our dinner. I couldn't be brave in a place like this, especially not when I was a stand-in for the girl he hoped to win. I suddenly wished he'd taken me bowling instead.

So distracted by my dismay, I almost didn't hear Martin's whispered, "Fuck me..."

I turned to look at him and found his eyes moving in a slow, stunned sweep up and down my dress—or rather, my body in my dress —and I cocked my head to the side. "That means you're surprised, yes?"

"Jesus Christ, Kaitlyn." His eyes lifted and searched mine, then he leaned forward and whispered in my ear, "This dress makes you look like you're naked under that black lace."

I shook my head and whispered back, wanting to defend myself, "I'm not naked, though. It's just skin-colored silk. Here, stick your finger through one of the holes."

"Oh God," he groaned and leaned away, shaking his head and gritting his teeth, his eyes on the floor as the maître d' approached.

I grimaced, wondering if my dress was obscene. I tried to stop my blush before it started and took a step back, letting Martin deal with the man while I dealt with my embarrassment. I wished I'd changed, but it was too late now.

Hell, I wished I'd stayed in the closet.

Soon we were being led to a very private table, completely hidden from view by several cleverly placed screens. Martin's hand was on my back and I felt stiff and unsteady. The maître d' moved to pull out my chair but Martin frowned at him, then stared him down until he backed away. Martin moved to pull out my chair; as he did, he looked fierce and a tad frustrated.

I took my seat hurriedly then accepted the offered menu, only half paying attention as the maître d' recited the chef's specials. I was too busy looking for prices. There were none. My stomach sunk.

Then we were alone.

I glanced up at Martin and found him concentrating on his menu. He was frowning and his eyes were darting over it too fast to be reading.

"Are you upset?" I asked, unable to stop myself.

He moved just his eyes to mine, his jaw set.

I continued, explaining, "I honestly thought the dress was fine. Sam told me it was fine. You know I'm not so good with dresses. This is the fourth dress I've owned in my entire life. The first time you saw me in a dress it was borrowed and—"

Martin lifted his hand and waved away my explanation. "Kaitlyn, it's...it's not the dress. I mean, it *is* the dress, but it's not the dress. Everything is fine. You look beautiful."

I twisted my lips to the side. "Is it obscene?"

He gave me a half smile, it was shaded with regret. "No. It's great. I'm sorry if I made you feel uncomfortable. I was just...surprised. You look very different tonight." His eyes swept down then darted back up.

I tried to return his smile. "You expected jeans and a concert T-shirt? Or my tuxedo?"

His half smile turned into a full smile, though it was small. "I was hoping for the red pants."

I sighed my relief and laughed, feeling better, seeing he was being sincere and wasn't upset.

The grin disappeared from his face when I laughed and he stared at me. I felt my smile wane as I stared back. All sound was replaced by the rushing of my blood through my heart.

Martin opened his mouth, was about to say something, but then the waiter appeared and broke the odd moment.

Our server repeated the specials and asked for our drink orders. I indicated that the tap water in my glass was perfectly fine. Martin frowned at me then ordered a bottle of wine for the table. It had a lot of consonants and sounded really expensive. I was surprised when I wasn't carded.

When the man left, Martin considered me for a beat, then said, "Dinner is on me tonight."

I was sipping my water when he made this proclamation, so I swallowed quickly and shook my head. "No. Absolutely not. We're splitting it right down the middle."

"I'm not asking, Parker."

"Don't be silly. We're f-friends. Friends split checks." I stumbled over the word *friends* because it felt deceitful. I didn't want to be his friend. I tried not to wince at the uncomfortable pang in my chest caused by my dishonesty.

He huffed. "Then who doesn't split checks?"

"I don't know. Everyone should split checks. I've never not split my check."

"Even on dates?" His tone was aloof as he asked the question, but I noted his eyes narrowed slightly.

I considered how to respond, because I hadn't been on a date. I didn't consider the dates my gay high school boyfriend and I had gone on to be dates; besides Carter and I had always split the check.

Martin and I had never gone on a date, and I'd turned down all offers from others since. I thought about being evasive and saying, *Yes, even on dates*, because that wasn't technically lying.

But it was stupid and childish and I didn't want to play games, even though I'd just spent ten minutes inadvertently eavesdropping while hiding in the front closet of my apartment during which my roommate drilled him with twenty inappropriate questions.

Distressed by this thought, I revealed, "I've never been on a date."

He was staring at me again. I stared back and gave him a tight smile.

"You haven't....? Since we broke up?"

I shook my head. "No. There's been no one."

"What about that guy in your band? Adam?"

"Abram. And no. We're not dating. We haven't dated."

He nodded thoughtfully and he shifted in his seat. "I think he's interested in you."

I shrugged, getting a weird premonition I was about to say something monumentally stupid in an effort to be honest, but without the wherewithal to stop myself. I was still caught in the tailwind of my earlier evening calamities.

Calamities paired with my abandoned confrontation plans meant that there was no telling what would erupt from my mouth.

"Oh?" I said, reaching for my water again.

I could feel it coming; it was like the shark in Jaws... circling...circling.

"Yeah. If you gave him even a small sign, I bet he'd ask you out."

I replaced my glass. "Well, I can't date anyone right now."

"Why not?"

Oh God, I was going to say it. Oh God.

"Because I'm still in love with you."

There it is!

Time slowed, then screeched to a halt.

I'd surprised him.

Hell, I'd surprised myself.

Of course I wanted to tell him, but not like this.

Not like this.

Not. Like. This.

NOT LIKE THIS!!!

Then all at once, time lurched forward.

His mouth parted slightly and his eyes widened; they moved over my shoulder and searched the screen behind me. I'd caught him completely off guard. I could see he was shocked, stunned speechless.

Meanwhile I was feeling the aftereffects of handing him my heart. I thought I was prepared. I wasn't. I was so definitely and definitively NOT PREPARED!

I felt immediately bruised and dirty. As well, I was experiencing honesty and courage remorse. The words hung out there, like underwear with skid marks on a clothesline.

The waiter returned at just that moment and asked if we were ready to order. Martin blinked furiously then turned his attention to the man and I saw he'd mostly recovered. He cleared his throat before gesturing to the menu to ask a question.

I stared at him while he ordered an appetizer, my stomach falling further with every calm syllable from his mouth. Meanwhile the single word running around my brain was: escape. Escape. ESCAPE!

Martin's eyes lifted, connected with mine, and in that split second I could read nothing of his thoughts—probably because mine were in such turmoil.

The waiter turned, poised to ask me if I wanted anything. Instead I stood abruptly, my chair almost falling backward.

"I'm sorry," I said to Martin first, then turned to the waiter. "I'm sorry, where is the ladies' room?" My voice was higher pitched than I would have liked, but I wasn't going to complain because the fact I could speak at all was a miracle.

The waiter smiled politely and had just finished his instructions when Martin stood as well, drawing my attention to him.

His eyes were narrowed, like he suspected foul play, and he said, "Kaitlyn..." His tone held a warning, and he paired this with an almost imperceptible head shake.

I gave him a tight smile, not quite making eye contact because...devastation.

I nodded noncommittally as I darted out of the privacy screens. "I'll be right back."

But that was a lie.

There was no way in hell I was going back.

In that moment I knew with a sudden, implacable force that I had been right. I would never be able to be *just friends* with Martin Sandeke. I would never be able to see him and not want everything from him. I would always be drawn to him. I also knew that being with Martin wasn't necessary for my happiness, but I could never be happy as just his friend.

I was passionate about him, and I couldn't be unselfish or reasonable *or* calm where he was concerned.

As I threaded my way through the twists and turns of the screens, I felt the first stinging tears behind my eyes. Finally I made it to the front and I plucked my coat from the rack by the front door, then bolted out of the restaurant.

My feet didn't hurt, but they would, because I was going to have to walk at least four blocks to find a taxi.

[17]

NUCLEAR CHEMISTRY

"Do you want to talk about it?"

I shook my head and blew my nose.

It was stuffy.

I'd been crying.

But I wasn't crying now.

Yet my nose was still stuffy.

"No."

"At least tell me what happened!" Sam shook her fists at me in frustration, grumbling, "I'm dying here. You have to give me something. Do I need to take a hit out on Martin Sandeke? I will, you know. I have some Russian cousins who need an outlet for their aggression."

I gave a pitiful laugh and shook my head. "No. It's not his fault. I just...I just said something stupid, then regretted it, then left."

"Oh." Her eyes moved over me. Sam seemed to be planning her strategy as I pulled off the shoes she'd loaned me and placed them next to the bed.

After escaping from the restaurant I flagged down a taxi six blocks away, started to cry, then paid the exorbitant cab fare, and started to cry even harder.

I snuck into the apartment. Sam didn't hear me as she was singing loudly in the shower, then lay on my bed and cried. I cried into my pillow, quietly, just like old times.

Despite my carefulness, Sam heard me and came to the door dressed only in a towel.

Now we were in my bedroom and I was a pitiful mess. So much for trying to be strong on my own.

"I never want to see him again," I said to no one. "Just thinking about the possibility makes me want to join the Peace Corps and fly to a far off third world country. Hopefully they'll have closets."

"What did you say? It couldn't have been that bad."

"I told him I was still in love with him."

"Oh...oh!" She gripped her towel tighter, her eyes large as saucers. "Holy shit. What did he say?"

"Nothing. He ordered an appetizer."

"*What?*" Now she sounded pissed.

"So I got up and excused myself for the bathroom, but I left instead. He was probably relieved when he figured out that I left. God, I am so stupid." My chin wobbled again and I held my forehead with my fingertips.

Yes, I felt remorse and the pain of rejection, but I also felt relief. At least now it was over. At least now I knew for certain. Despite the clumsiness of my confession I'd finally freed myself.

Now I could move on and stop wishing. I could pick my crumpled heart off the floor and stop stepping all over it.

Sam took a deep breath and was possibly about to give me some words of wisdom, but a pounding on the front door interrupted her.

We both sat up straight and stared at each other.

Then we heard Martin's raised voice.

"Kaitlyn, open the door. I know you're in there."

I stood abruptly, my hands balled into fists, a thunder bolt of white hot mortification slicing through me. I was suddenly sweating.

"Oh my God. What do I do?" I whispered, which was silly because he wouldn't be able to hear me all the way in my bedroom.

Sam looked at me, stunned. "Open the door...?"

I shook my head frantically. "No. No, I can't. I can't face him. Please don't make me."

She gave me a sad look. "Oh, Kaitlyn—"

"I mean it. Open this door," he bellowed from the hall. He sounded really, really angry.

"I'll just tell him to go away, that you don't want to see him," Sam offered.

"No. That won't work. I have to hide." I nodded at this thought because I was crazy. "Tell him I'm not here."

"You want me to let him in?"

"Yes. You get the door. Tell him I'm not back yet. He'll...well, he might want to wait for a bit, but you tell him to leave. He won't stay in the apartment if you—"

"I'm going to count to ten and then I'm going to break this door down."

We both jumped at the sound of his threat.

Sam shook her head, her mouth curved in a frown of knowing better. "He won't be able to break the door down," she whispered, "it's reinforced steel."

"Okay, I'll go hide—"

"One."

"—in the front closet."

"Two."

"You let him in."

"Three"

"Tell him I'm—"

"Four."

"—not here, not back yet."

"Five."

"He'll leave."

"Six."

"Then—"

"Seven."

"—we'll be all clear."

"Eight."

She nodded her understanding and I tiptoed out of my room, running as lightly as possible. Sam loitered behind.

"Nine."

Sam called out, "Just a minute, Sandeke. I was in the shower. Hold your ball sack!"

I went to the hall closet where I'd been hiding earlier and shut the door behind me, pressing myself backward into the folds of the coats. My hands were shaking.

"Ten."

I heard the door swing open.

I heard his steps thunder into the apartment.

I heard Sam shut the door.

I heard her follow him, shouting, "What are you doing?"

"Where is she?"

"Who?"

"Sam..." His voice sent a shiver down my spine. He was really mad. I didn't think he'd be angry.

"What?"

"Where is Kaitlyn?"

"Why? What did you do to her?" Sam was also angry.

They sounded faraway, so I guessed they were in my room. I also noticed Sam was trying not to lie if at all possible.

"I know she's here, Sam."

His steps came closer then farther away. In my mind's eye I saw him marching into Sam's bedroom, coming up empty, then moving on to the bathroom, kitchen, then living room.

"If she's here, then where is she, Martin?" Sam was staying on his heels. They walked past the closet again. It sounded like he was going back to my room.

There was quiet and I held my breath, clutching my hands in front of me. Then a really terrible, terrible thing happened. It made my blood run cold and my entire body freeze.

"If she's not here, Sam..." his tone was glacial, beyond incensed, "then why are the shoes she was wearing earlier next to her bed?"

Sam said nothing. I covered my face with my hands and closed my eyes. I was such an idiot. In the dictionary next to the word idiot was a picture of me. But it didn't matter. Nothing really mattered because he was going to find me and then I was going to expire from a broken heart and embarrassment.

Embarrassment, mortification, chagrin, unease, discomposure... GAH! The synonym game wasn't helping!

I heard footsteps.

He was coming.

I heard a hand on the doorknob.

He was there.

I heard the door swing open.

It was him.

I heard the light click on.

I couldn't open my eyes. I'd exhausted my courage earlier in the restaurant. I had none left.

But when I heard the door shut, I dropped my hands and I found myself face-to-face with a very irate Martin Sandeke.

That's right. He was in the closet with me and he'd just closed the door. I stared at him. I knew I looked panicked because some of his irateness ebbed and became cautiousness.

At length he said, "Parker."

"Sandeke," I responded automatically.

"What are you doing?"

"Uh…" I released the breath I'd been holding. My eyes darted to the door behind him and I betrayed the truth of it. "I'm hiding in the closet."

His brow was still furrowed, but his gaze relaxed slightly. When he spoke, he spoke very slowly, like he was trying not to frighten me. "Why are you hiding in the closet?"

"Why does anyone hide in a closet?" My voice was very small, my chin wobbled, and as new tears flooded my vision, he began to blur a little.

Martin lifted a single eyebrow and stalked closer, raising then showing me the palms of his hands. He was less than a foot away when he gently wrapped his long fingers around my upper arms.

"Do you hide in the closet often?" His voice was soft and his eyes moved over my face, likely taking in the smudged mascara and resultant raccoon eyes.

I realized abruptly that we'd had this conversation before. Except it was in a chemistry lab and I'd been unable to scratch an itch. Maybe I hadn't made as much progress as I thought. Maybe all these months of trying to be someone different, better, stronger, more passionate had been futile.

Or maybe it was Martin. Perhaps I'd always be the girl hiding in the science cabinet, hiding from Martin Sandeke.

"Sometimes." I choked on the word, my jaw clenched, and I willed the tears to recede. Instead one spilled down my cheek. His eyes followed its progress then moved back to mine.

"Is this an everyday thing?" he asked in a near whisper, his thumbs brushing lightly over the sleeves of my dress.

He was confusing me and I heaved a sob, my chin falling to my chest and said, "No. Only on special occasions, like when I make an idiot of myself and tell Martin Sandeke that I'm still in...in...in—"

I didn't finish because he slid his finger under my chin, lifted my face to his, and kissed me.

Oh boy, oh boy, oh boy, did he ever kiss me.

It was a devouring kiss, a hungry kiss, a demanding, a claiming, a merciless kiss. He crushed me to him and swept his tongue into my mouth, leaving me no chance to breathe or recover or think.

And it went on and on. Martin dipped his head to one side then the next, his hands roaming over my body, grabbing and squeezing and reaching for the hem of my dress, sliding his hand against the soft silk. It was only when his fingers connected with the straps of my garter belt did he lift his head and let me breathe. And that was only because he wanted to release a string of expletives as he confirmed I was, in fact, wearing thigh highs; and I was, in fact, wearing lacy panties.

"Fuck me," he finished, his eyes moving back to mine, turbulent yet determined.

Meanwhile I was trying catch my breath. "Martin, I—"

"Parker, I fucking love you. I've always loved you. I never stopped."

I could hardly believe his words. I felt suddenly weightless, over-whelmed, and bursting with such intense levels of joy I just barely contained my instinctual desire to do a jig.

He continued, sounding stern yet tender, "And you really, really pissed me off when you left tonight."

"I'm sorry I did that." I nodded, smiling because I was level one million happy.

"I forgive you." He returned my grin.

This made me frown. I wasn't the only one who'd been an idiot, so I pointed at his chest with my finger. "But, in all fairness, you ordered an appetizer."

"So?"

"So? So I tell you I love you and you order escargot."

Martin, still grinning, bent and kissed my neck, then bit it. It hurt a little and it felt wonderful. His breath was hot against my skin. "You shocked the hell out of me. I didn't know. I had no idea. I never know what you're thinking. You hide everything behind those gorgeous gray eyes..."

I'd missed his sharp teeth and leaned my head to one side to give him better access, pressed against him. I couldn't think. All I knew was we were in a closet kissing, his amorous hands were up my skirt, and the figurative Bunsen burner in my pants demanded satisfaction.

"Martin—"

"There has been no one else since you. No one." His mouth was hot on my skin, devouring me. "You're all I think about, all I want. You are everything."

Oh, gah! Right in the feels!

I braced my hands against his chest before he could capture my mouth again, needing to tell him the whole truth. "Listen, wait, I know we have a lot to discuss and this is all very sudden, but—"

"Sudden?" He reeled back a bit. His contemptuous tone and slightly horrified expression told me he disagreed.

"Yes, I mean—one minute we're friends, or we're working on

213

being friends, and the next minute I'm telling you I'm still in love with you..." I searched his eyes, made sure he was really looking at me. I wanted him to understand this wasn't temporary, that my feelings weren't going to change. "But, you need to know, this wasn't sudden for me. I made up my mind last week, after you explained things in New York, but before you came to the coffee shop. I want to be *with* you. I don't want to be just friends. That's not going to work for me."

His mouth hitched to the side and his hands on me tightened. "Kaitlyn, I decided we were never going to be just friends the moment you walked into chemistry lab last year. We were *never* going to be just friends. That wasn't ever going to work."

"But. But. You said—"

"I lied."

My mouth fell open.

He shrugged, showing me he did not regret this lie. "I was tired of waiting. I needed you to forgive me, show you I've changed, but I knew you wouldn't listen to me if I showed up at your door and demanded we get back together—which is what I wanted to do. Christmas was extremely frustrating because I saw you were taking my offer of friendship seriously, and you were trying to do the right thing."

"I did take it seriously. I wanted to be your safe place," I admitted with a new rush of emotion that stung my eyes. "I love you, I care about you, and I wanted to be there for you even if you didn't love me... But my pants kept getting in the way."

Martin smiled very briefly at the mention of my pants, but then he scowled. His tone became fierce and angry as he leaned farther away. "Don't ever think that I never loved you."

"I—"

"When you said that to me in New York, when you told me you didn't think I'd ever loved you, I swear to God I wanted to strangle you. I've never felt like such a failure."

"Oh, Martin, I promise, I didn't say it to hurt you. I didn't." It was important he believe me.

"I know. You didn't think I cared. I figured that out later, when you were asleep on top of me on the couch, after I acted like a fuckwad and suggested sex with no strings, wanting to hurt you back. I *am* sorry about that," he whispered, sounding truly remorseful.

Yet his hands, having now lifted my skirt completely over my hips, were currently taking liberties with the bare skin of my torso, my back, and delving into the lace of my underwear.

"I forgive you," I gasped, a hot cascade of chaotic need coursing through me, everywhere he touched igniting my arousal. My movements became jerky and frantic as I pushed away his jacket and coat, and grabbed for his zipper.

"Kaitlyn—"

"Everything is forgiven," I added in a rush, tired of talking. We weren't friends—well, we were friends. But now we would never be *just* friends. There was no reason we couldn't get started being more than friends.

Right. This. Second.

Martin caught my wrists, halting my progress, his breathing labored. "No, no—we're not doing this yet."

"But I need you, I need to feel you," I whined.

"Don't—"

I tried a different approach, lowering my voice and cupping his erection through his pants. "I love you. I want to make love to you. I need you inside me."

Martin groaned inelegantly, a despairing, needy sound. Pressing his lips against mine, he silenced me with the hot slide of his mouth, his invading tongue. Martin brought my hands to his sides and trapped them there.

My heart soared even as my lower belly flip-flopped then twisted with erotic anticipation. He released my wrists and one of his hands moved on my thigh and between my legs, shifting the lace panties to one side so he could touch my center. I inhaled sharply, arching at the contact, my eyes half closing.

"So wet for me...I love how you feel. I've missed you so fucking much." He sounded mesmerized and a little vicious. "Tell me how much you need me."

I couldn't form words because...sex.

"Say it." He paired this demand with a stroke of his finger. I realized he was unbuckling the belt of his pants with his other hand.

I shuddered in response to his skilled fingers, having to hold onto him "I need you, I need you so much," I barely managed to say.

I felt the words.

I felt them to my bones.

I never wanted to be separated from him again.

He was pressing me against the coats and my hands wound around his neck. His pants dropped to the floor, leaving him in boxer briefs. I reached for them frantically and pushed them down, freeing his penis.

I gripped it. Stroked it twice. I felt it, and it felt amazing, and right, and crucial.

He hissed, "You're still on birth control, yes?"

I nodded, rocking my hips into his hand, feeling him there, needing more.

He kissed my lips harshly, then said against them, "I haven't been with anyone but you. Not since the boat. Not for months before that. I haven't wanted anyone but you. I never want to be with anyone but you. You're all I can think about. Just you, only you."

I moaned. The time for coherent thought had officially passed. I understood what he was saying so I nodded my head, giving him permission to do what I'd been fantasizing about since it first happened.

"Please...please." I rubbed against him, wanting to completely give myself over to passion.

"I'm sorry I have to do this," he said. His voice held true regret. He then proceeded to tear my new lace underwear in two.

I didn't have time to react because the next thing he did was grab my bottom, lift me up, and turn my back against the wall. He then brought me down, filling me in one swift stroke. He rocked back then filled me again with another inelegant thrust of his hips, pinning me to the wall, spreading my legs wide, to his satisfaction.

My head fell to his shoulder. I closed my eyes. I felt.

I felt myself adjust to him.

I felt him stretch me.

The beautiful friction his body made with mine.

I felt my love for him, and my desire, asphyxiate and overwhelm me.

I felt our combined passion for each other and the insanity of it, how mad and reckless we were.

"Say it again." He moved in then out, slowly at first, but then increasing the tempo to a punishing pace. "Tell me again."

I knew what he wanted. "I love you."

"I want you in so many ways, so many ways—"

"Then take me."

He growled and my back hit the wall. I was uncomfortable and completely, irrevocably aroused. There was nothing smooth, practiced, or controlled about what we were doing. Only greedy and needful. Essential. It was all passion and no technique.

I was mindless with selfishness. I couldn't think past this moment because I wanted it so badly. So I'd taken it. It was raw, and it was real, and it was true. We both came quickly, hard, loud, and together. And I immediately wanted a repeat. Or a threepeat.

In the aftermath our ragged breaths married, and his mouth sought then mated with mine—slow, sensual, and loving. I whimpered, sore but needing him still. He laughed wickedly, grinding into me.

It's true. We'd just had sex in the front closet of my apartment while my roommate was in the next room, likely laughing her ass off. I didn't care. I had no regrets. Actually, quite the opposite.

When Martin carefully lowered and released me, my feet touched the ground and my legs were wobbly. I leaned heavily against the wall and tried to right my dress with clumsy fingers as he finished buttoning his pants, a devilish and satisfied smile claiming his features.

I opened my mouth to say something—that we should go make love on my bed now—but then he kissed me senseless once more, getting me hot and bothered in the closet all over again. Pulling away after several long, wonderful minutes, he whispered hotly against my ear, "The next time we make love, it will be in our home, in our bed, the one we share with each other."

He leaned away slightly, capturing my gaze, his dazzling gaze telling me he was serious.

"But—"

"Because I can't live without you anymore. I can't spend any more days and nights not knowing when I'll see you, hear you play, touch you. I won't settle for less." His tone was stern, implacable, as though he'd reached the end of his patience.

I exhaled my frustration, because I was already calculating how to get him totally naked tonight. "But you live in New York and I live here."

"Then I'll commute."

My head hit the wall behind me and I glared at him. I couldn't think. "This is not a decision to make right now. We need time, we need to talk—but later. Much later. Not tonight."

"No. Talk now." His eyes were uncompromising and belligerent, sharp and pointed, and I knew it would be nearly impossible to talk him out of this. But I didn't want to talk him out of it, I just wanted him to cede that we had time to discuss living arrangements later. Living arrangements, cities, zip codes, commuting—that could all wait.

But right now, I didn't want to think about being responsible. In fact, I didn't want to think at all. I wanted to focus on feeling and touching, and logic and reason be damned.

Passion for the win!

"Martin, Christmas was…it was good, I think, and last spring we had a beautiful week—"

"Don't you get it yet, Kaitlyn?" He sounded tortured, at his wit's end.

Martin's eyes captured mine and he held me, all of me, hostage with the savagery of his gaze. Martin's hands lifted to my face, his rough calluses against the smooth skin of my cheeks and jaw, his fingers threading slightly into the hair at my temples. When he spoke his voice was raw with months of hope and need and desperation.

"I don't want a beautiful week with you. I want a beautiful lifetime."

218

* * *

Much to the disappointment of my pants, Martin and I did not have the sex again that night.

I started referring to it as "the sex" in my brain while we were still in the closet, because sex with Martin wasn't ever going to be sex. It was THE sex. Everything with him felt like it should have a definite article (the) in front of it, as though all verbs became nouns and took on a special meaning.

The sex.

The cuddling.

The touching.

The whispers.

The laughter.

The words.

The feelings.

The teasing.

The love.

I couldn't wait.

But rather than "the sex," Martin pulled me away from Sam's rainbow of coats, out of the closet, and to my bedroom. While I straightened myself, he waited for me, throwing his coat, jacket, and tie to my desk chair. He watched me in the reflection of my dresser mirror, and I found I couldn't, nor did I want to, feel embarrassment when his gaze was so possessive and predatory.

When I faced him, he stalked to me, walked me backward until my legs met the edge of the mattress, all the while staring at me like *this* was Christmas morning and I was everything he'd ever wanted and hoped for.

I lay down first, he stretched over me, his lithe form above. I reached for him. I touched him. We kissed.

We kissed for a long time and his hands never strayed to the hot zones; though I could feel his want for me, his desire with every shift of his hips. And each time things became a bit frenzied he would retreat, breathing heavily and reining himself by placing whisper-soft kisses over my face, jaw, and neck. Or he'd just hold himself still above me, slowing his heart.

And I cherished him. I poured my desperate longing and care for Martin into my touch. I stroked his back lovingly and held him in a way I hoped communicated the gravity of my affection. I returned his kisses and gave him several of my own. I managed to untuck his shirt and slide my hands along the sides of his torso, memorizing and remembering the feel of his skin.

Eventually the urgency tapered, something in my soul soothed, and he rested beside me. I was tucked tightly against him, my head on his shoulder, my body curved into his side, his hands in my hair, and his lips at my forehead. We both basked in each other's presence along with a deep sense of decisive contentment.

And strangely, my mind was blank. I was truly in the *now*. Likely because the *now* was so very, very good.

But Martin had clearly been thinking, because he asked, "Why didn't you tell me when I came to the coffee shop last week?"

I turned into his shoulder and hid my face. "If you must know," came my muffled response, "I did decide to tell you. I was going to call you and schedule a time to meet. Then you came by my work and asked for girl advice. And tonight, we arrived at the restaurant and I assumed you were taking me there on a reconnaissance mission for your date."

"My date?"

"The girl? The one you like? The one you wanted advice about last week when I narrowly managed to refrain from stabbing you with my butter knife."

He groaned, shaking his head. I lifted my chin so I could see his face. When his eyes opened they were equal parts amused and frustrated.

"Kaitlyn, *you're* the girl. I never gave up, I just figured I needed to take a different approach. I kept fucking things up when you were in New York, even though I was trying to be so careful. I needed your advice because everything I did seemed to push you further away."

I smiled against his starched shirt. He smelled like Martin: expensive sandalwood-scented soap, and even more expensive aftershave.

I knew my smile and voice were dreamy as I said, "When I first saw you, after the show in New York early in December, I didn't know what to think. I hadn't expected to ever see you again. Eventually I thought you were trying to give me closure. But then, when you came to me a few weeks ago and wanted to discuss the terms of our friendship, I figured you wanting friendship meant you were indifferent to me, that you didn't want me anymore."

"No." He communicated so much with the single word, and it was a violent rejection of my assumptions. As well it imparted the depth of his frustration. "How could you possibly think I was indifferent to you?"

"Well, you said—our last night on the island—that you could never be friends with me because you'd never be *indifferent enough*. Drawing the logical conclusion, I assumed you were now indifferent enough to want friendship."

He heaved an exaggerated sigh. "I told you the truth on the island. Like I said in the closet, I never wanted to be just a friend. But, since you offered me nothing else, I was willing to settle for it—for a time— if it ultimately got me what I wanted."

This made me grin.

I felt his answering smile as he continued, "I thought you'd read the interviews. When I first saw you in New York after your show I was waiting for you to either tell me you'd moved on or tell me you felt the same. But then you were quiet. Evasive. So I thought, if I could just..." He shifted on the bed, holding me tighter. "When I found out you hadn't read anything, that you'd actually been avoiding all mentions of me, I realized how badly I'd fucked up. So when you came to New York for the week before Christmas I tried to give you your space."

"So you stayed away that week because you didn't want to push me?"

"Yes. I wanted you to see that I'd changed, that I wasn't...demanding."

"But you are demanding."

"Well, not as demanding."

I slipped my hand under his shirt, wanting to touch him. "So what happened? Why didn't you say something on Christmas?"

"I'd planned to. I thought, you would see the piano Christmas morning and then I'd *gently* explain about the foundation. You would forgive me, see I was right, and then we'd get back together."

I tried not to laugh. "Gently?"

He ignored me. "But you fell asleep in the car. And then took a shower and were sneaking around the apartment."

"I wasn't sneaking. I was trying to put your gifts by the fireplace."

Again, he ignored my statement. "And I couldn't sleep. I needed… to touch you, or have a strong drink. And then we drank and I was an asshole."

"Because I implied you never loved me."

Martin shifted to the side, glanced at me from the corner of his eye, and contradicted, "No. You didn't imply. You flat out said it. And I got so pissed."

He sounded angry now, just remembering it. I decided it was best to move the conversation forward.

"I finally read your interview from Men's Health where you called me The One."

"When?"

"After I got your text on New Year's."

He didn't respond right away, and when he did he said, "Huh."

He looked so handsome, lying in my bed thinking with his big head, so I brushed my lips against his. This of course led to us kissing like mad again.

When we finally pulled apart, Martin was above me once more and his breathing was labored. "Kaitlyn," he started, then stopped.

"What is it?" I reached for him, smoothed my hands over his jaw.

I saw his chest rise with an impressive inhale before he spoke. "I did choose you. You know that, right?"

I waited for him to continue. I wasn't certain what to make of his statement, to what—in specific—he was referring.

He shifted on the bed, turning onto his side and propping his head up, his arm bent at the elbow. His other hand gripped my hip.

"I didn't choose anything at first, after you...left. Like I told you last week, I kept thinking you were going to agree to see me in secret. In my mind, we weren't over, not at all. But when you didn't change your mind, nothing about revenge or seeing my father humiliated meant anything. I saw you were right and I walked away, though I think a part of me will always want to see him suffer."

I was quiet while he had his moment of anger. Martin's father was a bad guy. I knew the best Martin could hope for was indifference toward the man.

Eventually, he shook himself and continued, "I dropped out of university because you asked me to leave you alone, and I couldn't do that if I stayed on campus. But then I couldn't let you go, even when I didn't see you. So almost everything I did—setting up the foundation, the interviews, publicly calling my father a dickhead—was all about earning you back, earning your trust, hoping you would consider taking me back once I'd made everything right."

I felt my chin wobble and was relieved these threatening tears were happy ones.

"Oh, Martin." My voice was shaky, but I didn't mind. "Did you really call your father a dickhead?"

He nodded. "They didn't print that part, but he is a dickhead."

I laughed, wishing the newspaper had printed that Denver Sandeke was a dickhead. But I also wished for so much more.

"I wish I'd read your interview when it was printed. I wish I'd gone back to you after our initial fight and tried to work things out, find another way. I wish I hadn't been hiding in the closet all summer, avoiding all mentions of your name."

"I don't." He shook his head with a remarkable kind of certainty, like he knew all the secrets of the past and the future.

"You don't?"

"No. Because, even without you, I am happier than I've ever been. As soon as I walked away from my father, I started working on projects that interested me. You know those sketches on my drafting table? I'm inventing again. My purpose is now about what I want and not dictated by my hatred for him. If you hadn't called me on my bullshit, then..." He didn't finish the thought. Instead his eyes lost focus, as though he were imagining an unpleasant alternate reality.

I felt myself smile. Martin had been the catalyst for my choice to embrace my music and, as such, passion. He forced me out of my closet of expectations and purposeful obscurity. Even separated from him, I was happier in my life than I'd ever been before.

And, in that moment, I had a thought.

Maybe that's what real love is.

Maybe love, at its essence, is being a mirror for another person—for the good parts and the bad. Perhaps love is simply finding that one person who sees you clearly, cares for you deeply, challenges you and supports you, and subsequently helps you see and be your true self.

Love, I decided, is being a sidekick.

[18]
STRENGTHS OF COVALENT BONDS

"WHEN WILL YOU be home?"

He didn't answer right away.

In fact, he was noticeably quiet, as though he were enjoying the question, the moment, and everything it meant.

But I *knew* he was smiling.

I felt my automatic answering smile, the kamikaze leap of my heart, and the igniting Bunsen burner in my pants—a trifecta of happiness and anticipation—at his silence.

The last month had been bliss. BLISS I TELL YOU!

We dated. We went on dates. I saw him almost every day. Although I hated he had such a long commute. During the week when I had classes, Martin stayed with me at my place every night. My weekends were pretty tied up with shows and work. Sometimes we stayed in New Haven and sometimes we crashed at his place in New York. Yet wherever I slept, he slept too.

But notably, we'd only made love three more times since the closet, each time he swore it was the last until we moved in together, and I was frustrated. Pragmatically speaking, it's a crime against humanity to have a boyfriend as hot—body hot, brain hot, heart hot—as Martin Sandeke and *not* have the sex.

He was being stubborn, and though I'd been able to entice him a few times, he wanted to wait until we had our own place. Really, he was blackmailing my pants.

"Soon," he responded from the other end of the phone, his voice so low and lovely, and laced with meaning, the single word a promise.

I heard the urgent *vroooom* of his car and pressed my lips together so he wouldn't hear me laugh, but I was unable to keep the amusement out of my voice. "Really? How soon? Because I was thinking of running some errands."

"Parker, don't tease me."

Oh...sigh.

Tonight he was coming home to our home.

Home was a really, really small one-bedroom just two blocks from the apartment I'd shared with Sam...until yesterday. The timing had been perfect because her friend Kara ended up moving into my room.

Honestly, I didn't know what Sam was more excited about: me and Martin *finally* getting back together—as she put it—or the fact she didn't have to pack up her stuff and move into a three-bedroom. Of course, she also took an alarming amount of pleasure in tearing up my chore chart.

Regardless, today was my first day in our new apartment and tonight would be our first night in the apartment together. I hoped it would be sans underwear.

I leaned against the kitchen counter, my legs feeling a little wobbly, my heart feeling a lot full. "Fine. I'll wait for you. But soon better mean soon."

"Soon means soon." This was accompanied by another *vroooom.*

This time the sound made me frown.

"Don't kill yourself trying to get home."

"I won't."

"Remember, I have my weekly call with my parents in about ten minutes. It shouldn't last longer than a half hour, so you don't need to rush."

"I won't rush." Just as he said this I heard his car *vroooom.* Before I could interrogate him about it, he added, "And I picked up dinner."

"Oh! What did you get?"

"Tacos."

I grinned. Over the last month he'd frequently brought New York takeout for dinner. I suspected he did this in an attempt to win Sam over. It worked. The first time he arrived with lasagna from Little Italy she forgave him for everything.

I further suspected he picked up dinner so often because it was informally exempt from my sharing expenses rule.

Upon my insistence, we'd decided to split everything for our new apartment down the middle—rent, utilities, groceries, everything. Strangely, I didn't have to insist at all. Martin didn't argue. I surmised he recognized how important my financial independence was to me; he understood I needed to prove to myself I could make a living as a musician.

I did mostly lose our argument about furniture though. He didn't mind second-hand furniture, but he didn't like the idea of pressed particle board and plastic. He liked sturdy hardwood antiques—*real* furniture made from *real* materials—Mission or Shaker style and time-period. Most of the items that ended up filling our living space—a turn of the century walnut desk, matching end tables, mirror, and chest, art deco-stained glass lamps, and a black leather loveseat sofa with two matching club chairs—were well outside of my price range.

But he valued genuine and he valued comfort. In the end I relented because we kept my mattress. Honestly, the only items I was attached to were my keyboard, my guitar, and my mattress.

As well, he kept his New York apartment. He owned it outright and it made financial sense as an investment. Plus, it was fun to visit the city (and my piano) on the weekends.

I was about to question Martin further about the tacos when I heard the distinct sound of another *vroooom*.

"You're using your hands free, right?"

"Yes. I'm using the car's Bluetooth."

"Okay…just…just be careful." I worried. I didn't want him rushing through traffic and killing himself.

"I'll be careful. I love you, Kaitlyn."

"I love you, Martin. Bye."

"See you soon," he said instead of goodbye, and then he clicked off.

As I hung up my phone, still in a cotton candy haze of happiness, I realized that Martin never said goodbye. The entire time I'd known him, he'd never said the words to me.

Huh...

Aaaand I was smiling again.

I was still smiling when I opened my laptop and signed into Skype for the weekly call with my parents. I hadn't yet told them about Martin and me, but I did ask George to add an item to the agenda this week entitled, *Kaitlyn's new address*. I figured I'd give them the heads-up once we came to the topic. They would make note of it. We would move on.

That is not what happened.

As soon as the video image of my parents came up on my screen I could see that my mother wasn't smiling. This was atypical now that we did our calls via Skype. Usually she was happy to see me. Today she looked concerned and preoccupied.

Furthermore, she started speaking immediately. I didn't even get a chance to greet my father and George.

"Kaitlyn, some pictures were sent to me today from an associated press photographer of you and Martin Sandeke. And my office received calls from several newspapers asking about the status of your relationship."

My attention drifted to my dad. He looked grim, like he'd just recently argued with my mother. They didn't argue often, so I could tell when they did because he always looked grim afterward.

"Uhhh..." I gathered a steadying breath and said the first thing that came into my head. "Do you want to skip forward on the agenda?"

"The agenda?"

"Item number seven, my new address."

My father's eyes lifted, he was now looking at my image on the computer screen with curiosity. George was taking notes, appearing neutral as usual. My mother was obviously confused and a little stunned.

"What does your new address have to do with...?" I could see she'd answered her own question before she'd finished asking it.

I gave her a moment to absorb reality, my eyes flickering again to my dad. He was giving me a small smile.

"Oh, Kaitlyn." My mother shook her head, bringing my attention back to her. She looked concerned. "You didn't even consult with us about this."

I stared at her for a long moment, unsure how to respond, especially since old Kaitlyn and new Kaitlyn had two completely different instinctual reactions to her statement.

Old Kaitlyn was mortified I'd disappointed my mother.

New Kaitlyn was pissed.

New Kaitlyn won, though, and I felt myself flush with mortification and discomfort. "Mom, why would I consult with you on where I live?"

"Not where you live, it's with whom you live. Your decisions affect more than just yourself."

"That's right. They affect *Martin* and me." I started to sweat.

"Yes. They do affect you. Martin's father isn't likely to let the fact that his son absconded with one hundred twenty million dollars go. Eventually he's going to try to make Martin's life very difficult and you will be caught in the middle."

"Then we'll cross that bridge when we come to it. I have complete faith in Martin that he'll be able to deal with his father."

"But that's not the only factor. Kaitlyn, you must see," she leaned forward in her chair, her voice held a note of pleading, "my opponents will insinuate that you and Martin have been together this whole time. All the denials I made back in the spring will ring false."

"And I'm sure you have a staff that can help you handle these kinds of issues."

My mother sighed. It was not a pleased sigh. "Are you being purposefully obtuse?"

"No. Are you?" I said through clenched teeth.

She stared at me. Or rather, her face on the screen stared at me, and I couldn't tell if she actually saw me or saw a problem to be solved.

After staring for a good while, during which I refused to look away, she shifted in her seat, her eyes narrowing just slightly. "I am curious, how is it that—"

"Nope." I cut her off, feeling a spike of bravery paired with my spike of irritation. "No. You can be curious, but I'm not answering any of your questions. This is not a senate committee meeting and I am not under oath. I am an adult, as you like to remind me, capable of making my own decisions. As such, the identity of my boyfriend is my prerogative, who I live with and who I decide to love is my choice. I love Martin. What you do for a living is your prerogative. If your job has a problem with who I love, then maybe you should stand up and tell your job to mind its own business."

I could see my dad off to the left. He smirked then tried to cover it by rolling his lips between his teeth. When that was ineffective he hid his smile behind his hand.

George, as always, looked bored while taking notes. I could just imagine reading the meeting minutes later…

My mother's calm exterior fractured a little. She appeared to be frustrated, she also appeared to be reluctantly proud. Even so, she surprised the hiccup out of me when she finally said with another sigh. "Okay."

"Okay?"

"Okay."

"Clarify what you mean by *okay*."

"Okay, your points are valid ones. I cede that you are an adult and your decisions are your own. I apologize. I will issue a press release that who my adult daughter dates is no one's business but hers and has no bearing on my career."

"So, you're going to point out the obvious."

My dad chuckled like he couldn't help himself and shook his head.

To my mother's credit, she cracked a smile. "Yes. I'm going to point out the obvious. And I'm also going to redouble my efforts to respect your boundaries. But if Denver Sandeke ever…I mean…I hope you know that I…that—"

I took pity on her. "Mom, it's okay. I promise I'm not going to do anything— on purpose at least—that might cloud or take away from the work you're trying to do. You do good work."

"But again, Kaitlyn, Denver Sandeke is not to be underestimated."

"Yes. I agree. I promise I will let you know if Denver Sandeke ever shows his chinless face. But I have a life to live."

"And I want you to live it." Her eyes were full of uncharacteristic emotion and she appeared to be truly repentant. "We've made progress, you and I. And I don't want anything to jeopardize that progress."

"Me either." I nodded, giving her a warm smile, impressed with myself that I managed to keep my outward cool. I exhaled my relief, feeling like I'd just run a mile.

"Good."

"Good."

And it was. It was good. We were figuring this out, every call and interaction forging a new path, and I was immeasurably thankful she was just as invested as I was in making this work.

George eventually cleared his throat and said in a very George-esque way, "So, back to the agenda."

I was granted a reprieve to calm down. We restarted at the top of the agenda and covered various and sundry topics like where they were vacationing for summer recess, whether I would be home for spring break, and thank-you cards I needed to write to family members for Christmas gifts. My aunt Donna on my dad's side always became a bit twitchy if I didn't write a thank-you note.

Then we arrived at agenda topic number four. I tried not to grimace.

"Have you made a decision about performing in May? At the fundraiser and the benefit concert?" George prompted, rubbing the bridge of his nose where his glasses typically rested.

"No." I shook my head. "How soon do you need to know?"

I hadn't decided. On one hand I was warming to the idea of pushing myself out of my comfort zone. The benefit for Children's

Charities in particular sounded like it would be awesome. I liked that there would be kids there and I could compose something specifically for them.

On the other hand...

My mother leaned forward again, her tone was infinitely patient. "I wish you would do it. I think you'd really enjoy yourself."

I glanced at my dad and he spoke up as well. "Katy, you're amazing. It's important to share your talents. I agree with your mom."

"I still need some time." I frowned at them both.

My mother sighed, again frustrated. "You know we just want what's best for you. And I can't believe that you're happy serving coffee and playing weddings every weekend in that little band."

I felt my defenses raise. "Believe it. I'm happy. I'm happier than I've ever been. I don't need to be important—"

"You are important—"

"You know what I mean. I don't need to be notable. I love playing and composing music. And that's enough for me."

My dad placed his hand on my mother's arm and shook his head, then turned his attention back to me. "Just think about it. It's hard as your parents to see you with this remarkable talent, capable of great things, and not sharing it with the world or getting the attention you deserve."

I gave my father a hard look. When I flew home for Thanksgiving I'd played him some of my compositions. He couldn't have been more proud and excited. I figured that was only because he was my dad, he'd always been equivalent levels of proud no matter what I did—whether it be a finger painting or defrosting chicken.

"Just think about it," George chimed in. I was surprised to see him also giving me a pleading look.

"I said I would. I'm thinking about it. I just need some more time."

"We need to know by March first." George refocused his attention back to his notes and I was relieved the conversation moved on to the next topic.

The rest of the call was uneventful and we signed off with sincere *I love yous* and *I'll see you next week*. Although my father threw in at the very end, "I might have a business trip at the end of February in New England. Maybe I can take you and Martin out to dinner? Meet this boy who has captured your heart?"

I only managed to stutter and nod before the screen went blank. My dad was a sneak. Of course he tossed it out there like an afterthought. As far as he was concerned the issue was settled. He would meet Martin at the end of February.

I stared at my monitor and realized I was grinning. I was excited about the prospect. I couldn't wait for them to meet. I also wanted Martin and my mother to get along. They'd started out on the wrong foot and I knew—once they grew accustomed to each other—they'd probably hit it off.

The sound of Martin clearing his throat pulled me out of my thoughts. I glanced over my shoulder and found him standing in the doorway to the bedroom—our bedroom—a small smile lighting his face.

"Your dad is coming at the end of the month?" he asked, looking pleased peppered with petrified.

I jumped up from my place at the desk, but then meandered to him, liking how he looked after a day in his corner office—tie gone, jacket gone, shirt sleeves rolled to his elbows.

"How long were you listening at the door?" I asked as I ogled.

Martin reached for me, wrapped his arm around my waist, his grin growing as he admitted, "Long enough to hear you call me your boyfriend and tell your parents we're living together."

"Oh, so you've been prowling like a creepy lurker the whole time?"

"Yes..." He paused, and his face grew surprisingly solemn. "You should know, you're completely safe. My father isn't going to come after me. He's cut me off, but he won't do anything else."

"Why not? You've told me at least a dozen times how wicked he is. What would keep him from seeking revenge?"

"Because I had ways to collect information while I lived in his house. Bribing senators and corporate corruption aren't the worst of his sins."

My eyes widened as they moved between his. "Do I want to know?"

"No."

"So...you're blackmailing him?"

"Not actively. Let's just say he has incentive to leave us alone."

I tried not to smile. I tried and failed. "And you're not going to use this incentive for revenge?"

"Nope."

I narrowed my eyes on him and gave into the urge to say, "I'm really proud of you."

Martin grinned at me and stood a little taller, like I'd pinned a badge of awesome on his chest. We shared a stare of mutual admiration.

Then his gaze softened and sobered, and he said, "Thank you."

"For what?"

"For choosing me. With your parents just now, thank you for choosing us."

My heart did a funny little dance in my chest—both happy and sad —and I lifted my hands to his face. His was a man's face, his jaw stubbly and rough. I loved my man's face. I lifted to my tiptoes and gave him a soft kiss, and he tasted like coffee and mint gum.

Then I gently rubbed my nose against his before I leaned away. "You know I love you. But it was also the right thing to do. "

He smiled again. "And Kaitlyn Parker always does the right thing."

"Not always. For example, I've fiendishly hidden all of your clothes."

He lifted a single eyebrow in obvious delighted surprise. "Have you?"

"Yes."

"It's not that big of an apartment, I'm sure I could find them."

"Who said they're in this apartment?" I gave him a meaningful look.

The truth was, they were in the apartment. I'd hidden his boxes of clothes in the front closet.

His smile turned into a devilish grin, baring his wonderfully sharp teeth. "What about you?"

"What about me?"

His hands smoothed down my back, into my cotton yoga pants and underwear, gripping my bare bottom. "Should I hide your clothes?"

"No need. I plan to be naked for the next twelve hours."

He groaned. His mouth crashed down on mine, and he walked me backward toward the bathroom, his hands now turning greedy and searching. How we made it successfully into the tiled room was a miracle, especially since we were doing the clumsy de-panting dance on the way. Martin whipped off my top and found I was braless. This elicited a pleased growl as he pressed me against the sink. Meanwhile I worked on the buttons of his shirt.

Stupid business shirt with all the buttons.

We were in a frenzy, our hands covetous as our mouths mated. He slipped his fingers into the front of my underwear, teasing me but not touching where I needed.

I tilted my hips forward, trying to force him to ease my suffering.

"Touch me, Martin. Please."

His head bent and he captured my breast with his mouth, drawing tight circles around the center with his tongue.

I felt his hot breath against the wet spot he'd created when he answered, "First the shower. Then the kitchen table. Maybe the desk."

"What...what are you talking about?" I arched against him, my hands sliding down to his boxer briefs and stroking him through the fabric.

"All the places we're going to make love tonight."

A surprised laugh tumbled from my lips followed by a rough intake of breath as he parted me with his skilled fingers, rubbing my center.

"I thought..." I had to moan before I could continue; he was making me brainless. "I thought you wanted to start with our mattress."

"We've done that, thanks to your trickery," he responded darkly, referencing the three times I'd seduced him over the past month. Martin withdrew his hand just long enough to discard his shorts and reach into the shower to start the hot water. "I want to make memories on *all* the other surfaces."

I smiled, through my haze of love and lust for my Martin, and teased, "Starting with the shower?"

His eyes cut to mine as steam rolled out of the stall, his hands back on my body, peeling away my underwear. His expression and his voice were deadly serious as he said, "Yes. Because I have been thinking about it since Christmas and I need to take you against the wall while your perfect tits and perfect body are slippery and wet, sliding against me."

A flush of feral desire pooled in my belly, making my body feel tender and heavy. His words did that to me; his dirty talk made me feel wanton and bold.

Before I could think better of it I asked, "So you're going to fuck my sweet pussy?"

His mouth fell open with surprise and his eyes widened. Martin blinked at me, like he didn't quite trust his ears. Meanwhile—despite my boldness and arousal—I cringed, feeling silly, and peered at him through one eye.

"Did I say that right?" I asked, still cringing. "Because when you say it, it sounds sexy. But when I say it, it sounds weird and alarming —like a premeditated criminal action."

Then Martin laughed, an uncontrollable, deep rumble of pure happiness. He pulled my naked body against his naked body and hugged me. I could only smile and try not to blush or feel like a dirty talk failure.

"You are so perfect," he said against my neck when his laughter receded; he bit me—hard—like he wanted to devour me, then soothed the area with his tongue. "So fucking perfect."

I tensed, my belly twisting with delight, as his hands were growing amorous again.

"I'm perfectly weird you mean, and I don't like the word *pussy*," I whispered. "It has too many 'S' sounds."

"You're perfect and I love you." One callused hand lifted to my breast and roughly caressed it, pinching me. His other arm, still

236

wrapped around my middle, steered us into the shower and under the spray.

"I'm bad at dirty talk."

He didn't respond. Instead he pressed me against the wall and I was overwhelmed by sensations: the cold tile at my back, the hot water above, his roughened hands rubbing slippery soap over my stomach, thighs, and breasts, his sensational eyes capturing mine and wordlessly telling me he believed I was perfect.

I couldn't keep my hands off his actually perfect body nor did I try. The heat of my earlier embarrassment gave way to a new heat, a building promise between us.

His mouth was everywhere the soap wasn't and when he finished lathering, he held both my wrists in his hands and slid his body against mine, increasing my arousal exponentially until I was brainless.

"Repeat after me." Martin's voice was low, impatient and demanding, his tongue licking water droplets from my jaw as he released my wrists and smoothed his hands down my sides to my hips.

"I, Kaitlyn…"

"I, Kaitlyn..."

He lifted me as though it were the easiest thing in the world. My hands came to his shoulders and enjoyed how they bunched as he flexed his muscles. He spread my legs wide and rubbed his hardness against the yielding slickness of my center.

"Want you, Martin..."

"Want you, Martin—"

I sucked in a sudden breath as he pushed inside me, his face at my neck sucking and biting and licking.

"To take me in the shower…"

"To take…me…in…the shower…"

Everything about this act felt more crucial than I'd remembered, so much more necessary on a base and instinctual level.

"…and make love to me for hours."

"To…to…"

I couldn't finish. I didn't want to talk, I just wanted to feel. I glanced down at him and our bodies where they joined. I enjoyed the sight of our connection—his hard against my soft, my legs spread wide to accommodate his size. I watched my wet breasts moving up and down in time with his rhythm, bouncing in his face; his rigid and sculpted body curved toward mine as I arched away from the wall. It was the sight of us together—of me with him—that made me feel sexy, overwhelmed by how crazy hot we looked.

I wondered if we could install a mirror in the shower.

Aaaaand, with that thought I came—assaulted by water and steam, the slick sliding of his body with mine, and the realization this was the first of many happy—and sexy—memories.

* * *

WHEN WE CRAWLED into bed it was because we needed sleep. But instead of sleeping, we found ourselves facing each other naked, cuddling and touching, and discussing plans for the future. These plans ranged from the various trips we wanted to take together, to various places we wanted to have the sex—he wanted to christen all the showers in his apartment, meanwhile I wanted to lay claim to his desk at work—to a new gaming store that had opened in Times Square. Martin insisted he'd take me the next time we were in the city. We discussed that my father was visiting at the end of February and where we should take him for dinner.

"Don't worry," Martin squeezed me, "I'll be nice to your dad."

I let my amusement and confusion show on my face. "Well, I should certainly hope so."

He gave me a wry look. "You know what I mean. I've been practicing."

"Being nice?"

"Yes."

I rolled my lips between my teeth because his features held an expression of extreme consternation and I didn't think it would be wise to laugh at him. "How's that going for you?"

"It's been...difficult, but sometimes good."

"Difficult?"

"Yeah, like that annoying girl you work with at the coffee shop."

"You think Chelsea is annoying?" I was surprised. I'd never met anyone—especially a man—who thought she was anything but wonderful.

"She's vain and irritating. In fact, she reminds me of my mother, always expecting strangers to adore her."

I felt my eyebrows jump at his accurate—albeit simplified— description of my co-worker. Perhaps Martin's tendency to value perceived goodness and genuineness stemmed from his disdain for his mother.

After a beat Martin surprised me by changing the subject. "Do you want to perform at the benefit your parents were talking about? Yes or no?"

I hesitated, took a moment to trace my index finger over the line of his collarbone. "Kind of. But I don't want to do it because my parents think I need to be more impressive. I like playing in my *little band.* Just being around music every day is a dream come true. I don't need accolades and attention."

"But you saying no just because your parents think you need to be more impressive is allowing them to dictate what you do. If you're saying no because of what they think, that's just as bad as saying yes because of what they think."

I frowned at him and his sensible words. *Stupid sensible words.*

Meanwhile he smiled at me like he knew what I was thinking, and he knew I knew he was right. His smile turned smug.

"Fine," I admitted finally. "You're right. Is that what you wanted to hear?"

"No. I already knew I was right. I was hoping for something more like, *Oh, Martin, you are a sexy genius. I can't live without you and your big…head.*"

I couldn't help my sudden laugh, though I did smack him on the shoulder. He continued his smugly smiling ways and leaned forward to give me a kiss.

"Seriously though, do it if you want to do it. Or don't. But make the decision based on what you want to do, not to avoid or cater to someone else's expectations."

I nodded, feeling my chest flood with warmth and affection. He really was my mirror. He was on my side. We were a team. We moved in unison, toward a common goal, and it was a beautiful thing.

Martin's hands hadn't quite settled on my body. He'd move them every so often—from my hip to my thigh, from my thigh to my breast —like he was taking full advantage of his all-access pass. It had the byproduct of warming me up.

Apropos of nothing, I pushed, "But getting back to having the sex on your desk at work, what days next week are you free for lunch?"

He gave me a funny look, like he thought I'd been bluffing earlier. "You really want to do that?"

"Yes. Do you have walls or blinds?"

"Walls facing the rest of the office, but windows to the outside."

"Good."

"What's gotten into you?"

"Technically, you have—"

"Ha, ha."

"But, actually…nothing. I just like the sex. I like the sex with you. I like how sexy it makes me feel. I like the making out and the fore-play, and the orgasming. I like thinking about it and planning our next encounter. And, even though I am a girl, I don't think that makes me weird. I think it means I have a healthy sexual appetite, and I'm in love with the man I crave. I refuse to apologize for it."

His mouth hooked to the side. "I'd never ask you to apologize for it."

"Good. Because I won't."

Martin's eyes narrowed on me, like he was in deep thought, but his smile never wavered.

Then he said, "In the closet."

I waited for him to explain. When he just continued to look at me, his eyes heated with meaning, I prompted, "What about the closet?"

"Let's make love in the closet."

"But we've already done that."

"No. I mean all the closets. Every closet we can find."

I grinned. "Every closet?"

"Yes."

I threw my head back and laughed, thinking of all the closets in the world and how I'd struggled to avoid them, to avoid indulging my fears and reclusive inclinations, now that I'd found the courage to follow my heart. Little did I know following my heart would bring me right back to the closet.

But this time I would be with Martin and we would be making love. Or maybe we wouldn't.

Maybe we'd just be sharing a private moment alone.

Maybe we'd be hiding from the world—just a little—but that was okay.

Because the world could be unpleasant and overwhelming. A demanding place full of uncertainties and expectations and fears. I was coming to realize retreating, hiding from the world on occasion, was not a bad thing to do, as long as I didn't do it too often or because I was afraid of living my life.

Sharing a closet with Martin—closed away from everything else but our mutual love, respect, and devotion—might be a very healthy thing. We were a team, a perfectly situated pair of sidekicks.

And sharing a closet with my sidekick sounded like paradise.

~THE END~
Pre-Order Penny Reid's next release Marriage of Inconvenience coming 2018!
Pre-Order now!

Read on for a sneak peek of Penny Reid's latest work!

There are three things you need to know about Kat Tanner (aka Kathleen Tyson. . . and yes, she is *that* Kathleen Tyson): 1) She's determined to make good decisions, 2) She must get married ASAP, and 3) She knows how to knit.

Being a billionaire heiress isn't all it's cracked up to be. In fact, it sucks. Determined to live a quiet life, Kat Tanner changed her identity years ago and eschewed her family's legacy. But now, Kat's silver spoon past has finally caught up with her, and so have her youthful mistakes. To avoid imminent disaster, she must marry immediately; it is essential that the person she chooses have no romantic feelings for her whatsoever and be completely trustworthy.

Fortunately, she knows exactly who to ask. Dan O'Malley checks all the boxes: single, romantically indifferent to her, completely trustworthy. Sure, she might have a wee little crush on Dan the Security Man, but with clear rules, expectations, and a legally binding contract, Kat is certain she can make it through this debacle with her sanity—and heart—all in one piece.

Except, what happens when Dan O'Malley isn't as indifferent—or as trustworthy—as she thought?

Marriage of Inconvenience is book #7 in the *Knitting in the City* series and is **available for pre-order now!**

ABOUT THE AUTHOR

Penny Reid lives in Seattle, Washington with her husband, three kids, and an inordinate amount of yarn. She used to spend her days writing federal grant proposals as a biomedical researcher, but now she just writes books.

As of 2018, Penny has published 16 novels.

Come find me-
Mailing list signup: http://pennyreid.ninja/newsletter/ (get exclusive stories, sneak peeks, and pictures of cats knitting hats)
Facebook: http://www.facebook.com/PennyReidWriter
Instagram: https://www.instagram.com/reidromance/
Goodreads: http://www.goodreads.com/ReidRomance
Email: pennreid@gmail.com …hey, you! Email me ;-)
Blog: http://pennyreid.ninja
Twitter: https://twitter.com/ReidRomance
Ravelry: http://www.ravelry.com/people/ReidRomance (if you crochet or knit…!)

Read on for:
Penny Reid Book List

OTHER BOOKS BY PENNY REID

Knitting in the City Series

(Contemporary Romantic Comedy)

Neanderthal Seeks Human: A Smart Romance (#1)

Neanderthal Marries Human: A Smarter Romance (#1.5)

Friends without Benefits: An Unrequited Romance (#2)

Love Hacked: A Reluctant Romance (#3)

Beauty and the Mustache: A Philosophical Romance (#4)

Ninja at First Sight (#4.75)

Happily Ever Ninja: A Married Romance (#5)

Dating-ish: A Humanoid Romance (#6)

Marriage of Inconvenience: (#7)

Winston Brothers Series

(Contemporary Romantic Comedy, spinoff of *Beauty and the Mustache*)

Beauty and the Mustache (#0.5)

Truth or Beard (#1)

Grin and Beard It (#2)

Beard Science (#3)

Beard in Mind (#4)

Dr. Strange Beard (#5)

Beard with Me (#5.5, coming 2019)

Beard Necessities (#6, coming 2019)

Hypothesis Series

(New Adult Romantic Comedy)

Elements of Chemistry: ATTRACTION, HEAT, and CAPTURE (#1)

Laws of Physics: MOTION, SPACE, and TIME (#2, coming 2018)

Fundamentals of Biology: STRUCTURE, EVOLUTION, and GROWTH (#3, coming 2019)

Irish Players (Rugby) Series – by L.H. Cosway and Penny Reid

(Contemporary Sports Romance)

The Hooker and the Hermit (#1)

The Pixie and the Player (#2)

The Cad and the Co-ed (#3)

The Varlet and the Voyeur (#4)

Dear Professor Series

(New Adult Romantic Comedy)

Kissing Tolstoy (#1)

Kissing Galileo (#2, coming 2019)

36715031R00139

Made in the USA
Middletown, DE
17 February 2019